MYSTERY IN PALE GREEN

ADVENTURES IN THE WINE COUNTRY #11

DIANA STONE

1

DANGEROUS DRIVER

I'm Christmas shopping in San Luis Obispo. My car is full, except I'm freaking out about what to get Quinn. The search for "What to get your guy for Christmas" suggests cologne, watches, or golf equipment. He doesn't wear cologne, or at least not around me. Maybe some aftershave? He probably doesn't need another watch, and he doesn't golf. I can't give him tech equipment that he doesn't already own in smaller and better versions. HELP!

It needs to be thoughtful and interesting, not a soap that smells like beer—but maybe if it smells like lemons?

How about a braided leather bracelet? There's one I can get with with my name on a steel bead. I think my name engraved on a horseshoe nail would personalize it more, after all, I want it to be unique. I click to order it right now, and later I'll run by the jewelers with some horseshoe nails. Maybe it'll have the date on it, so I can give him one for each year, like a charm bracelet. Or maybe not. I'll worry about that next year.

Whew, I slump down for a few minutes to enjoy the peace. I'll get Travis, Adam, and Dave a bar of beer scented soap.

I'm driving the Subaru because it gets better mileage than my Ford dually. Right now, I'm zipping home at 67 mph, which is keeping up with the light traffic on the scenic highway, bordered by rolling hills on one side and views of the ocean on the other.

In the rear-view mirror, I see a black Suburban racing up. Damn. To be polite, I increase my speed to 70. He comes right onto my tail and stays there, only a few feet off the bumper.

Damn it. My car is small and easy to intimidate. If I'd been in my pickup, he could sit there all day while I'd be thinking "Screw you— I'm going fast enough."

He can wait for the passing lane two miles ahead, or he can cross over the double yellow line, since he's obviously in a rush, staying on my bumper like this.

I can't see the driver. My roof is too low, and he's too close, but I bet it's a man.

He backs off a few feet, giving me breathing room.

Then guns it—racing up and slamming into the back of my little car!

I grip the wheel, fighting to steer into the curve. Thank goodness I'm not sliding off the road. He didn't hit me right, or that would have happened. I quickly glance in my mirror and see that he has backed off—probably to be out of the way if I spin out. But I'm not.

I stomp on the gas and increase my speed to over 80 mph. That's faster than I'm comfortable driving on this stretch. He's closing the gap again. I see the dark shape eating up the distance between us.

My phone and Glock .45 are in my purse that flew to the floor. They could be anywhere down there. I can't out drive him and reach for my tools at the same time. I try to tap the button for the phone Bluetooth system, but I have to remember which one it is. Gram's is different from mine, and I haven't driven her car enough to be sure which one answers, hangs up, or dials.

He's close again, I press harder on the gas, while testing buttons for the phone.

That annoying voice slowly says, "Say a command or press the talk button to enter a number."

I press the button and shout, "Dial."

"Say a command or press the talk button to enter a number," it repeats.

Shit. I pressed the button *and* said 'Dial.' I have to say Dial without pressing the button.

I press the button and try again.

He's inches off my bumper. I need to prioritize. Calling the police won't save me in the next few minutes. I need to out drive the Suburban, stay safe, and not hurt anyone else.

The road winds and undulates like a country lane. If I can't outdrive him on the flat, I'll be dead on the uphill part. This car doesn't have the power to get away.

I'm coming up fast on a delivery truck. I can't pass because the line has changed to a double yellow, which means I can't see ahead well enough to know when it's safe.

On the left is a long, gravel parking area at a scenic overlook.

This may be my only chance.

Just before the end of the gravel, I swerve across the south-bound lane of traffic, nearly getting hit as I dive between two cars.

I aim for the gravel, and press the brakes *hard* while I'm still on the roadway to slow the momentum of the car. It starts skidding. I let it go for a bunch of yards, then I pull up on the parking brake, and yank the steering wheel to the left.

The tail swings around, and around, and around. Finally coming to a stop in a cloud of dust. My head is spinning. I can't see a thing through the gray clouds. I don't know which way I'm facing, nor do I know where the SUV is.

I inch forward and direct the car south, from the way I came. Cars have stopped as the cloud lingers in the roadway, obscuring visibility. I pull out and step on the gas. Now is the time to get away.

I calm down enough to press the right button, say "Dial" with an adrenaline infused voice, and finally get through to 911.

Can I describe the vehicle? It's a black Chevy SUV without a front plate. I couldn't see the driver, except he took up room in the front seat, suggesting a big man, rather than a woman. It's very little to go on.

I'm sure this isn't a random attack. Unless there's an angry driver who happens be on the same stretch of road as me. Though, it's possible; I tend to attract trouble.

I speed to the police station, finally feeling safe when I walk in the lobby. A deputy comes out to examine my caved-in bumper, looking for traces of paint, or other evidence. Occasionally, but not this time, the suspect's license plate stays attached to the victim's car. There isn't a transfer of paint, because the chrome bumper is what slammed into the car. He takes a written report, but unfortunately, that's all we can do.

A deputy who patrols Cambria follows me home. While I'm driving, I leave a message for Quinn who is off somewhere, fighting for our freedom. While I'm at it, I call Travis because he may know where Quinn is, but he isn't answering, either.

It looks like I won't be getting any help from my men.

I park at the back of my property, hiding the car on the far side of my truck. The deputy follows me to my door and sees me inside. That's fine for now, but what about tomorrow, and every day after?

2

A SIDE JOB

"Foxhunting—isn't that what English royalty did, back in the dark ages?"

"You mean before P.E.T.A.?" The group who advocates for animals.

"Yeah, I guess."

"It's more than that. I'm a member of the Santa Barbara Hunt. We chase coyote, not fox," she explains, as if a coyote is so much different from a fox.

"Do the hounds still rip them apart?"

"You disapprove?" I think she, in fact, disapproves of me.

"Well..." I pause to find the words. "I'm not a fan of that kind of..." I trail off, "sport."

"I've seen what a coyote can do to a lamb. Don't make me describe it," she says. "If we didn't get them, the farmer would trap or shoot the varmints, they're a menace. Besides, it's more natural this way."

More natural to be attacked by a pack of dogs? I figure she knows more about sheep farming than I do, so I don't make her tell me the gory details.

"Whether or not you approve isn't the point." She looks at me scornfully. "I'm here because I want to know if my husband is having an affair."

"And how does this involve me?" Don't blame me. I'm not sleeping with anyone but Quinn.

"I'd like you to ride with him."

"I don't jump."

"You're a good rider, you can fake it," she insists.

"I haven't jumped an obstacle higher than two-feet in the past fifteen years. How do you expect me to pop across a five-foot ditch?" I'm incredulous she thinks I have that ability. Maybe I should be flattered.

"I'll get you a babysitter. He'll jump all day and even make your dinner." She tries to bargain with me.

"Look, I can ride well, very well. But I've never galloped across miles of range land, leaping dry creek beds and fences.

"Maybe you didn't hear me—I said I'll put you on a steady horse. He's like a recliner, you won't even have to think. He'll do all the work." She looks frustrated. "I already told you. I need to prove my husband is cheating on me," she speaks louder, as if I'm hard of hearing.

"Why me?"

She sighs with such emotion I feel like a fool for not understanding her plight. "You're the kind of woman he likes: tall, thin, blonde, and you can ride." I get the feeling she hates me for this. "I'll pay you well."

"I don't need the money enough to be permanently disabled." I can imagine the damage as the horse misses a step and sends me flying over his head with a sudden stop at an oak tree. I'll never recover.

"You can ride at the back of the pack," she rolls her eyes. "You don't expect to ride at the front, do you?" Again, I get that look.

"The back, or the front, what does it matter—I can't jump!" Are you deaf?

"Five hundred dollars to get the proof," she hisses.

I shrug. "No thanks." I turn away.

"Five-hundred-dollars," she enunciates each word, "*every time* you get on a horse, plus expenses."

I feel myself start to waver; she's offering to pay me $500 to sit on a well-trained horse. That's a decent amount of money for something I've been doing my whole life. Perhaps I can ride that foxhunter after all. I'll take a few jumping lessons and have an experience I wouldn't otherwise have.

* * *

THAT WAS THIS MORNING, after a crappy night's sleep, because I was reliving the experience of the blacked-out SUV.

I had just finished my three-mile jog that *just happened* to take me past Mandy Crawford's Cambria Seaside Resort. I used to stay away from the place, which is hard to do, since it's only two hotels down from mine. But today I began a campaign to irritate her.

She's been recording my office conversations, and I want to know why. Maybe I can torment her enough to get her to react. How do I know she's recording me? Uh, because I'm recording her. No, it isn't strictly legal, but she started it.

By 10:00 AM I am in the office in time to meet Georgina Stamford of Santa Barbara. She is married to Lyle Stamford of Stamford Plumbing. She phoned yesterday requesting a meeting for this morning. I'm a boutique bed and breakfast owner, so I readily agreed. There's a lot of competition for tourist business in Cambria. Maybe she wants to discuss an air-conditioners' sales convention.

She regally strolls through the open French doors ten minutes late. My first impression is of wealth. She is in her mid-60s, and is impeccably dressed in a white linen blazer with the sleeves pushed up to her elbows. Her white capris are eye-squinting white. That means something right there. She has supreme confidence to wear that color. Does she wrap herself in plastic to keep clean?

I only wore white riding breeches at dressage shows, and by the time I got off the horse they had black stains from the saddle, green from her alfalfa-colored drool, and brown from touching everything dusty.

"I'm looking for Jessica," she uses her best, arrogant tone.

I hate to admit that's my name.

"I'm Jessica, and you must be Georgina Stamford?"

"Of course." Of course she's Georgina, or of course I'm Jessica?

"I was told you have long, blond hair," she emphasizes the word long.

"I did, until the Dog-Collar Killer dragged me around by my pony tail. I cut it off that same day." I reply, hoping to shock her.

I succeed.

She raises a single eyebrow, "That's a shame." She pauses. "I need you in long hair."

Nothing about a killer dragging me around, escaping, making the news. Nope, just she wants me to have long hair.

"And why is that?"

"Because I married a cheating bastard."

"Oh. I've been there too." We have something in common after all.

"Well this one is trying to get away with fifty million dollars of my money," she hisses.

I can tell she's really angry, because most people don't tell an hotelier how much they make, lose, or spend.

"So you came to book a room?" I ask, lightly.

"No," she snaps. "I want you to get that loser to chase your tail, and bring me proof." She lays her sun glasses on the counter. That tells me she's warming up to the subject and plans to stay for a few minutes.

"How much tail chasing do you need?"

"As much as I can get. My father, bless his soul, insisted on a prenup. Before we married, I only saw him as the most handsome man I'd ever met. I missed the part about him twisting me around his little finger, and chasing beautiful women at the hunt club." She takes a fortifying breath then continues. "I need a beautiful woman to protect my inheritance."

"I'm not really a beautiful woman," I reply demurely. I consider myself outdoorsy.

"No. You're not," she agrees.

Thanks.

"But you're attractive enough, and you're the best I can find at the last minute. Most of all, you're discreet," she lowers her voice and glances around.

Oops. I would be, but Mandy Crawford is listening with her transmitting device stuck to the underside of the counter. Georgina isn't booking rooms for a conference. This is personal, and I have to get her out of here.

"Let's step outside to discuss this," I hurry to the front, and head out the door, without looking to see if she's following. She will be; I'm moving like a truck, and she can't help but get caught in my draft.

A confused look cross her face, temporarily erasing the confident one. Well, that's interesting. She has a repertoire of emotions under that haughty exterior.

I stop on the small rise overlooking the ocean. "I'll be building the hot tub and a champagne bar here."

She glances around, politely. She isn't acting as powerful without the high counter between us. I'm 5'9" 135 pounds. She's four inches shorter and thin. She would have a nice face with few signs of middle-age, but she needs a nicer personality.

She said the cheating louse likes younger women. What a shame, he's ruining his marriage, as well as his career, to follow his lust.

"Why did you choose me?"

"Abigail Johansen said you're the best."

The conversation comes to a halt. Abbie; we met when she was engaged to man who planned to take everything she had—he was a psychopath as well as a thief. On the last night of his life, he was attacking my horses in the pasture with a butcher knife. He shot every round in his gun trying to kill me, but my trusty .38 had one bullet left, and my aim was true.

"Abbie likes me." That's putting it mildly.

"Yes, I got that." She loses some of her bad attitude.

"What do you have in mind?" I feel myself giving in.

"Not much. You just may have enough wit to get him interested in a quickie in the horse stall, and get photos of the act.

"Ohhh no," I drag out the word to emphasize how much she's out of bounds. "No sex. No criminal acts. No hands down my pants. I don't go that far." I make sure to lay the ground rules.

"Look, young lady, this isn't Victorian England. Can't you encourage him with your body, everyone else does?"

"No. Not everyone does. I don't need the job that badly. I'd be doing it because," I stop to wonder why I'm agreeing to it. "I guess, because your cheating husband touches a nerve with me, though foxhunting sounds like a weird, elitist sport."

She rolls her eyes for effect, but swallows her retort. "Thank you. Just ride the best you can, and get him to chase your tail."

"If he's a real horseman, I should be able to impress him with my riding."

"My dear, he's a man. He's impressed by an attractive woman in tight breeches," she corrects me.

It looks like I'll be riding to hounds in the near future.

"It'll be two weeks from Saturday." She smiles. "The horse you'll be riding is called a hireling. It's a term unique to foxhunting meaning to rent someone else's horse."

She slides a book out of her Hermes bag and passes it to me. "Study up on the terms so you'll fit in."

I open The Big Book of Foxhunting to the bookmarked, dictionary page. "Music" means the barking of the hounds. "Cry" is the music of the pack when they are running hard. This one gets me: "To 'sing' is when the hounds hold up their head and make a wonderful noise. They shouldn't be stopped from their anthem." I hated it when my neighbors used to let their dogs "sing!"

"Gone to ground" is when the fox has run into her burrow, but "earth stopping" is when the hunter blocked off her burrow when she's out at night, now she can't get back in when they chase her. The huntsman shouts "tally-ho" when the fox has been seen and the chase is on.

There are familiar words I've heard used in other situations such as "vixen" being the female fox.

"You can read that later. Make sure you do, or you'll embarrass yourself, and Lyle won't want you."

She's rather blunt, but I think that applies to most things, people don't want to look foolish, or to be seen with fools.

"Ok, I'll memorize it." It's easier to agree with her than to debate.

She opens her purse, digs around for a minute, and then hands me a white envelope. "Please count it."

It has $700 in crisp hundred dollar bills. I could see she was adding money from her wallet since I'd turned down her first offer.

3

JUMPING LESSONS

What did I just agree to? I'll be riding to hounds in two weeks.

How hard can it be?

I open the book and flip past pages of old photos with Lt. Colonel, Captain, or Lord Someone-Royal jumping hedges; jumping wide creeks where the landing side is sloppy, churned up ground. That's a recipe for a fall.

But this isn't England. We have rolling hills with very few creeks. The rain from last week has run off so there shouldn't be any boggy ground. I'll be on an experienced horse and wearing a helmet.

A search reveals only two stables in Paso Robles that have jumping lessons. My first call goes to voice mail. The second has been disconnected. Oh no.

I'm getting anxious. I don't have a clue how to jump. My other option is to return to Los Olivos and saddle up Bunny. She is athletic, and we've jumped a few obstacles on the trail. Am I going to be a self-taught foxhunter who has never jumped over two-feet? I'll be a "hill-topper," those riders who go through gates to ride around the jumps. I'm sure Lyle Stamford won't look twice at me if I do that.

I head to the lounge in the Garden cottage to start reading her book. And stressing over the photos—except the ones where the riders are on flat ground, with the rolling, green English countryside in the background. With a bunch of killer hounds running ahead of the "field."

After an hour, my head is swimming with these terms. So after the huntsman shouts "tally-ho" or maybe "holloa" when a fox is seen, it's unclear if that's when the riders start galloping after the fox, or if it's my cue to turn away because he is about to be killed. I like the term "loss;" that's when the hounds lost the scent they were following.

Thank heavens, The Santa Barbara Hunt Club also has trail rides. That would be a safer way to catch Mr. Stamford's eye, but would he be interested in *that* kind of woman? It's not as if I'm a chicken. I can ride a tough trail, up narrow goat-paths, and down slippery slopes. Bunny and I even jumped off a six-foot waterfall, though not by choice—a robber wearing a lion mask was chasing us.

I'm convinced I'm more of a trail rider.

A while later, I receive a return call from the only jumper trainer in Paso. I'm trying to enroll before asking the specifics.

"This is a group lesson package that is scheduled in the evenings, once a week, for six weeks. Our horses are safe and experienced," she explains. "What age is your child?"

"No kids. It's for me." Maybe I sound like a parent.

"Our lessons are geared toward children, I'm not certain we can make an exception," she hesitates.

"Please, I need to learn to jump. I'd like to ride with the Santa Barbara Hunt Club—very soon."

"Do you have experience with horses?"

For the next few minutes I expound on my past experience: breeding dressage horses; showing every weekend; and training some difficult ones I wish I didn't own. I leave out the part about cleaning corrals, sweating for hours in the heat, trimming and shoeing their feet. Yes, I can do a lot, and I have the bruises and scrapes to show for it.

She finally agrees to take me.

Without asking the cost, I thank her. Then I try to negotiate the six weeks down to three days.

"Miss Wilcox, that isn't as easy as it sounds. I have a heavy schedule. I'm booked solid, plus with the winter rains, some classes have had to be rescheduled," she hedges in a tone that is about to become the answer No.

"Can I pay you double?"

She's silent for a moment. "That might work," her tone becomes a Yes.

"Thank you!"

* * *

I'M KEEPING a folder with notes from my lessons. I'll read them just before I put my life on the line. Just kidding. I mean, I'll brush up on them before I have fun on a well-schooled horse.

The stable has a long, paved driveway which indicates someone spent a boatload of money on concrete; it doesn't come cheap. There are several nice cars, a bunch of regular ones, and a few pickups, indicating this is a busy stable for all income levels. I'm driving my Subaru with the crumpled bumper. I don't care about impressing anyone, as I'll only be here for a week.

The parking area is in front of a twenty-stall MD barn, and shaded by ubiquitous California pepper trees. MDs are modular, prefabricated barns, so common in California, and probably a lot of other places. You order the number of stalls you want, the truck arrives, the men put them together, and you have a complete barn in a week.

I walk up in my black Dehner boots, holding my riding helmet.

Emma is also in boots and breeches. She's at the cross-ties tightening the girth on a bay horse's saddle. I'm guessing she's my instructor based on her directions on where to find her. She's younger than me by a few years. That's okay, since I don't know how to jump. Anything she says will probably be more than I know.

"Hi, you must be Jess." She raises her hand in a half wave.

"Hi Emma." I walk up and stand next to her and the tall Thoroughbred.

"He's ready to go. You can adjust the stirrups when you get on."

"Great."

She unclips the ties, and leads him out without saying anything else. She wasn't the most talkative on the phone; this may be the way she is. We don't have to become friends; I only need to feel confident over three-foot jumps.

The arena is huge, with lots of jumps set up at various stride lengths. They're well cared for, and look freshly painted and straight. That's one thing, plus the arena footing is sand and she even has it watered for me. I guess that's what I get for $100 a lesson, and I'll be having my second one after an hour break. Yes, I said I'd pay her double, and it looks like she's starting right.

"What's his name?" I shout from his back.

"Clay."

I start by warming up Clay at the walk, and I check if he knows what leg-yields are. He has had some training and easily steps to the side from my leg pressure. He also stops and then walks forward easily. I pick up the trot after a few minutes and put him through the same routine. He is placid enough not to get annoyed by my tests. His canter is ground covering, and he goes like he's on auto-pilot, without my needing to constantly leg him to maintain his pace. So far, very good.

"Let's start with the cross-rail at the trot," she shouts over the sound of his footfalls.

I see her pointing at the miniature X. It looks about a foot high, this will be a piece of cake. We trot up, and he flows over it.

"Good. Pick up the canter and try it again."

I come at the jump, but the striding isn't perfect.

"You were a little passive there. That's okay. It was a long spot, but you have to go with him."

Oh great. I messed up on a one-foot jump.

I continue around in a nice, rhythmic canter and try again. This time I shorten the reins and take more control, since she doesn't like passive riding.

"He was more determined there. You were more committed three or four strides out, and he felt that."

I jump this a bunch more times, each direction. My instructions are to come in straight and keep a steady rhythm.

"You don't have a good eye for distance," she scolds. Then a few moments later adds, "That's alright, only about ten percent of riders do." She modifies her comment to include almost everyone else.

I stand Clay next to her, to give him a little break while she explains what I didn't do well, and how to correct it. I don't make too many excuses. This is why I'm not a jumper, I suck at it.

A few minutes later she directs me to the two-foot turquoise, vertical fence.

"Come around to the right, and don't let him slow down."

We come in straight, and I apply more leg. A stride later he leaps it from way back. Yikes! I almost get left behind.

"You got behind the motion. Try it again, but don't rush him."

We circle around again and come in at a slower pace. He jumps it clean. It feels like heaven. This is fantastic!

"Very nicely done," she praises.

A few more jumps, many more corrections, and even a few compliments. That ends my first jumping lesson in fifteen years.

Clay gets hosed off and put away for a snack before my next lesson. It's been an easy 45 minutes for him. He used to be a talented show jumper who has been now relegated to school-master, for beginners. He can clear four feet, but the most he usually does is pop across a three-foot, hollow wall.

"You realize," Emma begins, "The obstacles you'll be jumping in the field will be solid. These in the arena fall down with a whisper of a touch."

"I've been told I'll be riding a well-trained horse."

"For your sake, I hope so." She looks at me sideways.

That doesn't sound good.

You can't claim she's complimenting me to make a few dollars.

In the shade, I munch on a granola bar and have a bottle of water. I'm fueled and ready for the second lesson. I used to lead three trail rides a day when I worked for Nikki, but this is a bit more stressful.

She's at it again. "You bumped him in the mouth. You need to be softer."

"Yikes, and I thought I could ride," I shout from across the ring.

"Try to shorten and lengthen his stride."

That's something I can do.

"Compress him before the jump. Get his hind legs under him."

We sail over the two-foot oxer: two vertical jumps pushed together to make it wider.

"Very nice there. Super. Nicely done," she sounds pleased.

That's a miracle.

"Tomorrow we'll continue where we left off," she tells me as we walk to the barn.

I dismount and lead Clay to the barn. He was a good boy and deserves to get my butt off his back, rather than ride every last step.

Emma untacks him and hoses him off, then puts him in a turnout in the shade. I join them, so I don't look like someone who rides the horse then leaves, and lets her do the work.

"You can go. Unless you want to watch the group lesson."

"Oh, they're next? I'll stay. Maybe I'll pick up something."

I get out of her hair, and find a bench by the arena to watch the teens ride for the next hour. Then I head home.

My brain is jammed full. I picked up a tidbit about staying back in the saddle until his front legs start leaving the ground. That makes sense, I don't want to get ahead of the movement. If he stopped or ran out, my arms would be wrapped around his neck. Not that Clay *ever* stops or runs out, but it's the best way to ride.

4

───

WEDNESDAY

My cell rings. It's Georgina Stamford. "How were your jump lessons today?" I'm keeping her in the loop with what I'm doing.

"Pretty good. I rode a good horse, and I remembered things I knew fifteen years ago."

"That's good," she pauses, "because we're moving the time-table forward." Why is it people say 'we' when they want backup for something unpleasant?

"How much forward?"

"Tomorrow."

"Whaat?" I screech.

"The hunt meets on Wednesdays and Saturdays. The landowner's BBQ will be this Saturday. You need to be there, and I want him to see you a few days prior. That way, he can warm up to the idea of a fresh piece of meat."

"I wish you'd told me it would be THIS Wednesday!" I'm getting uptight.

"It can't be helped. I looked at the wrong date." She doesn't apologize, but at least she explains why.

"Tomorrow?" Thank goodness I have Janet to do the morning work. I should be home by check-in.

"Be in Los Alamos at 9:00 AM. Call David and tell him you want to rent his horse. Look for the white Ford truck hauling a six-horse, gooseneck trailer. The farm name is on the side: David Reynolds Stables. I'll email you the information."

"Ok. I'll call him."

"Thank you." she sounds relived.

And I feel sick.

I make the call telling Mr. Reynolds I got his name from Abbie Johansen in Los Olivos. I'm using her name because Georgina wanted to stay out of it. The horse is mine for tomorrow.

* * *

I CAN'T SLEEP, anxiety is keeping me awake. Maybe a snack will help; something with crunch, such as crackers; crackers dipped in salsa; honey grahams; grahams with jam; and even a few sips of my home-made, very potent limoncello. Nothing is helping and now I have a stomach ache.

Finally, I open the book on foxhunting and become intrigued.

Beyond the outdated dress and etiquette, it looks like a fun time for the riders, the hounds, and maybe the coyote—if he's smart enough and fast enough. Since there aren't any sheep farms in the area, I hope he gets away. I'll only be there long enough to catch the cheating husband so it's doubtful I'll see the demise of Reynard.

The clothes are the same that I wear in horse shows. The stock tie, that I had a hard time learning how to precisely loop, has a reason for being; it's a bandage. Hopefully I won't need it. The pin that holds it in place should be horizontal, like a tie clip. The Master of Fox Hounds (MFH) and his staff get to wear the pin vertical. I think their swagger will also differentiate them. I used to pin mine half way between the two. It probably made me look like a drunk. I'll have to look at everyone's tie clips now.

Looking at the Santa Barbara Hunt website, I really shouldn't be intimidated. They look like a bunch of hunter/jumper riders, and some are even in jeans and rumpled polo shirts. Those must be the trail riders and gate monitors.

I click on a blog written by a gal who spent several weeks driving across the U.S., from hunt to hunt. She had some zany experiences; from a dilapidated B&B to the savory barbecue lunches. From galloping across the open vistas of Albuquerque, New Mexico to the vast, grass prairies of Kansas. What I come away with is that I wouldn't run my mares over that ground riddled with squirrel holes and volcanic chunks of rock. And while it's fun to see beautiful open space, I don't like what happens to the wild animals.

No, I don't have a reason to feel intimidated. Foxhunters are people who enjoy their horses. They like to gallop across the hills, and dress up in the morning only to be covered with mud and sweat by noon. They have to take care of their horses, hope they didn't hurt themselves, and drive home like everyone else. I've been-there, done-that in other riding sports.

I put down the book, flip my iPad closed, and get a few hours' sleep.

* * *

MY ALARM RINGS EARLY. I make my microwave breakfast of scrambled eggs and a chopped potato. It takes seven minutes in total. The carbs and protein should keep me going for a while.

To look the part, I'm wearing my beige breeches and a white cotton shirt, topped with a black hunt coat. Styles change from longer and looser, to shorter and tighter coats. This one is tight, and will show off my slim waist and bottom, as the horse and I fly over the jumps in front of him. Thankfully, he isn't one of the elite who ride with the hunt master at the front. If he were, he'd miss the view.

My breeches have a deerskin inlay that runs from my seat to my knees. I'll stay glued on anything that rears, bucks, or bolts. I'll also coat the saddle seat in saddle-stick, a resin sap. I won't become separated from my steed under any circumstances!

I put on my boots now, so I won't have to fuss with pulling them on if he's right there. I need to look the part from the minute I step from my freshly washed Ford dually—that I worked on until 9:00 last night.

It will take an hour and twenty-two minutes to get there. That's what Google Maps tells me. I hurry out the door feeling my breakfast sitting, undigested, in my stomach. Why doesn't stomach acid work through stress?

The drive is fast and very pretty. I'm watching my rear view mirror. There isn't a black SUV in sight. Here's the exit. It's the same one that leads to Quinn's compound about twenty miles away. The land is rolling; scattered with oaks; with farms and vineyards, and lots of open space.

I pull into the vineyard and park close to the other rigs. It looks like horse show parking with horses tied to trailers. People are hurrying around in riding boots, saddling horses, brushing tails, and putting protective boots on their horses' legs.

My truck fits in with the others, and has the bonus of being clean. I park, then head toward the four-horse trailer with David Reynolds Stables painted on the side. It looks workmanlike and clean.

That's David Reynolds with the gray gelding who I think is my ride.

"Hi, are you David—I'm Jess?" I ask in a friendly tone.

"Jess, it's nice to meet you." He steps toward me with his hand out.

He's a rugged man who spends long days in the sun. He doesn't have the middle-aged paunch of someone who sits in an office chair. His boots aren't new, but are polished. His clothes are clean and well worn. Georgina said he's an excellent rider and is a whipper-in (someone who rounds up the stray hounds and helps keep the pack together) he's been in the sport for over twenty years, and is well respected. I'm already impressed without seeing him ride.

"This is Ryan." He turns toward the 17.1-hand gray. "He'll take care of you."

"Thanks. I'm a good rider, but yesterday was my first jumping lesson in fifteen years."

"You'll be fine," his eyes flick down my clean, but obviously not new breeches; to my polished, but well used boots. He forms an opinion that I can ride. "I don't see a problem."

"Thanks." Good, I passed his initial appraisal. I'm not concerned about my riding—until I get to a three-foot coop.

He tells me about Ryan's breeding: he's an eleven-year-old Oldenburg out of his imported, German mare.

"Thank you for letting me ride him!" I see the substantial size of his legs and feet. They're strong enough to handle years of jumping. He is fit and well-built for the job.

"I know Abbie by reputation, I'm glad she referred you."

She didn't really, but she did refer Georgina Stamford to me. "She mentioned a few people to look for, one is Lyle Stamford."

"He is over there by the oaks, on the big bay." He nods toward Lyle.

"Does he ride at the front or the middle of the group?"

"It depends on who he's riding with."

"Abbie also mentioned someone named Roxy, where is she?" She's the one he's having the affair with.

"That's the woman on the Thoroughbred by the water trough." He points to a woman on a rangy, bay gelding.

She looks like she fits in, but I'll have to see how she acts around him. Is her attitude cute and perky, or sexy and seductive? I can either act the same, or be different, depending on how he reacts.

It's time to go. I lead Ryan to the mounting block. He quietly stands while I step into the stirrup. I touch his neck, "Good boy."

I wait for David Reynolds, then follow his horse. I'm supposed to ride behind the staff in the field. I'll go along until I can find someone to talk with in the back.

"Jessica Wilcox." He pulls his horse to a stop in front of a man in a red coat. He turns to me and continues, "Please meet the Master of Foxhounds, Mr. Jameson Royce."

"Hello, Mr. Royce. Thank you for letting me ride with you today."

He removes his helmet, courteously. "I'm glad you can join us, I hope you enjoy it."

Someone else in a red coat, called pink, rides up to speak with him. He replaces the helmet on his head which ends our introduction.

I follow David around as he introduces me to various people. And now we come to HIM. I recognize his horse first. A tall, strong, bay gelding with two hind socks. Georgina told me he'd stand out from the rest.

"Lyle, I'd like you to meet Jessica Wilcox. She is a life-long equestrienne, and owns a boutique bed and breakfast hotel on Moonstone Bay in Cambria," he sounds impressed.

That's interesting, he certainly conveys my resume with aplomb. Maybe this is a name-dropping club.

Lyle Stamford removes his helmet, revealing red hair streaked with gray. That, along with his chiseled, handsome jaw, and weathered skin give him the look of a confident adventurer. This sport compliments that lifestyle, and he's definitely a looker.

"Hello, Lyle." I smile and move my shoulder forward to shake his hand with my gloved one.

I notice David hasn't given me the details about Lyle, or that he is president of Stamford Heating. Either he is slightly snubbing him, or doesn't want me to be impressed, or because it doesn't matter who he is—we're all here to enjoy our horses at the fox hunt.

Lyle nudges his horse closer and smiles down at me. He's a tall man on a tall horse. He must like that.

"Hello there." I wonder if his resonant voice is meant to make me melt as he takes my hand.

"You have a nice looking horse." I put on my own silky spin on the words while looking directly in his eyes with a hint of a smile. Then I casually stroke my cheek, like I had flour on it. I'd stroke my neck, but this choker is wrapped tight, covering half the available area.

He reaches down to adjust the belt on his breeches. I think he's reacting to me.

The huntsman shouts, "Tally-Ho," and the first group, which includes David, takes off across the meadow. "The hounds picked up the scent," he shouts to me over his shoulder.

I'm left with Lyle—until his girlfriend literally trots over to join us. That says something, otherwise she'd have the horse walk over. She's wearing a tight polo shirt that emphasizes her large *attributes* and slim waist. She has a dark tan, and has a long, white-blonde ponytail draped across her shoulder.

If this is what he likes, I'm left out in the boobs department. Mine are nowhere near what she has, and I whacked off my long hair. That leaves me with fewer devices. I'll have to see where her flaws lie.

"We're off." He briefly looks at me once more, then nudges his horse into a trot to catch up with the second group. She doesn't look at me at all. I guess that means I'm not a threat in her mind. That blonde ponytail goes over her back and flies around behind her.

I feel overdressed in this coat. She's in a polo shirt, and I'm in this garb. Most of the others are in hunt coats, so I guess it's alright. Lyle is wearing a brown, tweed coat which makes him look like a Brit on a big-game hunt. Or maybe Indiana Jones.

This might actually be fun.

I fall in behind the others. Besides catching the cheater, I'll meet people and enjoy my time.

5
———

BEAUTIFUL COUNTRYSIDE

I'm trying to slide to the back of the group to let the eager riders pass me, but Ryan wants to go. I've shortened my reins, holding him back, but he's clearly telling me we're too slow, and we should move ahead. Sorry Ryan, I want to see how to approach the jumps and what the other riders do. We're not going first, we're going after everyone else does their thing.

The huntsman follows the hounds into a low area. The whippers-in don't have anything to do at the moment, he doesn't need to guide the pack in the right direction, because they are hot on the trail of a coyote. The pace is fast. The dogs are barking with what has become their music, but I don't hear it as such. I've seen too many thrillers where a man is trying to escape from a pack of baying hounds. The music builds our tension as we see him running, wildly looking over his shoulder; he stumbles and falls, but valiantly hobbles on a sprained ankle. The camera cuts back to the dogs pulling at their leashes, their handlers carrying shotguns and wearing plaid shirts, looking very back-woods and inbred. Cut to the man splashing through a stream while pulling off his shirt and throwing it in the bushes to throw them off his scent. We are left clinging to the hope he can lose his deadly, sick pursuers.

Nope, baying hounds isn't music. I don't know that I'll ever over-come that vision.

Back to reality, I'm one of the pursuers, not that it makes me happy. The second group of riders is now heading up a hill. I heard the guy in front of me saying the view will be great from up there. That's apparently what the second group does... we watch the first group, who closely follow the dogs.

So far, so good.

He's right. The view from up here is special. The dogs are down below, in empty acreage, but there are rows of grapevines to the south as it gets closer to the Los Olivos wine country. There are row after row of vines, looking like a patchwork quilt. The sun it warm, the breeze cool, and my horse is standing quietly next to the others as they watch the hunt progress.

We follow the ridge line on the fire-road. Everything is good. I've found another woman to follow. She's middle-aged and may be less of a dare devil.

To avoid a locked gate, the group changes direction, paralleling a barbed wire fence which crosses to another hill. I can still see the dogs milling in a patch of high brush and scrub-oak. Suddenly, the coyote bursts out, followed by the bloodthirsty pack, then the huntsman and his band of men. Then the second group.

"Come on," Lyle shouts as he takes off at a canter with *his friend* on his tail. I guess it's time to catch up. He's leading us down the hill—

Toward wood panels leaning against the barbed wire fence.

Ryan heads directly toward the coop—he already knows where we're going.

I replay my jumping instructor shouting at me to stay in my balanced position until I feel the horse's shoulders rise. Here goes! I'm up and over, landing and continuing onward at a canter.

I made it—that jump must have been three-feet high! I'm ecsta-tic. My deerskin seat, resin, and riding ability kept me in the saddle. Plus Ryan is a marvelous horse.

What a rush. No wonder people love this.

I'm cantering along, way at the back, but slightly ahead of the old and befuddled who are only trotting. I'll move up as I feel more secure, but there's no reason to push it and end up in the emergency room. I'll take it jump by jump. I may move back to the trail riders and open and close the gates.

So far, Lyle and his woman have left me in the dust. I see them standing with the big group in the distance.

Most important to me, we're coming to another jump, a fallen oak. I could skirt around it but I can see the huntsman has called a halt to forward progress. The two groups are milling around and some are watching me as I come in with the last of the riders. It's gone quiet; they lost the coyote; the group is waiting for the pack to pick up the scent.

Back to the log—Ryan pricks his ears, he wants to take it. I think I can. It's about three-feet, round and solid. I can do this.

I close my fingers on the reins as he wants to increase speed, but I let him pick his spot. He leaves the ground, I lean forward, give him the reins, and yippee—another clear jump. And it felt effortless.

David Reynolds is standing with the first group, but he heads over to me as soon as I come down to a walk. "You're doing okay?"

"Yes—he's a wonderful horse," I reach down to stroke Ryan's neck. He pricks his ears forward at my touch.

"He has a long history in the sport. My daughter successfully hunted him on the east coast for several years. Then she moved him into the show ring. He did well there too, since he is steady and consistent. Unfortunately, he hasn't been ridden as much as I'd like. Would you like to keep him tuned up?

"You're suggesting I ride him more than just a few times?"

"You're a good rider; you kept him balanced over the oak. He was getting strong, but you held him in just right."

"Thank you. I'd like to ride him again." For as long as Georgina is paying me to risk my life.

Roxy squeals in laughter, bringing attention to herself. David glances at the two, "She's hot for him. You may want to stay away." He pulls out his small silver flask of brandy. "When the hounds check, it's time for a swig. This is a fun part of the ride." He unstraps it from his waist and goes to hand it to me.

"Ah, thanks, but I'd better pass. I need to keep my wits for this game."

So he knows something about Lyle and the bimbo, it's obvious the way she's posing and laughing that she's making use of her feminine wiles.

"Come on, Ryan, let's poke our noses where they don't belong." I direct him toward Lyle.

The girl has turned her horse away and has moved into the shade. Lyle is taking a gulp of his brandy. Strangely, his tweed coat looks at fresh as when he put it on this morning. How do some people do that?

I make sure to show how excited I am after flying over that jump. "That was a blast. It beats riding in the arena any day of the week!" I'm grinning and happy—acting much more than I usually would.

He gives me a long, slow smile. "I saw you clear the oak. You're good."

That's a lie. I'm not good, but he's flirting.

"Thanks, but I can't take all the credit. The horse makes me look good," I share the compliment like a good horseman should.

"Aren't you a doll," he takes another quick swig.

"I've seen you from the back. You have a good seat." My comment has a double meaning.

"I wish I could say the same. Maybe you should ride up here with me."

"That's sounds exciting." I do something dumb. I cross my right leg over the saddle, and hook it over the horse's withers. Now it looks like I could be riding side saddle. It's very casual and sexy—as long as Ryan doesn't move too fast and make me fall off.

"You've been riding for a while." He notices my leg, as he replaces the cap on the flask.

"Since I was a kid. How about you?"

"After I became company president it freed up my time. Now I can ride the entire hunt season." He removes his helmet, places it in front of him, and runs his hands through this lush hair. Yes, he still has it, and it looks good. And he knows it. How many balding guys have ever removed their caps to run their hand through a few strands? None.

"You have a nice head of hair," I comment with a breathless tone.

"Lyle!" The bimbo jogs her horse up to him. "I need a drink," she huffs, arching her back, and placing one hand on her hip. This emphasizes her goods.

"Roxy, you've had plenty. You don't want to ride drunk," he lectures.

"Please," she whines. "I'm so very thirsty. You know how exercise makes me glow." She pulls the white ponytail over her shoulder and strokes it.

Is there anything I can do to out-perform this Roxy show? I don't think so.

"Here." He pulls it off his waist. "Keep it for a while."

She reaches for it by leaning over and arching more. "Thanks honey. I just need to wet my lips."

Damn, she's good. I glance at his face. He seems to reacting in a predictably male way.

I can't do anything to top this. I'm too new to his world. So I sit quietly to watch and learn.

There is a yell from the whipper-in causing the hunt master to shout, "Tally-Ho" as he bursts after the hounds. The rest of the staff are hot on his tail. I swing my leg back where it should be. Lyle tells Roxy to keep the booze, and he takes off at a canter. He isn't waiting for her. Huh. That's something.

I briefly consider befriending her. Can I possibly get any information from her? Or should I try to get him on my own? All I need is proof he's cheating. It doesn't have to be with me. Roxy will do fine.

She's strapping the flask around her waist. I hold Ryan back, and say, "This is my first time hunting. I guess I need to bring something to wet my whistle next time."

She looks at me, then deliberately turns her head and abruptly kicks the horse into a trot.

"So much for that," I mutter to the only ears that are listening to me—Ryan's.

It's time to move up my game. I'll stay closer to those two. It means more jumps. I lived through two. Let's see what happens next.

The scent must be strong, because the pack is in full cry. I only know it is full cry rather than just barking because another rider grinned and said that. I hope the coyote is a smart one. I certainly won't be hanging around for the kill. Someone in charge, decades or a century ago, changed the word from kill, maim, or destroy to "break up, or chop the fox." They sound disgusting when you know what they mean.

I understand there may be a need for population control of coyotes, feral boars, or foxes, but I don't want any part of the process. And it looks so elitist to be riding in scarlet hunt coats. Like the wealthy Brits used to do while stomping through the farmer's fields. Things have changed since those days. Now the local hunt riders are careful to go around planted crops. They maintain the jumps and make sure all gates are left the way they were found: either open, or closed.

Maybe I have read too many historical romance books about scullery maids and the household staff laboring hard for the gentry. England in the 1930's was still entrenched in the class system. "She doesn't know her place," and "She's getting above herself," are two phrases that my grandmother heard. I'm glad I'm a twenty-first century woman in the U.S.

After another jump, I think I can handle the three-foot coops. People say that height is inviting. I guess so, if I'm on Ryan.

Lyle and Roxy are several yards in front of me. I've been moving up; not blasting by, but carefully passing people after I've been riding with them for a few minutes. My confidence is growing, as is my trust in the training and ability of my horse.

The group canters to the top of another hill while the hunt master pushes through the undergrowth, following his dogs through the canyon. Up here, we have a spectacular view. There's no doubt we're in wine country, with rolling vineyards planted in precise rows around a few centurion oak trees. I am so privileged to be here! I hope it takes a while to get the dirt on Lyle. It won't be a hardship except for the drive.

It's a grand adventure worthy of any European world trips. I don't remember the name, but a trip a wealthy young man would take before settling down to the family business. Oh that's right, it's called the grand tour.

Well, it doesn't get any grander than this.

Thankfully for the coyote, he got away; apparently that isn't unusual.

After three hours of seeing the countryside by horseback, the master announces it is lunch time. I haven't had another chance to speak with Lyle. Hopefully I'll get it over potluck.

I walk along with David for the fifteen minute ride back to his trailer. It's important to show everyone I've been accepted by one of the top riders. It's who-you-know that counts, and I want to be able to chat and be accepted during my investigation.

"What have you said about me to the rest of the group?" I inquire.

"I haven't said anything. They know you're on my horse, but it isn't unusual to have someone ride him."

"Would it help my assimilation if they thought I was more of a friend than just a casual acquaintance?"

"Like a girlfriend"

"No, no. I just hate to be seen as a newbie."

"What do you have in mind?"

"To give myself more cache, maybe I could be a friend, someone with standing in your esteemed opinion."

He laughs. "That takes a while, but I can pretend." He reconsiders, "You ride pretty well for never doing this before. So maybe it won't be that hard."

"Thanks for the compliment and for moving me up in your faux ranking system."

He laughs.

I like making a man laugh, it means I got through his armor, unless it's a fake laugh. I don't know which one this is, but everyone else will think I'm humorous and charming; except Roxy. She and Lyle are a few horse lengths behind us. I hope I scored points with Lyle by getting David to laugh.

Before we get to the trailers, I jump off Ryan and loosen the girth. I've been in the saddle for three hours. His back needs to cool down before I strip off the saddle, exposing it to the air. No one else is doing this. Well, I guess their boots aren't made for walking. That puts that song in my mind. The one by Nancy Sinatra. Ha—Boots, get walking.

We tie up at David's trailer. I hope this is it for the day. I'd rather not spend another few hours in the saddle. I'd like to go home and check my business.

"Did you bring anything for lunch?"

"Yes, I was told about the potluck." I make sure not to say Georgina told me.

He strips the saddle from his horse, so I do the same. I brush the dried sweat from Ryan's sleek, shaved coat. It wouldn't be possible to ride a horse for hours, jumping and galloping in a shaggy winter coat.

A few minutes later, we're converging on the picnic area with our ice chests. I brought five packs of fancy cheese from the shop in town. I've already sliced them and have boxes of crackers. I made sure to bring high-end cheese to show my class, or my pretend-class. I buy the cheap stuff for myself and that's probably wrong.

At the table, I strip off the plastic covers from my plates. I've labeled each one, to be sure everyone knows what they are. Then I fan out the crackers.

This is a standing brunch. There are a row of tables enough for the bowls and platters, but the only chairs are if you brought your own. Some riders did, but others didn't.

There are bowls of cut fruit. There are also sandwiches on little buns. Salads, and beans, chips and dip. Thirty people may eat a lot, but we all bring a lot.

I hadn't planned on staying glued to David's side, but it's working out alright. He's mingling well, and I'm getting to meet those who rode in the first group. With a full plate of everything I normally don't eat for fear of gaining weight, I tag along.

Most of us have removed our hunt attire: the coats, definitely our helmets, and some of us, our boots. David kept his boots on, so I am as well. Roxy has hers off and is wearing flip-flops. I guess she won't be dealing with her horse after lunch. And her hair is perfect. It looks like she wasn't wearing a helmet for three hours.

Mine is mid-neck length; so I fluffed it with wet hands, and then scrunched it to make curls. I like my fun and wild short haired look.

As we get close to the couple, I notice she's pouting. It turns into a scowl as she stabs at the fruit on her paper plate.

"Hey Lyle, how's that air-conditioner working in your trailer?" David asks.

"It's good. My horses travel in comfort. It's my business, I can hardly let them sweat on a hot day, now can I?" He chuckles and takes a swig from his flask. He must have finished eating and has moved on in the festivities.

"Jessica, what do you think of the hunt, is it everything you thought?" he politely asks.

"I love it. What a great way to see the wine country, on the back of a cantering horse!"

"It's in my blood, twice a week, rain or shine," he holds up his flask as if to say "cheers."

"I might consider it, but I have a business to run in Cambria."

"You mean your hotel?"

"That's the short version." I pause and change my tone to one of pride. "I own five boutique cottages on Moonstone Beach. Nearly every night I get full occupancy. It's a lot of fun, in a beautiful location." I know I'm glowing with happiness. I'm in love with my job, and being on the craggy beach on the central coast gives me major bragging rights.

"I don't like Cambria. There's nothing to do," Roxy snips, while nibbling on a tiny piece of watermelon.

"Some people are better suited for Disneyland." I accidentally give her a sorrowful look.

The men look about ready to pop, holding in their laughter. In fact, Lyle does burst. He bends over and slaps his thigh. "You got that right!" He is smiling like I said something amazing.

She spins and walks off in a huff.

He looks over his shoulder and shrugs.

"I'm sorry," I actually sound sorry, but I'm not. She's a snippy, skinny creature having an affair with a married man.

The conversation moves on and I join in where I can. I'm trying to sound both fun, and intelligent at the same time. It takes some work to pull off. It's all timing. Knowing when to make a comment and where to put the emphasis. It's also a game I can lose if they don't like me.

David likes me, or maybe he likes the fun, so he's encouraging my antics. Lyle keeps sipping his brandy, ensuring that I'll sound funnier by the minute. You gotta love alcohol, I'm sure the comedians do.

Brunch winds down. Everyone packs up their food and supplies. Horses are loaded in the trailers, heading for home.

For my first time foxhunting, I'm overjoyed by how well it went. David made it smooth and enjoyable, and his help was invaluable.

When I arrive home I type up the report. I'm not immediately sending it to Georgina, but it's ready to substantiate what I did today.

Everything is quiet at the homestead. Before bed, I sit on the window seat, with my knees up, leaning against the wall. The window is open, letting in the sound of crashing waves. It's clear tonight, making sound carry. When I first moved here, I didn't like the incessant waves, but now I feel it's a constant in my life. They will always be here, something I can depend on.

I'm watching the road. There aren't any cars creeping past, specifically not a black SUV turning in my driveway.

But I haven't heard from Quinn. What's up with that? I'm on my own. I can handle it, I always do. It goes to show, I shouldn't get too comfortable relying on a man.

6

MIA CHECKS IN

I wake with the same thoughts about Quinn as when I went to sleep. I'm not as annoyed, but I have questions. Was another one of his Russian enemies driving that SUV?

Where is he, and why haven't we been as close as we had been? I'm upset that he took a government job in the Middle East, or somewhere. Or he didn't go anywhere. Over the past week I've been replaying and analyzing his words. All because he softly said the Russians won't come after me again. He didn't elaborate and allowed the subject to change.

So why was he landing at the air force base as if he was returning from a mission? If he 'took care' of them, he wouldn't have flown anywhere because they're supposedly thirty miles from here, in jail.

I'm no fool, so I made a call to inquire with Detective Taylor. He said the two brutes held in the local FBI building were transferred to a different federal facility, pending trial. I asked what kind of other facility, since they're already at the FBI building. He looked into it but couldn't get answers.

"I reached a dead end. I don't know where they went after they left Santa Maria," he reports.

"Hmm. And what about Mikhail Dedkov, is he still in the hospital?"

"After he stabilized, he was also sent to the FBI building in Santa Maria. And it's the same thing, he's been transferred out. I spoke with their investigator and was told it's classified."

"I hope that doesn't mean they're having a good-old-time in the Greek islands. I heard he has a yacht there."

"I don't know what to tell you. I'm at an impasse. My contact at the bureau hasn't seen this before."

"Thanks. Hopefully this means they're out of my hair for a while." I try to make their transfer sound like a good thing, instead of unsettling.

"I hope so." He pauses, "So how's it going with you?"

"I'm alright. I've been looking into a cheating husband who rides to the hounds. I went on my first hunt yesterday."

"Sounds interesting."

"Fortunately I stayed on the horse, and the coyote got away. So my day ended well."

"Give me a call sometime, okay?" He uses his unofficial tone.

"Thanks. I might do that." I smile, because this is a 'round-about way of asking me out. I'm the one who called, but he's suggesting I call him for personal reasons.

This brings be back to what Q said, "They won't come after you again."

Does this mean they're deep in the bowels of Guantanamo Bay, or that it's on a need to know basis, and the FBI investigator wasn't in the loop?

I'll ask him, otherwise I may never know; but I'll only ask by whispering it on the beach, where we can't be overheard; not by phone, text, or email. It will give him a chance to tell me the truth. It may not even be clandestine. They may have been specially transferred to a facility for enemy-of-state assholes.

It doesn't mean Quinn took them out by hand. He would have had help. You don't walk into an FBI facility, kill three Russians in a cell, and then invisibly walk out.

* * *

By afternoon check-in I'm desperate to speak with a normal guest. I've had enough of cheating husbands, dangerous Russian operatives, and a boyfriend who is always doing something secretive. It's a bit overwhelming. And, yes, I do believe he's truthful about working for the government, and I know it's our government. But there are other parts of our government that are less than friendly. The FBI is one thing, but he could be deeper by going to other countries as a "contractor" or he may be recalled to the Army. It can get down-right frightening, like the CIA. I don't like that part. People don't make it to old age in that job, and that includes their family, and friends —*and me!*

I'm expecting Mia Huntington to arrive anytime. From what she told me, I know she is an art major at UCLA and is doing independent study on Hearst Castle. I'm not sure what the art angle is, but there is plenty of it on that hill. Everything from the magnificent Spanish castle and guest houses, to the paintings. What I like best are the swimming pools—who isn't impressed with the Neptune pool?

She's prompt—which is unusual, since she drove straight through from L.A.

"Whew, that's a long trip." She rolls her suitcase through the open French doors. "Especially through Santa Barbara. It slowed to about 2 miles-an-hour." She leans her elbows on the counter and takes a deep breath.

"I know, that's a bad stretch," I commiserate.

"On a good note, I didn't get a ticket when I stomped on the gas for the rest of the trip," she laughs.

"You're lucky." I wonder how fast she was going. Oh well, that isn't my problem anymore.

"Neh, I just pull up my skirt and flash some leg," she chuckles, "that always works on the boys in blue."

That wouldn't have worked with one of my partners. He loved to write those tickets; it made his day.

"I haven't tried that," I reply, straight-faced.

"You're cute enough, take it from me, it'll work for you too." She smiles knowingly.

"Do you cry?" No one did that to me. Of course, they were probably pissed off to get a female officer.

"No tears, but I have a wide range, from innocent to seductive. I only have a few seconds to figure out which type of guy he is."

"I bet you're good at reading people."

"The best." She grins. "My little red Carrera likes to go fast, so I get a lot of practice."

She's a bundle of fun. I can appreciate her even though I'm 180 degrees the opposite. I don't drive 125 mph, nor do I come from a fantastically wealthy family. She's taking art classes at a top university because she doesn't know what else to do, and her parents insisted she get a bachelor's degree from UCLA if she wants to keep the car.

"Come on, I'll walk you to your room." I pick up the card keys and wave her out the door.

"This is a cute place. The only reason Mom let me come is because your reviews are good and you passed her sniff-test. She watches me like a hawk."

I can't help but ask, "Do you need watching?"

"Well." She ponders for a moment. "Yes. I did some crazy things when I was young."

That cracks me up. She's twenty-one now, so I'd still call her young. I'm not going to pry, but her mother phoned a few days ago to see if I would keep an eye on her daughter. I didn't agree to be a chaperone, but I said I'd be watchful around the cottages. There are a few bars in town, so if she's in the mood, she might play. I told her mother that too.

"So you're going to Hearst Castle tomorrow?" I change the subject.

"Yeah. I have to find something that catches my eye. I have five essays I need to write this coming quarter. You see, the professor is a sweetie, he'll give me an A if I try hard and include lots of pictures. My friend just took his class and told me the secrets." She steps into the room as I unlock the door. "Hey, this is adorable. It looks like dear old Mom picked right," she sounds pleased.

"Thanks. You can leave the windows open at night if you want to hear the ocean." I push aside the sheer white curtain to show her the locking mechanism. "No one can slide through this. Plus I have surveillance outside."

"Uh huh, that would make Mom happy. Our place is a fortress." She looks around the room, "I like how it's decorated, very beachy." She nods her approval.

"Thanks. I live on the property, up at the front, across from the Garden cottage. If you need anything, call or knock on my door."

"Okay, will do." She lugs her suitcase onto the bedspread. I cringe as the wheels leave a dark mark on the material.

She doesn't say anything, or maybe she doesn't notice.

"If you want to eat out, here's a book with a ton of places." I touch it, but keep talking. "I have my favorites, depending if you want fine dining, burgers, seafood… there's a varied selection."

Her phone dings with a text. She looks at it. "I should get this."

That's my signal to go. "Have a good afternoon." I step outside and close the door.

What do I think of the girl? I don't have an opinion beyond that she seems a bit entitled; but that's what you get when you rent a room for $250 a night. I'm not complaining.

I haven't even made it to the bend in the path when I hear her shouting at someone on the phone. "I never want to see you again. Don't you dare come up here."

Oh great, problems with a boyfriend or girlfriend, I can't tell which. This may get messy if she is loud tonight.

Her mother hinted that Mia is a handful. I hope she doesn't become *my* handful.

* * *

THE PROBLEM with being a light sleeper is I wake at the slightest sound. This time it's the whine of a Porsche downshifting from racing speed to idle. She has to go slowly across the dip where Moonstone Beach Drive meets my driveway. She accelerates to her parking space by her cottage, and then breaks hard.

Okay, maybe I'm nosy, or call me inquisitive. I roll out of bed and take a few steps to the security closet. I'll see what I can gather from her evening on the town lasting into the wee hours of the morning. My system is good enough that I can clearly see her in a short skirt, tiny top, and high heels. But she isn't alone. She seems to have picked up a handsome guy. He joins her at the front of the car and grabs her hips as they hurry to Pine cottage.

Young love. So much for studying art. I hope she closes her windows to keep the noise in.

I'm up at 7:00 a.m. The sky is getting light, but winter sun isn't as demanding as in the summer. I see Janet's car in the lot. Good, I won't have to make breakfast for the guests. Five rooms means at least ten people, if Mia wants her overnight guest to eat too. I'm not a bed and breakfast owner because of my love of cooking and cleaning. I inherited Greenstone Cottage from my grandmother. I like real estate, owning a business, and especially the location directly across the street from Moonstone Beach. I can't think of a nicer beach, and that includes miles of white sand in the tropics. I like our green beach stones and volcanic rock. It's a rugged and invigorating coast.

I cruise into the lounge and adjoining kitchenette to find Janet making the cottage fries and chopping fresh fruit for our breakfast layout.

"I thought I'd make French toast. I got the bug after watching a cooking show last night," she says, while slicing strawberries.

"That sounds delicious. I'll go for a run then come back and have a slice." I grab a berry, "Thanks. I appreciate your creativity in the kitchen!"

"I like to try new things," she reaches over to stir the potatoes.

"I couldn't be happier. I hope you know that." I look at her with a serious expression.

"Yes, you make that clear every day," she chuckles.

"Good. Okay, off I go. Let me know if anything goes right or wrong!"

Huh, there's that handsome guy from Mia's room waiting at the driveway. I mill around for a few moments until a car pulls up and he gets in the back seat. He's probably getting a ride back to the bar for his car. Wow, that's certainly a one-night-stand.

For a while, I was only jogging eastward, to avoid Mandy Crawford's fancy resort two hotels west of mine. But now I'm running right in front of her resort, not even on the boardwalk across the street. I'm deliberately letting myself be seen. Though Mandy is never here at this hour. But still, it makes me feel better that I'm no longer in hiding.

With Phil Crowne's death at her resort, Evan the roofer's involvement, and the listening device she planted in my office, she can hardly say I'm a bad member of the community. But that's exactly what she's saying and surreptitiously causing trouble. I'm trying to get her to make the wrong move, then I'll nail her with evidence, and hopefully make her look like the fool.

Mia meanders into the lounge at 10:45. "Jess, where's breakfast—I just got up?"

"We serve breakfast from 7:30 until 10:00. I can get you some cut fruit, but Janet isn't in the kitchen any longer." And I'm not going to make eggs, potatoes and French toast.

"Well darn it." She looks at me expectantly.

I keep a bland look on my face. "I suggest the French bakery in town or stop by the market on Main. They make a very nice soup of the day." I smile indicating that's my answer.

She pouts. "But I have a tour at Hearst Castle at noon. I won't have time."

"Hearst has wonderful food. You'll be fine."

"All right," she sighs. "Hey, um. If you see a guy hanging around, he shouldn't be here."

My eyebrows shoot up. "Hanging around," I repeat. I find it's best to repeat rather than guess whether she means a stalker, an ex-boyfriend, or that guy from last night.

"Yeah, he won't leave me alone." She puts her hand on her hip in annoyance.

I get the feeling she likes to get people worked up, but I won't play. "Would you care to elaborate?"

"I'm doing a little house cleaning. My ex-boyfriend refuses to believe I don't want him anymore."

"Does he know you're here?"

"Yeah, I think so. He said he would be taking me to dinner tonight."

"In Beverly Hills or in Cambria?"

"He didn't say, but he told me to dress warm."

"That could be anywhere—even Alaska," I joke a bit.

"You're right. He may fly me up there for fresh salmon."

"Seriously? That's like flying your live-in up to see the total eclipse of the sun." I almost sing the lyrics.

"Maybe I should find out." She pulls out her phone and speaks into the text, "Where do you plan on taking me?"

She's intently watching the screen, but he doesn't reply within a few seconds. She looks up and says "See ya," and flounces out of the office. A few minutes later, I hear her red Porsche zip down the driveway.

Yes, she's a wild one.

I stay busy all afternoon, not thinking about Mia and her ex-boyfriend. Until I get a call on my cell.

"Jess, I'm in trouble!" It's Mia, breathless.

"What's wrong?" I'm ready to jump into action.

"My car won't start," she wails.

Oh. It's safe to slow my heart rate. "Have you called a tow truck?"

"Not really."

"Who is the insurer?"

"I don't know, it's in my phone. Do you think I should call them?"

"Yes. I don't know anything about cars. Maybe he can see if it's the battery."

"Okay, I'll call them and call you right back." She clicks off.

And this girl is on her own? I guess she'll be learning a few things.

I don't hear anything, so thirty minutes later I call her. "How's it going?"

"The guy says the battery is fine. There's something wrong with the electrical system. He's loading it on a truck to take to a mechanic in Cambria."

"I don't think we have Porsche mechanics." That's too specialized for this town.

"His brother knows cars."

"Okay." She's letting his brother tinker with her $90,000 car? "Have you called your mother?"

"No, that's why I'm calling you. She'll freak out and make me come home," she explains.

"I suggest calling her to let her know the car is having problems, but you're fine, and handling it. Maybe you can rent another, or get a ride service to take you around? She'll probably be upset if you let an unauthorized mechanic touch it."

"You're probably right. I better call her right now. Bye."

* * *

At BEDTIME, after watching the surveillance video, I take a walk through the complex of five cottages. The Garden cottage, which contains the office and lounge, is secure. I feed the outside cats a snack. There's a buzzing sound somewhere around here I can't identify. It's above the tall Monterrey pine trees. It doesn't sound like bees, it sounds mechanical. The electric lines are on the east side, but they aren't making any sound. Oh bother, I hope it isn't something requiring maintenance.

I send Mia a text to make sure she's okay. She replies she got a rental, and her car is in the shop in Paso Robles. She's listening to live music at a dive bar. Fine, now I can go to bed without worrying that I should have advised her.

"Is your ex-boyfriend with you?" I remember to ask.

"No way. I'm with the locals."

7

LANDOWNER'S BRUNCH

It's early Saturday morning. I'm gulping down a breakfast of protein and carbs so I'll have enough energy to gallop up and down hills for hours on end. I'm heading to Santa Ynez for another day of endangering my life. I'm being facetious, I mostly feel okay on Ryan. He kept me safe just like Georgina Stamford said he would.

These days, hunt clubs are aware their freedom to gallop across thousands of acres could be taken away by the landowners without notice. So the riders are very careful to observe all rules and to keep their footprint as light as possible. Twice a year, the club sponsors a landowner's brunch to show their appreciation. Today, we're having one; it's like an upscale potluck.

They said to bring something that goes with the holidays, so I'm bringing limoncello cake. I asked David how much to bring, and was told fifty people had RSVP'd. That's a lot of baking. Uh, it would be, except I bought three pound cakes at the French bakery in town, then poured my homemade limoncello over the top. To say it has alcohol is putting it mildly; it's swimming in the stuff.

I taste a slice and instantly feel the wonderful, calming effect of the lemony goodness. If someone doesn't, that makes more for me to bring home. Germs won't survive the high percentage of alcohol.

And if a fly lands on it, oh well, I'll live. That's why I have an immune system, I have to give it something to do. Like the saying goes, "use it or lose it."

Maybe.

I have my .45 tucked under my leg. I'll be ready if someone tries to run my truck off the road. I doubt they'll try, unless they're in an 18-wheeler.

The traffic is light at this hour, so I'm able to enjoy the scenery along the coast, past Morro Bay with its round volcanos. Then inland through the rolling hills of San Luis Obispo. I love this part of the country! The communities along the way are small and touristy because of the natural beauty.

I exit the freeway and drive past rolling hills snaked with groves of oaks. It's such beautiful, open land, but if I wanted to own a chunk, it wouldn't be an option. The price is high, even out here, miles from the nearest town.

The posted sign reminds me the worker's entrance is a few yards ahead. I drive slowly to limit the dust next to the building that houses the wine presses, tanks, and bottling equipment. There's David's rig, under the oaks. He parks there to capture the afternoon shade. I pull up next to him. I'm keeping up appearances with my truck. I'm not driving the Subaru to this foxhunters' party.

It's promising to be a warm day, but I'm wearing a form-fitting spandex riding shirt. I love the zipper because it looks like a snaffle bit which I have suggestively lowered to reveal a few inches of my long neck. And I'm absolutely not wearing a running bra. The last thing I need is to smash and compress what Roxy is enhancing. The shirt is holding in my body heat, but the style sure makes me look sexy. I'm already sweating at 9:00 a.m., but if that's what I have to do to catch the roving eye of Lyle Stamford, then I'll suffer.

Ryan is relaxing at the trailer, already saddled. David has his foot propped up on the running board, buffing his riding boot to a brilliant shine. Mine are already dusty by the time I get to the horse.

"Good morning, David." I grin. "I could get used to this service. I just show up and my horse is already saddled."

He leans toward me and whispers, "I had a chat with Abbie about you. You're a good little rider, you've already impressed a few people here."

"Thanks for telling me. It makes me feel better." So he checked me out with Abbie. I guess he wants to know who is renting his horse.

We mount up and join the mass of anxious riders. Today is a popular ride. The crowd is double what we had on Wednesday.

The horn toots three times—signifying something.

"They're searching the covert," David translates.

I'm anxious too—about big jumps, and seeing the coyote killed by blood-thirsty hounds. I won't be close enough to watch, but I bet the pack will be loud and boisterous. Maybe the riders too? But maybe not. Most people who ride love animals. I may find out today if my theory is correct or not.

"Tally-Ho!" shouts the hunt master.

Half the group bursts into a flat-out gallop. What the hell, don't they warm up first?

Ryan is pushing past a lot of other horses. I thought he was too big to be this fast.

This isn't at all like Wednesday. That was tame, this is insane.

About twenty of us are charging toward a six-foot wide obstacle. How are we all going to fit? Actually, there are two jumpable areas with panels set up as four-foot high "chicken coops" across the barbed wire. Holy shit. I'm going to die right here.

I don't have the ability to do anything. I can't turn him away, or slow him down. I am in the middle of a tight bunch of crazy riders intent on getting there first. I hope my horse is as athletic as he is competitive. I do my best to maintain his balance, but he insists he knows more than I do.

Ryan noses between two others so we get there first. He sails over the jump. It comes and goes beneath us in a flash—not that I looked down. You never look down. Always focus on the next obstacle, because you're upon it faster than you'd think.

It almost felt like he didn't jump, he just sailed across, in a slight arc. He lands further out than the rest, and increases his speed, now we are almost on the tail of the first group. I'll be in trouble if we invade the elite crowd.

Thank goodness for my deerskin breeches and sticky resin; I'm secure in the saddle. My confidence is growing, though I'm still afraid of coming upon something gnarly.

The ground slopes downward, going into a canyon. I bring my shoulders back and tug on the reins to rate his speed. I'm used to riding my chestnut mare who stumbles, and is always looking twice at things which frighten her. But Ryan isn't Juliette. He rounds his back, tucks his haunches under himself, and is as balanced as if he were on the flat ground. This horse is amazing.

If we were galloping, this trail would be more dangerous. So I slow to a trot to navigate around the low hanging tree limbs without getting my head knocked off.

He leaps a seasonal stream, almost unseating me. I thought he'd splash through it, but I guess not.

The leader of my group canters to the top of the hill so we can have a view of the hounds working through the vineyard. It's easy to see the scarlet coats of the master and whippers-in as they follow the pack.

The barking is at a distance, but still annoying. Um, I mean the cry of the hounds is music to my ears.

The rest of the group has caught up with us front-runners. Including Lyle and Roxy.

"Good riding," he compliments with just two words.

"Thanks. That was fun." I grin at him.

We're watching the pack move around the hill, following the small canyon. There's no need to go anywhere at this point. Lyle whips out his flask and takes a sip, then recaps it and lets it slide back into place. He's getting in the spirit, but I think DUI on a horse is also a crime. I knew what it was when I worked in Shadow Hills. That's a part of the San Fernando Valley where a lot of drugstore cowboys had houses with horse-property. They'd ride to the local bar and drink for a few hours while their horses stood patiently tied to the hitching rail.

Roxy moves her horse between us and briefly glares at me before turning her back and saying something to Lyle that I can't hear.

It's obvious she's intimidated by me. Does that mean she's on shaky ground with him, or that she's too new in their relationship, or maybe she's just the jealous type? It may not have anything to do with me.

I also turn away, and pretend to watch the hounds. I can't chase him; men like to pursue. See how much they enjoy chasing the poor coyote.

But they destroy it when they catch it. I wonder if that has any significance.

Good—they lost the scent. Their barks changed timbre. From up here, I can see the stream with the sycamore trees growing in the dampest part. The coyote must have been smart enough to escape through the water.

The imbibers pull out their flasks and visibly relax while the men and women in scarlet coats follow separate groups of hounds on a mission to find their prey once again. *Take your time.*

I find someone to talk with about the hunt and horses. It's quite nice on our hill, watching the scene below; it's like being on a trail ride, kind of. For me, it's stressful running and jumping. I'd rather ride with the old-folks at the back. Or maybe not. I certainly wouldn't catch Lyle Stamford's eye if I did. I'm sure he likes the chase, and while I'm out front, he's sort of chasing me.

Damn, they found the coyote. The hounds change their bark, a shout goes up, and we're off again. This time I'm following Lyle and the bimbo. Closely watching him, I see he rides well. He demonstrates that at the barbed wire fence at the bottom of the hill. Roxy sails over it too. I'm next, but Ryan takes off earlier than I was expecting, leaving me to the whims of fate. The only thing keeping me on is my death-grip on the reins. Yes, I know, reins are for steering, not for balance. Sorry Ryan.

The hunt goes on and on, jump after jump. I'm either behind

them, hoping to learn something by watching them, or I'm in front —to show Lyle my ass. Yup, that's what I've been told. Some of the men like watching women jump so they can see their behinds. It must be a nuisance for men to be so full of testosterone it gets them hot seeing that.

Finally, it's time for lunch. The coyote escaped once more. I don't know the ratio of catches to escapes, but this is a good day for me. It's a scene I am happy to miss.

I find two women to ride with as we head back to the trailers.

"That guy Lyle is nice looking. Is he married to the woman who's glued to his side?" I casually inquire.

"No he's married to someone else. I've only seen her a couple of weeks. She's chasing him."

"Oh, too bad. A good looking man who rides is a plus in my book," I laugh.

"I know what you mean. My husband lets me do what I want, but he never gets on a horse."

Roxy has only been here for a couple of weeks. She obviously rides well enough to stay up with him. Maybe he met her somewhere else. I guess that's all I know for now.

At the trailer, I sponge off Ryan with liniment in a bucket of water, making him smell like wintergreen. When David is ready to go to lunch I go get my cakes on their glass plater and follow him.

It will be under the oaks. It's already crowded with riders setting their casseroles and platters on the serving tables. There is going to be a ton to eat, and I will be sampling most of it. Tomorrow I can diet, today I'll splurge!

It's festive with white tablecloths that have printed borders of green wreaths and pine cones. Each table has two small pots of poinsettia and ornaments that besides being festive, also stop them from flying away. It would be a disaster if a table cloth swept toward a horse like a flapping ghost.

I head down the food line, passing chafing dishes of turkey and ham. Someone even brought homemade boar sausage from when they got a feral one instead of a coyote. The side dishes range from the usual green bean casseroles to butternut squash and quiches.

The dessert table is where I set out my three limoncello cakes and the ingredient card I made explaining what is inside. The others look good too: Lots of banana bread, pumpkin spice bread, and brownies with colorful sprinkles on top.

I mill around, chatting with the other dessert people as they organize their delicious, high-calorie treats. Already, we have developed a camaraderie and have plenty to talk about. It's easy to come together while discussing how to make our cakes. Although I bought mine, I get kudos for making the limoncello.

The final dishes have been set down, and the hungry riders eagerly move toward the serving line. I step aside to let a few people move ahead of me, and conveniently, I end up right in front of Lyle. I smile at him in surprise. Roxy is behind him, scowling.

I bet she's on a diet, so I'll set my food-meter the other way. "Oh this looks great!" I glance at him with my face glowing in desire as I take a wedge of quiche. Yeah, I know, I may be going overboard with my emotional display. I should tone it down, otherwise I'll run out of excitement with the amount of food here.

By the end of the row, my plate is piled high. I would feel like a glutton, except that hers only has a slice of turkey breast and a few leaves of lettuce. I lean toward Lyle and whisper, "I hope this doesn't mean I'm a pig." I glance at my plate, then flick my eyes to hers.

"You don't need to worry, you look terrific," he softly says while giving me one of *those* smiles.

You're married, you jerk. He is, except I need him to latch on to me.

I stay close to him when he's looking for a place to sit. Roxy is talking with David. Oh good, he has her attention, so that leaves Lyle for me.

"Where are you sitting—may I join you guys?" I make sure to look at my plate so I seem more interested in eating than stalking him.

He sees Roxy is occupied with David, but waves her over as he heads to a table with a couple who didn't ride. The MFH Master of Fox hounds—hunt master, is seated next to them. No one is eating. The master is taking a swig from his flask, the man is nursing a tumbler of something strong, and his wife has a colorful cocktail.

"Hello Paul and Michelle, it's great to see you. Your ranch is beautiful as always!" Lyle uses a tone of someone comfortable speaking to the wealthy.

"Merry Christmas, Lyle. It's good seeing you again this year. Is Georgina with you?" The woman asks, perhaps not innocently, as she glances at me.

"Georgie is at a charity auction this morning. I'm riding alone." He smiles, then makes a bee-line to sit next to the hunt master.

I can see he isn't going to introduce me. I figure I have nothing to lose so I say, "Good morning. This is only my second time out, I'm riding David Reynolds' horse. It's been a pleasure to gallop across your property."

She stiffly replies, "We like to open it up for the hunt."

I sit across from her so I don't have to ask permission to sit next to her. I probably should have asked, but I'll assume she'll say yes. She knows Lyle's wife, so maybe I can get something from her.

David seems to have captured Roxy's attention. They're talking about showing horses on the Santa Barbara Circuit. That should leave Lyle free for me—except he's schmoozing with the hunt master and the landowner.

I make the most of it by speaking with the wife. "This is a lovely setting, it's a nice change for me. I live in Cambria," I reach out with my friendly vibe.

"Oh." She is surprised. "Cambria is a nice little town," she agrees, but makes it sound beneath her.

"Yes, it's cute. I have a hotel on Moonstone Beach. I like the atmosphere, though there isn't a lot to do." I call my cottages a hotel, since it sounds grander than a B&B, which could mean I rent out one room of a two-room house.

"Are you friends with Lyle?" she blatantly asks.

"No. That girl is." I nod to Roxy, but I don't look at her, so she isn't alerted. She and David are still deep in conversation about the top trainers in the area.

"I see." She scowls into her drink.

I lean forward and say, "I heard by the grapevine they're a couple."

She wrinkles her brow. "He's married to my friend," she growls.

"Good looking men like to expand their territory," I murmur an honest assessment.

Her expression hints at having experienced that. She quickly replaces the flash of sadness with a hard look, but doesn't continue the conversation. She turns toward her husband, joining him and the hunt master discussing their property.

So, what now? I take a few bites to give myself something to do. At least David is next to me on the right, even though he's still talking with Roxy.

Lyle is extremely complimentary, schmoozing for business. This isn't working well for my investigation. I've almost finished my lunch, and he's been busy with the other men. A whipper-in is sitting on my other side. He gave me a nice greeting then started on about the wonders of his hounds. This is the movers and shakers table. Here come two more of the male whippers-in with their plates.

This is the problem with being new, everyone has their friends, and I'm the odd one out at the head table. I haven't anything to say about hounds. I don't know anything about their care and feeding, though I soon find out they require a lot of exercise to stay fit. It's a lot of work to maintain a healthy pack of thirty dogs that are ready to hunt twice a week.

The hour hand slowly moves around the dial; time passes, but not quickly. I've listened and smiled, but become worn out with this. I'm an outsider. Perhaps sitting at the royal table was a mistake. If Lyle ever stops talking and goes for dessert I'll follow him.

Finally, the landowner and hunt master get up and head for the bar serving the drinks. Lyle follows. I wait, then head in that direction, dropping my plate in the garbage can when I see they're only getting alcohol, not seconds of lunch. I turn on the voice recording on my phone, and get my place in the short line behind Lyle as the other big-wigs place their order.

Lyle gets a whiskey and coke then surprises me by asking what I'd like. Oh shoot, I don't know. If I drink, I can't drive, but I'm so full, it will be a long time before it takes effect. "What you're having sounds good, but with half the whiskey."

He give me a flirty look, "Come on, enjoy yourself. You rode well today, you deserve it."

I change tactics mid-flight. "Sure, why not? Make it just like yours," I grin.

He tells the man to put my drink on his tab.

"I'll get my purse and reimburse you," I start to go.

He places his hand on my arm, "Don't worry about it, you can owe me." He takes a gulp of his drink and hands me mine as he moves to a place free from prying ears.

"Repaying you could be an interesting proposition." I run with his suggestion, which may not have meant anything, but I intend to make it something.

He looks slightly surprised. "It was a manner of speaking. I'm married." It almost sounds true.

"Oh, and what about Miss. Roxy over there?" I take a sip while looking up at him with unblinking eyes.

"We're not together," he insists.

"So that leaves room for me." Ha—where did that come from? I'm never that quick with a reply.

"You're a beautiful woman; interesting, intelligent, and a good rider. I wish I could take you up on your offer." He actually sounds sad.

"You can't handle a sweet dalliance?" I put my hand on my hip and blink at him.

"You're driving me crazy. I wish I could." He rubs his brow and looks distressed.

"Who's going to know?" I arch my back and run my free hand through my hair.

He watches me with longing. "Jess, you're a beautiful woman. You can get any man you want, but that man isn't me. I'm married and can't mess that up."

They always say "you can get any man you want" when they're turning you down.

"What does she have that I don't?" I don't pout, but I look perplexed.

"She's fun to flirt with on the hunt. You'd be a life-changing event. I can't do that right now."

"So you don't want to flirt with me like you do with her?"

"You're better than that. And I'm not doing anything with her, much to her chagrin," he chuckles.

"So you're leading her on?"

"I'm enjoying watching her pursue me."

"Thanks for being honest. I think you're an interesting and attractive man, and you can ride too!"

"It's mutual admiration, but you need to look elsewhere. David is single. He isn't as amazing as I am, but..." He shrugs and looks helpless.

I study him for a moment. "You know, I appreciate what you told me. I had an experience that made me distrust men. You've gone a long way toward restoring it."

"Thank you for telling me. I think your man was a fool, and you're quite a catch."

With that, he nods to the tables, "If you want a toy, you need look no further than the man you're getting your hireling from." David Reynolds.

There he is with Roxy. She just flipped her ponytail over her shoulder. Yeah, it looks like the two of them are hitting it off.

My limoncello cakes are popular. There are plenty of goodies on the dessert table, but I see mine quickly disappear after riders return for seconds and thirds of their favorites. I take a seat with a dessert aficionado and her friends and get a baking lesson.

A while later, I'm swiping the remains of raspberry filling off my plate when I notice Roxy sauntering away from David's horse trailer.

She heads over to her rig, unties her horse, and loads him in the trailer.

At the same time, David comes out from behind the trailer, running his hands through his hair. The dressing room door is on the far side, preventing me from seeing if they'd been inside. To me, it looks like she and David had a thing, since she can't get anywhere with Lyle Stamford.

I say good bye to the hunt master, and Lyle. Then I retrieve my empty platter and head over to David who is chatting with a small group.

"Thanks very much. I'm heading out. Would you like a hand with Ryan?"

"No, he's a breeze to load. See you next Wednesday?" he asks.

"I'm not sure. I'll let you know. He's a neat horse, lots of fun."

"Glad you like him," he nods with a smile.

Driving home, I have lots of time to speak with Georgina.

I get through and go into great detail about the ride, lunch and my impressions. "David was good enough to keep your husband's supposed girlfriend, Roxy, occupied. It gave me time to speak with your husband."

"Uh huh?" she prompts.

"I very much doubt that he's cheating on you with her. I even came on pretty strong, making it clear I was interested in him. He complimented my beauty, my intelligence, and riding ability, but he turned me down. He said sorry, but he's married."

"Damn," she mutters softly under her breath.

"He bought me a drink, and I told him I'd like to repay him. He didn't fall for it. Nothing worked."

"Hmm."

"I did see something interesting. When I was leaving, I saw Roxy leaving David Reynolds' trailer. A minute later, he came from the same side running his hands through his hair. I didn't see them come out of the dressing room because it was on the other side of the rig."

"Are you saying what I think you are?" Her tone has a hard edge.

"I'm not positive, but it looked possible."

"Okay. Thank you for the good work. I don't think there is anything more you can do. Lyle must be keeping it in his pants."

"Yeah, I'm sure he is, at least at the hunt club."

"Thank you." She clicks the phone off.

She didn't seem too happy about it. Maybe she wants him to be cheating so she can keep half the money. It's just a thought, but if she were doing this for altruistic reasons, I'd think she'd be relieved.

* * *

JUST BEFORE BED, Georgina Stamford calls.

"You didn't earn the money. You didn't prove he was cheating on me."

"What—how can I prove he's cheating if he isn't?"

"I think you need to do a little more work to make it fair."

"Oh?"

What does she expect me to do—he isn't interested.

"Look into David Reynolds. Find out if he's having a fling with that bimbo."

"I know we didn't discuss how much I was to do, but I think I proved he wasn't cheating at the hunt. Although it was interesting, and I learned about foxhunting."

"You didn't do a lot of work. You did a good job, I'm not saying you didn't, but I think another day might be fair—don't you?

She's waiting for my reply. She's a good negotiator.

"I guess I can go once more. Hopefully I won't crash into a jump."

"You'll be fine," she dismisses my reply. "Call David." She hesitates. "Don't tell him you know me, but I want to know about his activities."

"You thought Lyle was cheating, but you want me search for evidence that Roxy is having an affair with David?"

"Yes."

"Okay. I'll go on Wednesday." I hesitate, "And please transfer money to PayPal or send a check for the horse rental and two days investigation."

"Sure." She pauses. "See if you can get David Reynolds to sleep with you." She quickly hangs up.

What—is she stupid? I told her I won't sleep with anyone! Does she think by repeatedly telling me that I'll change my mind?

Lying in bed, the pieces start falling into place, into a different picture of the jigsaw puzzle. Why does she care if David, who is single, is having an affair with Roxy? And why would she want me to get him into bed? Am I imagining something that isn't there? Am I too suspicious?

8

FOLLOWING

I'm drifting off to sleep when someone starts pounding on my door. "Jessica. Help me!" A woman is shrieking. It sounds like Mia

I grab my .45 and hurry to the door. First, I look through the window, and see her illuminated by the Christmas lights wrapped around my porch railing. I don't see anyone behind her, using her as a human-shield to get in.

I pull open the door. "What's wrong?"

"He's following me!" She looks over her shoulder.

"Who?" I'm about to yank her inside.

"My ex-boyfriend."

"Where is he?" I step out of the way and let her in.

She stands there, not moving. "I don't know, but his drone is buzzing my head."

"Huh? Do you want to clarify that?"

"Just now, I was standing out front, watching the moon on the water. As I was going back to my cottage, a drone came out of nowhere and almost flew into me. I ran, and it followed me."

"Where is it now?" I turn off the lights and step outside. It's all quiet, except for the distant waves. Some of the other cottages have their inside lights on; I bet she woke half the guests. And I don't see a drone.

"How do you know it's your ex?"

"He was following me at home for two weeks. It swooped down on me like it wanted to attack. It has to be him."

"I guess he knows you're here now. Is he dangerous?"

"Well...," she stretches the word. "Mom doesn't like him, said he's no-good."

"Has he made any demands, texted you, or called?"

"Yes. Last night he sent a text saying 'I see you.'"

"Have you made a report with the Beverly Hills police?"

"Yes. This is the first time he used a drone. I guess he doesn't want to confront me right here. But the next time I see it, I'll try to hit it down and smash it to pieces." She is recovering and thinking about fighting back.

"I'll walk you to your cottage." I step into my running shoes, grab a flash light from the drawer, and secure my door.

It's quiet. I don't hear anything yet. Has it landed, or gone away? Is it watching from a perch? I don't like drones. They look like futuristic, artificial intelligence that wants to kill humans. The Pine cottage is the last one down the winding path. I trimmed the bushes lower after the last incident with Phil Crowne. I didn't want criminals having a place to hide. Now maybe I should put up netting to stop drones flying in.

"I'm calling the police tomorrow and adding this to the list of things he's doing to me," she is angry. That's good, it's better than being fearful.

"Good idea. Are you going to Hearst Castle again tomorrow?"

"My parents have a foundation membership so I'll be swimming in the Neptune Pool tomorrow. Do you know only a handful of members can swim in it—and I'm one of them?"

Of course she is.

"Wow, that's great. The pool is breathtaking." It's sparkling blue with black lines of inlaid tiles on the bottom. Roman columns, arcades, and marble statues surround it. There's an actual Roman temple displayed for an inspiring view.

"I know. I'm lucky," she sounds like she appreciates it.

"Are you going to be okay tonight?"

"Yeah. That stupid drone scared me, but Axel hasn't been dangerous. I'm sure he won't really try to hurt me. He wants me back."

"Axel. That sounds like a dangerous name. Is he a rock star?" I muse.

"No, he's a Harley mechanic. He likes to think he's mean, but I've met meaner."

"You like bad-boys?"

"Sure do. I like bikers, tattoos and leather."

I'd say she's an idiot, but I like bad-boys too. In my case, it's good bad-boys: military and police. Those who can handle themselves against soldiers of other nations and dangerous criminals.

She closes the door, and I head back to my cottage.

I hear that buzzing sound in the distance. It's coming closer. Now I know what it is... a drone!

I start looking in the trees, down the path... There it is, in the parking lot, hovering with its running lights on. Watching.

The FAA considers them aircraft, so you can't shoot them down, but I'll see what I can do about it.

I shine my high-powered flashlight at it, hopefully blinding the guy watching through the camera. I have my .45 in my pocket, but I won't let him know I'm armed. I don't threaten with my weapon when I have no legal ability to use it. It would make me look like a fool.

The drone follows me at a distance as I walk down the path between the tall pines. Maybe I can string a net with micro-filament. Its camera may not see it, so I could disable it. Unfortunately, if it's cheap enough, the guy would buy another.

I step up to my dark cottage. The drone comes down from the top of the trees. It's buzzing about twenty feet away at head height. It looks like an alien invader, angry that I helped the other female human. And now I want to kill it.

I shine my light at it again. It's a stand-off. I don't move, it doesn't move. Axel is showing how tough he is to stalk me, when his little girlfriend is in her cottage.

"You're a tough one, hiding behind a drone!" I shout at it.

I step backward, keeping my light in its face, until I get to my door. Then I slip inside and close it tight. Now I'm fighting with a drone as if it's alive. Mia is becoming something of a problem.

I hear it hovering outside the window, it moves around to the front window, the lights bright in the darkness. Great. Just great.

As I knew it would, it takes hours to get to sleep. With the adrenaline running through my system, and my anger at the man at the controls, I'm awake. Plus I'm online, searching the FAA rules about shooting them down, their limitations, cameras, and weaknesses.

9

SUNDAY MORNING

"I'm sorry. I just got back in town. I know it's a poor excuse." That's the text I see when I wake to the drizzling rain blowing against the window.

It's about time Quinn got in touch with me. I don't know whether to be happy, or tell him it's over. What kind of relationship is this? I don't want to seem clingy, but I think I've proven I am anything but that.

I immediately reply because that's what people do when they get a text. "I'm having a hard time. Things are turning problematic, and I could use a hand. That's probably not what you want to hear. Plus I'm frustrated about us." I press send, and there it goes, into the hands of fate.

I texted that I needed a hand. Yeah, I could use several. Plus a bunch of his friends and a few weapons to terminate this situation, whatever it may be. While I pride myself in handling my own problems, I don't know whose are landing on me. Is it Mia's ex-boyfriend, one of the Russians, or someone I pissed off?

At least it's drizzling. That means the drone won't be flying today. I read a few things last night that will be beneficial to fighting back. If it's following me, I want to bring it down. Meaning, I want to crash it to the ground. That's illegal, but having it buzzing after me, and staring me down in the wee hours of the night isn't acceptable.

If Mia's ex-boyfriend is behind the controls, then it will be gone when she leaves next week.

I just remembered, today she's going swimming in Hearst's Neptune Pool. They're usually only open four times a year for their foundation members. This is a special fundraiser, it costs more, has a late-afternoon Christmas dinner, and is going to be cold. I bet people will tip-toe into the shallow end, then only continue up to their knees, shrieking like little girls in the frigid water. They won't be teaming up to play volley ball.

Instead of going jogging today, I'll take a short break after the past few weeks—I'll take the time to sit with a cup of hot chocolate for an hour to recharge. I mix in holiday spices and add a squirt of whipped cream. My brain doesn't shut off, but it gets time to think more clearly.

What's going on with the SUV that slammed into me? I haven't heard from the investigator. I'll call Detective Taylor on Monday. Actually, I could text him today. I have his private number.

"Hi Josh. Have you heard anything about a black Chevy SUV trying to run me off the highway? He slammed into the back of my little car and rode my tail until I was able to lose him by spinning out at the Estero Bay view point just before Harmony."

He doesn't immediately reply, so I dress in my artsy innkeeper clothes and head to the Garden lounge for breakfast. Janet is off today, but her cousin Claire works two days a week. There is no way I'd want to cook a delicious breakfast and then clean five cottages. I have to do the books, run the place, and keep everyone happy. Plus I have to ride to hounds, for what I'd hoped was $500 a ride, but may be considerably less since I don't think her husband is cheating. You'd think she'd be happy.

Everything is running well. The couple from Rose cottage are having an early breakfast. I stop by for a brief hello, but end up taking a seat and chatting about their plans for the day.

I love my new job. It's wonderful to offer beautiful cottages and a tasty breakfast to my guests. I like sharing stories and listening to their adventures and plans. I'm not sure I could have a better life.

After they leave, I do necessary billing and computer work in the office until 9:30. Then I wrap things up and head back to the lounge to be sociable.

Mia is there, eating with the couple staying in the Lilac cottage. I swing past, saying hello and good morning. They're discussing the Hearst dynasty and the Patty Hearst kidnapping. "What a surprise when she robbed a bank with a machine gun a few months later," says the older gentleman.

I don't add my opinion about why President Carter pardoned her. I head toward the kitchen to say good morning to Claire. I bring her up to date with who is checking out and which rooms need to be freshened up. Then I dish up a large serving spoon of scrambled eggs, and another of cottage fries. I know they have more calories than fruit, but I need the energy today. A dash of salt and pepper make the crispy bits taste great.

I've started covering Mandy's listening device in my office. I remove the cover when what I have to say isn't private. I need to come up with something fake-newsworthy for her to run with.

"Claire, have you heard any gossip about Mandy Crawford in town?" She knows Mandy is out to get me, because she is friends with the head housekeeper. She doesn't know my office has been bugged, that's my secret. I feel the fewer people who know, the less likely it is to get back to the source.

"Oh, I forgot. It's been a few days, but several guests got food poisoning from their shrimp cocktails."

"I didn't know she had those. Do they go with breakfast?"

"They're a new addition to the champagne bar."

"Hmm. I need to get moving on my Bellini bar and hot tub."

"You really should. It's a shame not to make use of the view out front. Your grandmother didn't want to rip out the plants." She looks out the window at the rise overlooking the ocean.

"Yeah, well, plants can grow back, or be moved. A hot tub will be a nice addition."

"And I have another piece of information—" She hesitates as if wondering if she should say anything.

I look up from pondering about the native plant garden I'm going to dig up and replace with a tub and stepping stones.

"She said *you* were seen going behind the bar."

"What?" I jerk back to Claire.

"That's what Margo said."

"Who's Margo?"

"The head of housekeeping."

"I haven't been behind the champagne bar." I only went behind the bar in the office to plant my listening device.

"That's what Margo was told, and they said to tell everyone. They want the word spread around that you did it."

"What day were they sick? I'll check my schedule to prove I was somewhere else."

"I don't know and if I ask too many questions it may look suspicious. She's my friend, but you're my boss."

She worked for Gram for a while, and her cousin Janet has worked for us for years. We take care of our employees and make sure they're well paid and appreciated. I haven't listened to my own device for over a week. There will be a ton of conversations to wade through.

"Thanks for telling me. I didn't do anything to her shrimp, just so you know."

"I know. You're a good woman. Margo doesn't like Mrs. Crawford, but she worked her way up and plans on staying until she retires."

"Can you find out when they started serving the cocktails; I'm guessing sometime last week? That way I can look at my schedule and pray I have an alibi."

"I'll see what I can find out," she agrees.

"I'm glad I have you. Thank you for trusting me."

"You're welcome and good luck."

* * *

I WHIP out my phone and check Facebook. If she had something new, but didn't have time to change her website, she would at least announce it across social media. Ah-ha here it is. "Join us for Fresh Shrimp Cocktails overlooking Moonstone Beach. Today and every day. Don't settle for less than the best."

That was posted on Wednesday. It generated several Likes. Luckily, Wednesday I was at the hunt. I have proof of that. Now, to see when the guests got sick. I wonder if Yelp has any comments. After spending a few minutes going through various review sites, I can't find anything about it. I wonder if the Health Department was notified. Maybe Mandy made it go away by promising the sick people a free night.

As I head back through the lounge, Mia waves me over. "Jess. Can you tell us what you'll be serving for Christmas breakfast?"

"We'll be having a feast with individual quiche, gingerbread French toast, and champagne mimosas. I will also have a pot of homemade soup available all day, because many restaurants will be closed."

"That's great. We come up every year at this time. Your grandmother always took care of us," says another guest.

"And I will continue to do the same!" I smile at the memories of Gram's Christmases in Cambria. "Unfortunately, I couldn't spend as much time here as I wanted during the holidays. The town is always beautifully lit, the shops are decorated and offer cookies—it's so festive. It's a nostalgic time of year for me."

"For us too!" My guests nod and agree.

"If you like mulled wine, I'll be leaving a bottle and glasses beside the fireplace in the evening, along with cookies. And something more nourishing during the day."

"It sounds perfect." My two older guests look happy with this.

I think it'll work nicely, it'll be my tribute to Gram. Maybe she'll be watching.

Mia is going to the castle today for the pool party. I have a full house of guests for the week. Janet and I will be busy preparing for Christmas breakfast. At least the cottages will only need straightening, with fresh towels, rather than deep cleaning like if new guests were checking in. That means Janet will have time to cook and bake. Nine people hanging around, eating and drinking, will take some planning and dish washing.

I have our list and make notes when I think of something I need to ask her. She's the expert, and I treat her as such. I may be the owner, but I don't lord it over her.

Couples from Rosemary and Sage come in as I head out the French door into the drizzle sweeping in from the ocean. "Good morning. It's a bit chilly, isn't it?"

"Yes, but I slept like a baby," the lady replies.

"I'm glad to hear that. I hope you enjoy breakfast."

The gas fireplace is crackling and the scent of cooking is inviting. With light music in the background, and Mia and a older couple chatting, the lounge feels welcoming.

The second I get into my cottage, I hurry to the security closet, pull down the folding table, and drag up a chair. I have hours of listening to slog through for the words: shrimp cocktail, sick, Jessica, Greenstone Cottage.

One hour passes, and another. It's been busy at The Seaside Resort. I've been rewinding and listening, then again rewinding and listening, as I try to hear distant conversations.

Ah, here we are: Wednesday evening. "Room 215 just called. They claim the shrimp cocktails poisoned them."

"Not another one!" Mandy's voice.

"Sorry. I told them it's probably the flu. I told him exactly what you said—that we follow the strictest protocol for food safety."

"How many is this now?"

"Four rooms, but *only* six guests."

"*Only*," Mandy shouts. "*Only* six are six too many. Fire the woman who left the bowl out all day."

"Yes ma'am."

There's a long silence. I almost fast-forward thinking the call ended.

"Tomorrow morning, if they don't come down to breakfast, send one of our sympathy cards. Don't admit to anything, and don't promise anything. Write that we value them as our guests and look forward to welcoming them to our presidential club."

"Okay, I got it."

"You have to stop employee gossip. Tell them we investigated the allegations, and fortunately the surveillance video shows our competitor pouring a vial of something into the bowl of shrimp."

"Um-hmm. I'm writing it down," she quietly murmurs. A few seconds later she giggles. "Let me guess which competitor."

"You got it—we'll blame darling Jessica and her granny," she sneers.

I feel sick—as if they dumped a bucket of diseased shrimp on my head. How can they hate me so much? I haven't done anything to them. I've only been at Greenstones for a month.

10

THE REASON

The holiday has become a nightmare.

The stress of the past few weeks is overwhelming me. I do the best job I can with everything I do. I'm not a neurotic perfectionist, but I believe in a job well done, one that I can be proud of. One that I don't hesitate to say I did, that I created, and that I stand by.

What is going on with God, Karma or whoever lets this happen to an innocent person? I do know bad things happen to good people. It happens to be my turn now.

I turn off the receiver and slouch down in the chair. I know I'm crying when Cami meows, then jumps on the table. She walks back and forth, wafting her tail in my face. Cats seem to be attuned to the need for a friend.

For a long time I sit, just sit. My brain is stuck replaying the same conversation over and over. I don't even have to move when my alarm chimes a reminder to go to the office for check-in. All my guests are staying. I don't have anyone new to meet.

The dreary afternoon passes into a cold evening. I'm supposed to set out the Port and cookies. I hope there aren't any guests in the lounge. It will be a struggle to be festive if there are.

I rinse my face, grab my raincoat, and dash across. The tree is lit, and the lights are twinkling a happy welcome, but no one is here yet. This is the best thing that has happened to me all afternoon. I turn up the fireplace to a lot more than a flicker, then straighten the magazines on the table. I set out the wine and cookies, and include some brownies. I top off the hot water, brew more coffee, and make sure there are enough tea bags to provide a variety of options.

Then I hurry back to my kitchen table with a brownie and a glass of Port.

The alcohol thaws my frozen emotions, and the sugar gives me needed energy. I suppose I should formulate a plan of attack. I can't sit and wait for their next step. I've heard all that stuff about a good defense being a great offense.

I still need time to formulate a plan. I probably need real food to keep my brain firing correctly. At this point, I'm not ready to hear more of their hatred. I have to be stronger to withstand that.

It isn't until hours later that I'm ready to hear the rest of their conversation. Then it will be time to plan my offensive strategy.

I return to the security console, adjust my chair, and click Play on the receiver.

"I wonder how long it will take." I can hear Mandy's smile.

"She's young, but with what you have planned, I can't see her lasting more than a month," the manager replies.

"I tend to agree, but somehow she managed to get the city to resurface her driveway."

"Maybe she boinked the supervisor."

No, I did not!

"I think she's smarter than she looks," Mandy replies.

I press Stop to breathe and take a few minutes to get over these slurs. I rewind and continue listening. I know they're planning something. They expect me to cave-in to their pressure, but are finding me stronger than they thought.

What are they planning? And what is their motive?

"If I were the betting type, I'd say she freaks out."

"I hope so. I want that little goldmine." Mandy Crawford just revealed her motive.

She wants Greenstone Cottage.

11

CHRISTMAS MORNING

The phone calls start rolling in.

"Merry Christmas Jess." Mom sings a few bars from a carol.

"Thank you. Merry Christmas and Happy New Year to you," I reply, sounding friendly.

"What's wrong?"

"How do you know—why do you think something is wrong?"

"Because you sound distracted, and no one ever says Happy New Year on Christmas morning. It's too early."

"Oh. Thank you for the advice."

"So?"

"Where are you now?" I think she's vacationing somewhere in Colorado.

"I'm in Durango, staying at a B&B on a river; I love this place. Christmas music serenades me in every shop, and they have those little twinkly lights framing the windows. When I drive down the main street, arches of lights and snowflakes run from post to post. Every tree is decorated, making the town look like a scene from a Hallmark movie. It's even snowing right now—everywhere looks so festive, I miss that about southern California," she sighs.

"I don't miss the snow."

"You've never lived in the snow."

"Exactly, and I don't plan to."

"Why are you grumpy—isn't Quinn with you?" She isn't offended as she searches for the reason.

"Nope, he's off somewhere, saving America. But that's not the reason I'm testy. Last night, I found out Mandy Crawford is spreading lies about me so she can get Greenstones for herself. She said it's a goldmine."

"The witch!"

"Exactly. I was falling apart listening to her, but I'm better now. The problem is I can't fight back because I heard it on my illegal recording."

"Can you get your information anywhere else?"

"Well, yes. Claire heard that Mandy fired an employee."

"So find that employee. She may be angry enough to tell you something you can use. Pay her if you need to, but be aware, Mandy may go after her claiming she's lying."

"Mandy is powerful and has attorneys on retainer at the corporate level."

"I have attorney friends too."

"Ok, thanks."

"Make sure everything you say and print is lawful. You can still get sued, but she will be unlikely to win."

"I should have gone to law school so I could counter these crooks instead of being taken advantage of."

"It's never too late…"

"I'm a bed and breakfast owner now, but I'll keep it in mind for another lifetime."

"Date an attorney, but make sure he's in the right specialty."

"I may do that if Quinn doesn't appear soon."

"He's a good one. I'd keep him around," she suggests.

"I know but that's the point—he isn't around."

"Then make a decision. If you need a man around, then go find one. If you can wait, then keep him and try to work it out." It sounds logical.

"Those are good words of advice." I pause while I think. "I don't *need* a man, but I'd like one that's here more often, one I can rely on—but he is rarely here."

"Then rely on yourself and change your expectations."

"Yeah. I guess so."

"You're not exactly an easy woman to live with. Look at the trouble you get into. Nothing ever happens in the wine country, yet you manage to find killers, robbers, and schemers in every vineyard. What normal man could and would stand for that?" she uses her lecturing mother tone.

"Fine. I'll consider changing my expectations. Maybe you're right."

"I'm not saying it's entirely your problem. Maybe he could confide in you more, or include you in his plans."

"Thanks, that makes sense."

"You're welcome, and Merry Christmas. I'm on my way to brunch. Are you all right listening to my advice?" She carefully asks.

"Yes. I am. You're usually right."

It helps, and she *is* usually right. I suppose that comes with living twenty years longer.

I call Nikki to wish her a Merry Christmas. We only chat for a few minutes, because she and Travis are unwrapping gifts and having a French toast breakfast with Monica and Charlie. I feel melancholy—left out of the fun with friends and family.

"Come join us. It's only an hour away," Nikki enthusiastically suggests. "Here, I'll put you on speaker."

"Merry Christmas," shout Monica, Charlie, and Travis. Each in their own happy tone.

I'm getting teary-eyed. Maybe I should go there.

"Get in your car and come visit. I'm making more food than we can eat in three days," Monica shouts.

"I have guests. I need to go show my face." Even to my ears I don't sound happy about it.

"Our door is always open. You know where we are, we'll be here all day," Monica continues.

"Thanks. I might do that!"

Nikki comes back on and takes if off speaker. "Do you think you'll come?"

"Umm—."

"Ok, I know how it is. You're kind of stuck there. We'd really like to see you."

"The fun will be over by the time I get there."

"Yeah, maybe a little less fun. We can reheat things, but I know what you mean." She whispers, "In reality, we'll probably be doing our own thing in an hour."

"Whew," I exhale. "Thanks for saying that. I feel better about not coming."

"You're okay where you are. Go visit your guests and show them the Cambria spirit. Make sure you get out of your house. You need companionship," she suggests.

"Quinn isn't here. I have no idea where he is."

"Travis got back yesterday from parts unknown, he can't say where. I guess if I want to keep him, I have to accept it."

"He's worth keeping."

"And so is your man."

"Yeah. You're right," I sigh.

We end on speaker phone shouting Merry Christmas to one another.

* * *

No, I'm not wearing a Christmas sweater. My mother wears them which embarrassed me like crazy when I was a kid. I'm wearing a light-green caftan with a tasseled brown belt. It's very expensive, but I haven't had a reason to wear it before. I like the way it flows across my feminine curves because the fabric is 100% silk. If I get a spot of food on it I'll freak out. I'm probably out of touch with the younger generation, but I don't care. They're not the ones staying at Greenstones.

I check the lounge video feed and see it's filling with guests. Janet came in to set up for the brunch. And by the way, I paid her double. I want to keep her very happy to come to work!

Stepping through the French door, I'm hit with the scent of savory quiche, and the sweetness of French toast and ginger. Mmm, I already feel better. The light music in the background is a mix of Zamfir flute music and some Christmas music without words. I didn't want to go overboard on the holiday theme. By now, everyone has surely heard Jingle Bells a hundred times in the past few weeks.

The fir tree in the corner looks cheerful and provides a natural scent to add to the smell of fresh breakfast. The crystal ornaments are catching the light and sending colorful prisms into the room. The gas flames in the fireplace are flickering, and the heater is pumping hot air into the room. It's still raining outside, but inside is warm, friendly and festive.

My guests are serving themselves at the well-stocked buffet table and returning to their chairs with plates piled high. Everyone is mingling with each other. Their seats are turned as they chat with their fellow travelers. I don't know how this could get more perfect.

Granted, I did move the tables so they weren't so distant. I pulled them away from the walls, out of the corners, and made more of a conversation pit. And it worked. Oh my goodness, yes, it worked.

I stand for a few minutes listening to Mia. Then I perch on the arm of the couch and listen.

She is describing her first swim in the Neptune Pool. "It was freezing—like an ice bath. I'm surprised there weren't any glaciers floating around, but I wasn't going to miss my only chance to go swimming in that pool."

"Were you the only one?"

"No. There were a lot of us who took the plunge," she laughs.

"Did you walk around the grounds? I love the marble statues and colonnades." The guest from Sage cottage describes what she has seen on her tours. She smiles as she recalls the views from each terrace. "Did you know the architect, Julia Morgan, is the woman who designed, engineered, and decorated the entire castle? Can you believe it, a woman, back in the 1920s? I'm so impressed William Randolph Hearst was such a progressive man to hire her."

"We didn't get a tour, but I was able to go everywhere in the pool area. I couldn't see the ocean because it was raining; heavy waves that kept sweeping through, in cold sheets of downpour. They had a giant tent that made up the dining area, so that's where I went to have Kahlua and coffee. To be honest, I was so cold, I just wanted to get warm," she hugs her shoulders and sniffs.

"Oh dear. They shouldn't have had a party in December," a lady muses.

"You're right." Another sniff from Mia. "But it was worth every second."

I move toward the buffet and pull a red plate off the stack. There's no way I'm going to miss this spread. I may not have cooked it, but I bought it, and joined Janet in planning what we were going to serve. No, I'm not skimping or dieting today. I'll make two trips. This first one is for the spinach and leek quiche, and the goat cheese with ham and kale tartlet. I drop a scoop of roasted rosemary potatoes on the side.

I return to my perch on the arm of the couch. It's in the right place to be central to the conversation.

"Pull up a chair, Jess. Please join us," one of the guests suggests.

The man from Rosemary gets up from the table and gets an extra chair from the side. He slides it in next to his wife and steps back with his hands on the back, ready to help when I take a seat.

"Thanks very much!" I finish my first course at the table.

The conversation continues with the castle tours. I let them talk, because I've only been on two, and that was when I was a kid. I'd better go check them out so I can offer suggestions to my guests.

The door opens, letting in a gust of chilly, rainy air. We all turn to look. What a great Christmas present: Quinn has arrived. And he looks amazing in a fitness-emphasizing thin black sweater and jeans. His black hair is damp and wavy to his shoulders. He has just the right three-day growth of goatee to make him devastatingly handsome.

Across the table Mia murmurs, "Oh!" as the conversation stops.

"Merry Christmas, everyone!" he grins and steps forward a few feet.

I stand up with a smile. "Good morning. What a surprise! Quinn, I'd like you to meet my friends." I sweep my arm out to the smiling guests. "Everyone, this is Quinn, my boyfriend. I hadn't realized he was coming by today."

"What a nice surprise. Lucky you!" Mia speaks loud enough for all to hear.

"Yes, I agree," I reply with appreciation as I head to the door to give him a hug, and lead him to the table.

I guess I'm temporarily over my snit.

I get a chair from the office, and we squeeze in together as the conversation returns to Hearst Castle. It's a topic we all know something about, and is safe for a group of people with a wide array of opinions. This is something to keep in mind: it may be easy to lose clients if I have an objectionable viewpoint. They aren't friends, they're customers, and therefore my opinion isn't useful.

The party winds down when we are too full to eat another bite and lethargy takes over.

"Not that you're interested at the moment, but I'll have a pot of soup, and locally baked bread when you eventually get hungry, maybe around 5:00," I let the group know.

When the last person walks out the door, Quinn steps closer with a questioning look.

I smile, kind of shy, kind of uncomfortable, then I hug him. He wraps his arms around me and holds me tight for a long while. I feel his heart thumping beneath his muscular chest. He seems to be feeling something. I'm glad to know that.

"We'll talk at your place," he quietly says.

I nod and start tidying the room. He helps move the chairs back in place, and brings the plates to the kitchen. I wash them and pack away the leftovers.

I look at the refrigerator and scowl.

"What?" He immediately notices my stillness.

"I'm thinking about food tampering."

I lock the kitchen door on our way out. Usually I leave it unlocked for guests to leave plates or glasses.

12

NOT THE TALK

"Can we talk, are you in the mood?" I hesitantly inquire.

"Yes. I'd like to. There's a lot we need to work out," he sounds sad.

Is that sad like he messed up not talking sooner, or *sad* like good-bye? Suddenly I feel sick.

"Come on, let's sit here." He takes my hand and leads me to the window seat. I sit on one side with my knees pulled to my chest, he's on the other. The rain is coming down, but I like the rain, so it isn't a bad omen.

He smiles while looking in my eyes. He has such beautiful, dark brown eyes. Just like a horse. I chuckle, then start laughing, and I can't stop.

He keeps a firm hold on my hand and simply waits. I guess it's better than crying.

I finally clear my throat, smiling ridiculously that has nothing to do with anything we are going to discuss.

"I'm sorry, I uh, had had a lot of crap heaped on me the past few weeks." I explain it away.

"And I haven't been here, but I've been responsible for some of it," he's apologetic.

"Yes, you are, but there's more. This could go on all night if you're willing. It won't be a man-bashing fest. I've seen videos that insist men have no idea how to talk, don't know what to do, say, or think; and would rather walk barefoot across broken glass than discuss relationships with a woman."

"I was raised by an intelligent woman who treated me like an adult when I began to walk."

"You remember that far back." I make a joke, trying to return to normal.

"Maybe I was a little older." He smiles, softening his features.

"Okay," I take a deep breath, let it out, and begin. "A lot has been going on since the Russians were in town. The summary is that someone in a blacked-out SUV tried very hard to run me off the road. He slammed into the back of Gram's little car, but luckily didn't hit me right, because I didn't spin out."

His face loses all expression.

"Second: a drone is running amok on my property, and either following Mia, or me.

"Third: The owner of the resort two doors down is waging a smear campaign against me. I went through hours of surveillance recording and found out why. She wants to own Greenstones."

He's quiet, scowling, and thinking. I've said my part, now I'm waiting for his response. We'll talk about his part in my life later.

"Tomorrow, I'll bring in Adam. I'll also look into whether I'm responsible for the SUV incident. We'll plan a retaliatory strike against Mandy Crawford. She won't succeed in running you out of town. The weather has forecast another two days of rain which will ground the drone. I'll get additional hidden cameras that the pilot hasn't found. I'll track him down and put a stop to it," his voice is cold.

"That sounds wonderful. I can see my problems melt away with you and Adam helping me."

"They'll melt all right. Like a snow cone in the sun," he sounds resolute.

"Thanks. It's been tough facing this alone." I'm putting it mildly because I'm speaking to a military man.

He moves to the same side of the seat and quietly pulls me into his arms.

Finally, he speaks. "I know you still have questions and concerns. What would you like to know? I'll tell you what I can, or part of the story."

My major concern, my #1 fear: "Will the Russians try again?"

"No."

I want to ask if he's sure, but that makes it sound like I don't trust his answer. I consider asking if they're in Guantanamo; in FBI custody in a hidden compound; if they'll eventually be traded for U.S. soldiers; how did he get them transferred; and where are they now? How does he know they won't come after me again? Can he guarantee my safety?

I settle on the shortest question. He told me a few weeks ago they wouldn't bother me again. So I ask. "Are they alive?"

"No," he whispers in my ear.

Silence.

"Oh." It's the only word that comes to mind.

Oh. Damn. That's kind of scary. Maybe I shouldn't be quite as worried about things. He seems to be able to handle any situation. Who is this man I am in love with?

I guess he didn't go to the Middle East. He went thirty miles down the road. Or maybe, they were released and he followed them out of the country. Whatever... I don't think I should ask. But I do.

"Should I ask where and how?

"It's probably better not to know." He gently squeezes my arm. "But it was a decision made by men at a very high level."

I'm glad he's on our side.

"I'm fine with that answer. Thank you for telling me. I'm relieved." I know I'll feel the weight slide off me as soon as I get time to process it.

"So as you can see, the SUV that hit you was someone else."

"Yes. But why?"

"You weren't driving like an old lady?"

"No. I was keeping up with traffic."

"I'll get you in a safer car, one with guts. And it'll be tricked out with cameras."

"I hope this wasn't a one-time incident. I want to catch him."

"Do you really think it is? It sounds planned to me. In fact, it could have something to do with the drone."

"Hmm. That's a thought."

"Like I said, with me and Adam, he or they don't stand a chance. Don't worry, I'm not being foolhardy. I know what we're capable of, and our enemies are terrified of us."

"That's good. Thank you."

"I'll come up with a plan. We'll discuss it and implement it."

"You sound so official. I came from a police background, but yours sounds deadlier."

"Of course. You were bound by the rules of law. I get to skirt them."

"Not really while on U.S. soil," I comment.

"No." He agrees, but it sounds like a casual no, with a shrug.

I'm glad he doesn't ask if I'd prefer he play by the rules. Those rules don't keep people safe. That's my opinion. Bad guys don't play fair—I wonder if it's stupid to be bound by the same rules they ignore.

"Would you like to talk about the other things that are bothering you?" He continues.

"When you're here, it's like paradise. Then you leave at a moment's notice, and I can't reach you. When you return, you're cold for a while until you get used to life here again. I'd like to know a bit more of where you're going. Or maybe don't tell me it's a certain place, but then it ends up being another."

I shake my head to signal that's not what I wanted to say.

"That doesn't sound right. I guess what I mean is when I need you for friendship or help, you're not there. It makes it impossible—I mean, difficult to rely on you."

"I don't have a lot of say when they call me or where I go. I can't tell you, and it's best you don't know."

"It didn't seem to make a difference whether I knew about the

Russians or not. They still came to get me. I bet it's the same with other things. They will think you told me—so you might as well, so I have advance warning if something goes down," I counter his statement.

He thinks on it. "I'll tell you everything I can, and hint at some things I can't. Will that help?"

"Yes. Thank you. I wanted to get this off my chest."

"There is reason for that rule. No one wants an angry significant other spilling-the-beans to the enemy if they're pissed off, or bragging to a friend."

"I understand, but even the top players spill-the-beans to their mistress. That's why they have interesting women in the CIA."

"There are interesting men who play for the other side."

"I'm sure. Can you tell me, for example, that you're going somewhere in the desert, or the snow, or the jungle. That way I'll have a mental picture of where you are."

"And if you hear on the news that a major oil refinery was sabotaged in the desert, won't you assume it's me?"

"Yes."

"But it may not be. And if a friend comments on it, you might let something slip."

"I see your point."

"If possible, I will contact you more frequently when I'm away. It won't be during the operation because I need to keep a clear head on my work. Plus, it is often impossible, or could have deadly consequences."

"Ok."

We're quiet for a few minutes. Then I have another question.

"Why aren't you starting the survival school—and are you upset about that?"

"Things are heating up again, worldwide. They'll be calling me at inconvenient times. At first I was angered that I had to shelve my plans, but I've come to terms with it now. I'm one of the best and I'd like to continue doing it."

"You're impressive. I respect and admire you—that isn't something that I feel about most people. Many have big flaws, but you don't seem to. I guess the biggest is that you're good at what you do, which keeps you in high demand."

"Are you okay with my life? I don't have any plans on changing it. I want you to know I'm not choosing my job over you, but it's something inherent in me I don't want to give up." He looks slightly forlorn.

"I get it. I'm alright with it. I don't need you to become my partner in the hotel business."

"You seem to like having me as your private security expert," he chuckles.

"Yeah, I sure do. I'll sleep well tonight."

"Maybe, or maybe not." He leans in for a passionate kiss that makes me glad I didn't say I wouldn't see him again.

"I have something for you." He goes to his bag and comes out with small, wrapped box. "I wanted to talk to you before giving you a gift. I didn't want to influence you right away." He smiles and hands me the little box.

"I have something for you too!" I jump off the seat and dash to get it. "Who wants to open theirs first?"

"I will." He looks eager as he rips off the paper. "Wow, look at this." He examines the bracelet with my name engraved on the flat part of the horseshoe nail. "I love it. It's unique, and so *you*." He pull me into his lap, and kisses me, leaving no doubt he is happy.

As he snaps it on, he looks radiant, like I gave him the best gift in the world. "Now, here's what I got for you."

"Thank you." I pull off the ribbon, and carefully rip the paper. "Oh, they're beautiful!"

Diamond studs. "They look great with anything," I murmur.

"Or nothing," he whispers.

"Let's see..." I put them in my ears and then lead him to the bedroom.

13

CHRISTMAS DAY

I don't get much sleep, but it sure is nice having him back. It's glorious to hear the rain on the roof and splashing in the puddles. The window is open a few inches, letting in the fresh, chilly air as we snuggle under the covers.

A while later, Quinn returns to the kitchen table to plan. He's good at that, it's one of his skills I admire.

A while after that I trudge out. I need to set up the soup in the lounge for guests who might want a bowl or two on a rainy afternoon.

"Adam will be here by 6:00. He's stopping by my place to pick up what we need."

"And what do we need?"

"Additional cameras, transmitters, GPS devices, and one of my drones." He smiles broadly.

"Wow, that's enough to take down all my enemies. I'll be back in a few minutes." I grab an umbrella and hurry through the rain to the lounge feeling great.

It's busier than I expected. I leave the umbrella outside and step into the friendly room. Everyone looks up—I guess they're anticipating my arrival with food.

"Hi everyone. I'll bring out the light dinner in a few minutes." I pick up the empty cookie plate on the way to the kitchen. "I guess you liked them?"

"Sure did, and the sandwiches too."

"I'll refill everything to keep you going all night." I smile at the lady.

I'm pleased to see two couples playing the survival-skills card game. That's funny, I re-gifted it to Gram from when I was on the police department. I'm glad it's getting good use today. The wife from the Rose room is reading, while her husband plays chess against himself.

"I see you've found the games. There's also Clue and Risk in the cabinet if you want to stay up all night." Gram made sure to have lots of board games available for rainy days.

I set out the hot pot and bowls on the serving cart. Then heat what Janet calls her hearty winter vegetable soup. And just in case, I bought a quart of tortellini soup from the specialty market. While they're warming, I shake out a bag of crackers into a bowl. I would have skipped the cheese, because it gets dry and unappetizing if left out too long. But with a full house, I slice both the block of Cheddar, and the Edam. Then I cut into the loaf of rustic bread and also a long baguette.

The coffee urn is running low, so I dump the last of it, and brew fresh. It's a quality holiday blend in decaf and regular. Plus hot water for tea and cocoa.

I wheel out the cheese, crackers, and hot drinks out first, to give them something to start with. My second trip a few minutes later has the big hot pots of soup and the bread.

A few days ago I'd decided to include lasagna. I'm not doing turkey, stuffing, and such. I thought tasty, easy to prepare food would work fine—just in case everyone went out. I didn't want to go to a lot of work, but have no one here to appreciate it.

Everyone moves toward the sideboard, even the chess player.

"Has Mia been here this afternoon?" I look up from arranging the plates.

"No, I don't think so."

I'll send her a text to see if she caught a cold from swimming. She might need something brought to her cottage.

"Have a nice evening. I'll refresh the goodies later. Port and mulled-wine will be on the menu, along with a few other delights."

"We'll be right here. Between the food, and our new friends, there's no reason to sit in our rooms."

"I'm glad." I really am! This is a perfect Christmas Day. My guests are happy, and I have Quinn back for a while.

* * *

ON THE WAY OUT, I turn up the path to check the parking area where Mia parks. A minute later, I see her red Porsche there. As I swing back by her cottage, there's the Do Not Disturb sign on the lever. I won't—just in case she's sleeping, or wants privacy. So I'll go home and send a text from there.

"The sandwiches for lunch were a hit with the guests. I just put out lasagna and soup for a light dinner," I say to Quinn who is still at work. I kick off my shoes and head for the bedroom to change out of this silk stain-magnet. "I also have lasagna for us." I raise my voice from the closet.

"You may want to look at this first."

"Look at what?" I slide a long sleeved T-shirt over yoga pants, then head to the security room to see what Q is talking about. He's sitting at the desk with a pen poised over a clipboard.

"Are you aware that the drone was controlled by a man in a black SUV?"

"No! How did you figure that out?"

"I replayed the security footage. The drone located two of the visible cameras, but missed those at the street I camouflaged as a pinecones." He presses a button to stop the footage and looks up.

"I didn't know I had those."

"I put two at the front I didn't think you would need, but they turned out to be useful."

"How far back did you go?"

"To the evening of the drone incident." He hits play at the right place. "This street cam shows a black Chevy SUV slowly drive past and park down the road by the bridge."

"That's almost a mile away! How are we supposed to catch him when he can hide so far?"

"I rewound all the video until I was able to follow it to the source. It takes patience," he agrees. "See this—along the roadside?"

The video has lost resolution, but I can see a tall-ish, slender man in dark clothes step out and place a drone on the ground. As soon as it's airborne he gets back in the vehicle. "No front license plate. How annoying," I grumble.

"You can see the running lights fly past all the other hotels on the beach. It swings onto your property at the front path. See here." He changes to another feed. "It buzzes down and almost collides with Mia."

"That's when she came screaming to my door."

"Then it went to the parking lot and flew around. You came out here, and confronted it." I see the video of me shouting at the stupid thing while I shined my flashlight in its eyes. "I tried to blind it, but I really wanted to smash it with a baseball bat."

"It's a camera, sweetie. It doesn't have eyes." He leans over and kisses my cheek.

"Yeah well. I still wanted to kill it." We watch as it buzzes around my cottage, hovering at each window, making me angry and stressed, inside.

"Understandable," he murmurs, then changes the feed, returning to the street view of the SUV in the distance. "Look at this." A black four-door car pulls up next to the drone operator. It isn't the police investigating a car parked on an empty street. It has to be his friend or accomplice.

Another ten minutes pass. We see the drone return to its home base. The slender man picks it up, then drives north, away from my cottage. The four-door car drives toward us.

"Look—it has a front license plate!"

He zooms in and captures it.

"This was exactly a week ago. Nothing has happened since then."

"I'll run the plate to see if it's anyone you know. It could be Mia's ex-boyfriend, but I doubt it."

"It won't help if neither of us know the owner of the sedan."

"Unfortunately, I think you're right."

* * *

THE LASAGNA IS DELICIOUS. I got two trays from my new favorite restaurant, happily for me, its name is '500 Calories.' Based on the flavor of the cheese, and the freshness of the ingredients, I'd say it's 500 calories for a half-serving, but I'm not complaining tonight. Quinn is here and he loves it. I almost feel guilty that I didn't make it myself. His mother, a restauranteur, would have made it better. I guess I could have spent hours slicing zucchini, grating the cheese, and hand-picking the home-grown basil. Yeah, but I was running a bed and breakfast, and trying to make sure I keep it up to my grandmother's standards.

I also pour us a glass of my homemade mulled wine. I added sugar, allspice and cloves. It's nice. I keep taking a sip, and another. It's relaxing me. I can finally relax because I have Quinn here to keep watch.

"Sweetie?" He touches my hand.

"Hmm?"

"I appreciate you. I know it isn't easy being with me. I'm always away and I can't explain much. I know many women wouldn't be able to handle it."

"Thank you for acknowledging my sacrifice. I won't mince my words, it has been hard on me. But you are also an amazing man who I wouldn't be able to find again if I looked for the rest of my life."

I'm sure I'd be able to find someone, like Detective Josh Taylor, but he wouldn't be nearly as fantastic. I've come a long way in the past six months. I have to laugh over how I fell for Jack Courtland and his fancy winery. I've been blessed—if you're into religion, and blessed—if you're into Karma. Both ways, the word is the same, and the result is the same!

"You know, you aren't supposed to profess that to a man. We already have big egos, and some tend to stray."

"Do you stray?" I jump on that immediately.

"No. I generally don't have enough respect for the women I see out there, and I have too much respect for myself," he sounds introspective.

"Mmm," I murmur to acknowledge what he said.

He puts his fork down and reaches over to grip my hand. "I'm not perfect, but I will never do anything stupid in our relationship, or in my life. I could never find anyone else who fits me as well as you do." He sees my questioning expression. "Yes, that includes beautiful lady-spies on the French Riviera." He grins.

I don't know if he's joking about the Riviera or if it's an example.

"I may need to wear a sequined gown with a knife in a black, lace garter more often," I joke to cover my unease.

"That's what keeps me around… your humor, feistiness, and you have a strong sense of self."

"Oh. Thanks, that's good to know." To give me something to do, I pick up my fork and slide it under a fat square of lasagna. Chewing isn't sexy, but oh well.

My phone dings a text.

"It can wait. I hate to jump every time someone wants to communicate. In the old days, people would leave a message on the house phone, and not receive a reply until the other one got home from work."

"Times have changed and you have guests now," he reminds me.

"Ok, thanks." I was only doing that so he wouldn't feel second best.

The text is from Mia: "Axel made my friend tell him where I am. He's driving up here. What should I do?"

"When will he arrive?"

"Ten minutes."

Oh brother. She could have told me sooner. I immediately call her.

"Hi Mia. So what would you like me to do about it? Is he angry?"

"I don't know what he's thinking. He easily gets jealous. How about if I borrow your boyfriend?"

"Uh, no. He doesn't need to get involved in a domestic spat."

"It was just a thought," she pouts. "He looks like he can handle it."

More than you know. But I say, "It's best to avoid domestic disputes."

"What should I do?"

"If you don't want to see him, load up your bag and drive out of here in the next few minutes."

"But I like it here. I don't want to go."

"Your window of time is closing. Is there anything else you might want to do about it?"

"I don't want to be alone in my room with him."

She isn't coming in mine.

"If he's going to be loud and obnoxious, I'm sure the other guests don't want to deal with him in the lounge at Christmas."

"What should I do?" Her voice takes on a high note.

Get out of here. But I don't say that. No one wants a fight at their place. That includes restaurants and other hotels. Hmmm. She could go to Mandy's!

"Well, there is a larger hotel, only two doors to the west. They have a large communal room and lots of people around. There's a security guard on staff. He patrols all night, and they also have surveillance cameras. There are usually two workers at the front desk. Maybe you should check in there."

"A security guard? That sounds like a great idea. Ok, I'm throwing my stuff in my bag."

Less than five minutes later, we hear her Porsche speed out the driveway and decelerate a few yards away into Mandy's parking lot.

"I think I just avoided a lot of shouting and door slamming," I muse.

"Do you have something you'd like to say to Mandy's transmitter in your office?"

"Sure, I'd love to, but I don't know what fabrication I can come up with."

"How about the truth and something nice?"

"Why? How does that help me?"

"It won't hurt, and you got Mia out of your hair. You'll see how Mandy and company respond if you act like a fellow hotel owner rather than a competitor. There have been a lot of wars started over a misunderstanding."

"Fine. I'll go do it." I head out the door.

But I don't make it to the Garden cottage because here comes Axel. It can't be anyone else but him, looking Goth in a black trench coat, long black hair, and piercings. Charming.

"Hello, can I help you?" I put on my friendly but professional innkeeper's voice.

"Hello ma'am. I'm looking for Mia Huntington. I believe she's staying here," he has an English accent.

"I'm afraid she checked out a short while ago. Was she expecting you?"

"Yes. She's my girlfriend, but she sometimes likes to break up with me. This is one of those times."

"I'm sorry about that. She seems like a nice girl."

"She is. Thank you for your time." He turns to go. "Do you know where she went?"

Oh dear.

I shrug and try to look helpless. "I couldn't say. Before you go, would you like a cookie?" My answer is screwy, but I didn't actually lie. Well, not really.

"No thank you. I must be on my way." He returns to the parking lot and I hear his own Porsche drive out. He can't be poor.

Quinn comes outside. "He isn't at all what I imagined."

"No. He's multidimensional."

"That's one way of putting it," he laughs.

I delay a few moments longer to look around. After scanning for danger, I enjoy the soft sound of water dripping off the pine needles. The air is fresh and the plants are releasing their pungent scents.

The clouds have almost gone. The night sky is inky-black, interspersed with gusts of wind. It's a perfect setting for Axel the Goth. Except he doesn't seem too bad, and it isn't just the accent and the Porsche. Or maybe it is, but he's polite as well.

"He can still be an ex-boyfriend. Until she changes her mind and she moves him back to boyfriend status," I remind him.

"Come on, let's go tell Mandy Crawford about Mia."

We enter the Garden cottage. The room is now empty. Everyone piled their plates on the serving cart and left the tables tidy. The chairs are pushed in and it looks like they care. There's only one cookie left, and the wine decanter is nearly empty. I'd say they enjoyed their evening.

Quinn has unlocked the office, so I follow him in. We look at each other and nod. We'll play the good cop/ bad cop routine.

I stand behind the counter and begin, "Mia wanted time away from her boyfriend, that's why she came here. The other day, her friend told him where she was. So I suggested she go to Mandy's resort. It has the quality she expects."

"Are you sure you want to support your competitor?" Quinn asks.

"Yes, I do. The resort has the right environment for my client."

"Isn't she known to be a—I know you don't like the word—a bitch?

"Yes, I've heard that and been told to watch out for her. But she's a strong woman and I respect that."

"Jess, I'm telling you, I know her type. She'll do her best to ruin you."

14

WHERE'S AXEL?

No, we don't get too much sleep. Not only because we were making up for the days he's been away, but because he can't sleep—of all things. I thought I was the only one. He's been replaying hours of surveillance video, including checking on Mandy's office.

I wake at 3:00 to find him in the kitchen having seconds of lasagna. I flop into a chair, squinting at the strong light.

"I guess they didn't talk tonight," I grumble.

"Go back to bed, sweetie. I have other things I need to do," he suggests nicely.

"Oh, you mean for your boss?" The clandestine employer.

"I'm afraid so. It's going to be a busy year."

I drag myself up, give him a kiss on the cheek; take a forkful of lasagna, and head back to bed.

* * *

Q is sound asleep when I wake. I figure he won't stay that way through my rolling around, so I get out of bed and head to the kitchen. It's as good a place as any.

At least the fox hunt has been cancelled for today. In England, you'd still be riding, since if it was cancelled every time it rained, you'd never get on a horse. I'm happy to be a wimp.

It's too early to worry about the guests, and I bet Mandy hasn't listened to the recording. So what should I do—maybe go for a run? The next storm hasn't blown in yet, it's still off the coast, waiting.

The drizzle starts halfway through my run, so I cut it short by looping through the picnic area by the bridge. The parking lot is empty except for an immaculate black Porsche. I don't see anyone hanging around, but I wonder if it's Axel's. The windows have the darkest of tint. Because of that, I'd have to get right up beside it to see in, and I'm not sure I want to. I could try looking through the windshield, but...

I make my decision, I'll jog by without poking my nose into their business. I glance at the license plate and hope to remember it when I get home, playing a memory games that often fails. "8THN765." By the time I come up with words to correlate with the letters I've forgotten the rest of the numbers.

I run back to the street without sensing movement from within.

As I pass Mandy's resort, I wonder if I should swing through to see if Mia's red Porsche is there. It would be easy to see, but do I want her wrath, or one of the managers? No.

Quinn is up when I return. "I hope you weren't worried. I left a note on the bedroom door."

He looks up from a plastic gizmo in his hands and smiles, "I saw it. I was following you with this."

I take a closer look. It's a drone controller, I saw something like it online while researching. "I thought they couldn't fly in the rain."

"Mine can. This is high-end and weatherproof."

"Of course it is!" I have to laugh. Q has the best.

"That Porsche you were wondering about?"

"You can read my mind too?"

"Your stride changed. I could tell when you slowed, read the license plate, and thought about checking it out."

"Impressive. Yes, that's what I did. How about when I got to Mandy's driveway. What did you read there?"

"I stopped watching you and looked for the red Porsche. It's parked on the far side of the resort, under a tree."

"Thanks, I was thinking about looking, but decided against it."

"I figured."

"Is it still flying around?" I lean over to look at his phone app.

"Yes, I'm monitoring the area."

"And?"

"All quiet this morning, but I'm wondering about the Porsche. I'll buzz over the ocean and have a look through the windshield."

He moves the toggle to gain altitude, then sends it back to the picnic area where he wants to remain high enough to be unseen. The view is beautiful. It's like a documentary, seeing the coastline and road from this medium height. I see the allure of having a drone, it gives you the eyes of an eagle.

"No one's in the car," he comments.

"So where is he?"

"Beats me." He slowly patrols over the park area, then takes a lap around the property to the east.

It starts to rain in earnest. "I'm going to jump in the shower to warm up—or cool down. One of those."

"I'll land this baby in your back yard. It doesn't look like much is happening at the moment."

* * *

LATER IN THE AFTERNOON, Quinn is doing his work, so I settle down to listen to the receiver in Mandy's office. I fast forward. I stop at the part where the daytime manager is saying "The man in 201 is a sexy Italian. I'm trying to figure out a reason to knock on his door. Maybe I'll see if he needs clean towels."

"Don't embarrass yourself," Mandy remarks.

"I know, but he's gorgeous."

"Maybe he's gay."

"I don't think so. He looked like he appreciated what he saw."

"Sweetie, you know I love you, but you're twenty pounds overweight, and you need a face lift. I doubt he's looking at you that way," she remarks caustically. So much for calling her sweetie.

Oh my goodness—I can't believe she said that. She's a witch to everyone. I stop the replay. "Quinn, are you free? Mandy is a total cow to her friends too."

"What happened?" He shouts from the office.

I dash in there and tell him.

"Now you know not to take her so seriously. One day, someone will pay her back for being so cruel."

"You're right. I guess I feel better." I go back to the security room, sit at the fold-down table, and press play again.

Thirty minutes later, I hear this. "Your least favorite innkeeper just sent us a guest."

"As long as they don't get killed like that guy looking for the gold."

"No, this is some girl with an ex-boyfriend hanging around. Jessica said she recommended us because we are a beautiful resort worthy of her expensive client."

That's not exactly what I said, but it's close enough.

"She's a fool if she thinks kissing my ass me will prevent the takeover."

"She doesn't know about it. Maybe she's being nice."

"Nice people finish last," she cackles.

I wonder how long this manager will stay around after being verbally abused. If she wants to keep her job, she may have to deal with it.

* * *

It was a quiet day, until I received this text: "Jess. Axel needs help."

Is she an idiot? If you need help, don't text an innkeeper, call 911.

I call back, skipping the text. "What's going on?"

"We spent the night together, but this morning after breakfast he vanished."

So much for her needing to get away from him. I just lost several nights' income by sending her away.

"Do you happen to know his license plate?"

"No. Wait a sec—I think it begins with an 8," she sounds pleased.

Oh brother. That isn't much help.

"And approximately what time did you finish breakfast?"

"I don't know, I'm on vacation."

"Did you get in a fight?"

"No. Everything is fine."

"Even though you raced out of my place like a scared woman?" I was going to say like a bat out of hell, but I refrained.

"Maybe I overreacted, but he's gone now. I haven't seen him for a long time."

"How long?"

"Hours, all day."

"Is his car parked close to yours?"

"I don't know."

"Go look," my voice takes on a certain tone I'm sure her mother uses.

"Ok, I'm walking."

The door opens and I hear shuffling. "No. I don't see his car."

"It's a black Porsche, right?"

"Of course. He only wears black and only drives black." She says it like I should have known.

"Is the car registered to him?"

"I don't know."

"You didn't see him drive away? Did he walk? What was the last thing he said?"

"He said he was going to get a shrimp cocktail for us."

"They have a bar down at the patio. So he left and never returned?"

"Exactly."

"That's odd. I saw a black Porsche at the park on this morning on my run. I wonder if it's still there. I suggest calling the police. They'll take a report and check with DMV to see if he is the registered owner. If he is, the car license plate can be shown as belonging to a missing person."

"Ok, I'll call them, but I want to come back to your place. There are dangerous people here."

"Sure come back. I'll be here for the next hour." I have news for her, there are dangerous people everywhere.

Quinn has been listening. "I'll send up the drone for a quick flyover." He carries it into the rain and watches it take off, then returns to monitor what it finds. The Porsche has gone. That was hours ago, I guess it would be, but it's strange that Axel went for a cocktail and never returned.

An hour passes while I putter around the office and set out more cookies. I'm not providing a meal like I did yesterday. The restaurants are back to full capacity, and everyone is out and about, despite the rain.

Mia hasn't arrived and could take all day for all I know, so I head to town to pick up a few things. There are a ton of people walking around for the after-Christmas sales. One shop pulls me in by displaying a crystal horse ornament. It's a beauty, and even though it's only 10% off, I get it.

Then I dash back to get another for Nikki. She's crazy about horses too.

Ding. It's a text from Mia. "I'm in your lounge. Where are you? I need to get in my cottage."

Heavens. "It's been two hours since you said you'd be over right away." How annoying.

"I was busy," she whines.

"Hang out for a few minutes. I'll tell Quinn to keep an eye out for you. Help yourself to the cookies and Port wine."

"Fine. I'll be here getting fat and drunk. Send in that hunk of a man so I can have some fun."

I ignore the comment. I'm sure she wants to get a rise out of me. Her mother must know how to handle her. Or maybe not. She grew up and turned into this. Mommy let her run wild.

I text Quinn to let him know the darling, I mean my guest, is in the lounge and ask him to keep an eye out to make sure no one kidnaps her.

"I heard her drive in. There's no sneaking around in that car."

Ding. Another text from the grown child. "Hey, I forgot. I invited a gorgeous Italian man to join me. Don't send in your man. I don't need two of them vying for my attention."

I'm standing in a line at the counter to get more soup-of-the-day from the market. It's spicy lentil. I also want a frozen pizza. This is as far ahead as I can plan for quick eats. I need to get a few pounds of dried lentils, beans, and quinoa to make my own good food.

"Quinn, she invited an Italian man to join her in the lounge and doesn't want you there. She said she doesn't want two gorgeous men at one time. Yes, you read that right."

"I'll stay far away," he replies.

15

HECTOR

Mia's red Porsche is parked crooked in the check-in area. Of course.

An expensive, black Audi is parked correctly, in the next space.

After lugging the food into the house, I go straight to the lounge. There's Mia and the Italian. I guess Axel no longer matters.

I unlock the office, flip on the lights and get the computer going. Then I catch up on email and reply to a guest's comments on a social media site. She still hasn't come in, so I head into the lounge. There she is, on the couch in front of the roaring fireplace, lying back against the Italian. The bottle of Port is empty and the cookies have gone. She wasn't kidding about munching through everything.

I stand in front of her, feeling like a guardian of sorts.

"Hi Mia." I wait for her to focus her dreamy, drunken eyes. "I can give you your room card now if you'd like." I hold it up for her inspection.

"Sure. Leave it on my purse." She slowly waves her hand somewhere, but not where her purse is.

"Did you get this smashed on my wine?" I'm stressing.

"No. I love the champagne bar. You should get one," she advises.

"Yes, I'm planning on it."

I flick my eyes behind her and evaluate her new friend. He's exceptionally good looking. That's the first strike against him. The second is, while she's leaning against his chest and can't see his expression, he has been watching me without breaking eye contact. He even smiles suggestively. The jerk.

"Hello. I'm Jessica Wilcox." I politely introduce myself, without stepping closer to shake his hand or being overtly friendly. I am polite; after all, he is her guest.

His voice also sounds infused with alcohol. "I'm Hector." He untangles one hand from around her waist and runs it through his lush, black hair.

I'll give him credit for having nice hair. And a nice car, and nice clothes. But that's it. This isn't what the usual guests in Cambria are like. Well, maybe they are, but I think they come in couples. I don't actually know. Oh well. Come one, come all.

I break off eye contact to look for her purse. It's on the table by the empty cookie plate. I'm about to leave the key on top of it, when I realize it's an expensive designer bag. I pick it up and bring it to the table in front of her.

"I've brought your purse. It's right here with the key on top." I wait until she opens her eyes, then I point down to it.

"Um-hmm," she acknowledges then lets her lids close.

I don't even look at Hector, the handsome Italian. I've had enough of him. He brings back memories of Luca in Chianti, when I was there for three days investigating a winery for Jack.

Quinn needn't worry about Mia chasing him tonight. Maybe he wasn't worried, but I was irritated.

* * *

I LOCK the office and head back to the cottage. Q is there, working at the kitchen table.

"Are you ready for dinner?" He asks, with hope in his voice.

"Sure!"

"How about soup and pizza?" He smiles, knowingly.

"That sounds good."

That's what I picked up today. I'm not much of a nurture-with-food kind of woman. I nurture, but not by cooking for hours. And if I do, then I want tons of thanks in return for my hard work.

The meal is tasty, perhaps not for the nutritionally aware, but I don't always have to eat organic. Though I'm not sure about Quinn. He has to be in top form to stay alive.

"Are you worried about eating pizza—will it pose a problem when you're fighting for your life?"

"Neh, I'm young and healthy enough to withstand an indiscretion now and again."

I have the live feed from the lounge coming through the open security room door. The volume way down, I absolutely don't want to hear her giggling. Yuck. But I want it high enough to know when she leaves. Finally, at 6:30, she must have recovered enough to get hungry. They head out, and I hear the word 'dinner.'"

Looking at the rest of the camera feed, I see that she goes directly to her cottage; and he goes to the parking lot, leans against his car, and calls someone. I can't help it, I turn up the volume on my very good system.

"She's taking a leak. You gotta be kidding?" He's listening, then says. "She offered. It would be mean to say no," he laughs. "See you later."

Quinn comes over to listen. "Sounds like he'll be getting some tonight," he comments.

"Yeah, I think so. I wonder what will happen if Axel comes by."

"Who knows, he's a strange one, he may be okay with it."

* * *

JUST AFTER 2 A.M. we're wakened by pounding on my front door.

"Jessica. Jessica. Wake up!" It's Mia.

"Oh hell. What now?" I roll out of bed and hurry to the door. Mia is alone out there.

"What's wrong?" Those are my first words after I turn the knob.

"Axel was found at the side of the road!"

"Dead?"

"No. He's dazed and frozen solid," she's hysterical.

"Come inside." I stand aside to let her in. "How do you know?"

"The cops just called," she sobs. "I should have known he wouldn't leave me!"

"How did he get wherever he is?"

"He said a guy slugged him and forced him into his car, drove him up a long road, beat him up, then shoved him out and drove away."

"Wow. So that's what happened to him."

"It took him all day and night to get to the road. My poor love. He fought for his life in the pouring rain."

"Where is he now?"

"At the hospital in Paso Robles. Will you take me to him?"

Uh.

"Please. I have to go to him!" She begs.

I inhale and answer, "No. Get that Hector guy or call a ride."

"Hector is sleeping and I don't like Uber."

"Then drive yourself."

"It's dark."

"You never go out after dark?" Yeah, right.

"I'm too upset."

"Mia, you have a car. Drive slowly and go see him. He's alive and he's fine," I lecture like a mother.

"That's not fair. I need help. Why won't you drive me?"

"Because it's the middle of the night and you have a car. Be an adult and drive there."

"I'm going back to the Seaside Resort. They're nicer than you." She jerks open the door and marches out into the drizzle. She turns with a glare, "They know how to treat someone like me."

I close the door and lock it behind her.

"She's a handful," Quinn shouts from the bedroom.

"No kidding!"

An hour later, a Porsche engine revs a few times by my back

fence. For someone in a rush to see her precious Axel, she took a long time getting out of here. I don't know if she'll return, or if she has her things. I'll find out after the 11 a.m. check-out.

I wonder if her new boy-toy is still there. I couldn't be bothered to check the parking lot surveillance feed.

* * *

THE RAIN CLEARS out in the early hours. The sun is shining, and it promises to be a beautiful day with white clouds and a brilliant, blue sky.

I head into the lounge at 9:00 when I see it's filling up. Janet is heaping the warming pans with scrambled eggs, cottage fries, and pancakes.

"Hello, good morning!" I breeze in and join the others at the line. Quinn will be here in a minute.

The door opens. I look up as that Hector guy strides in. What is he doing here? He stands behind me in line.

"Has Mia returned?" I ask while I recover.

"No. I haven't seen her." He smirks while reaching around me for a plate.

"Then what are you doing helping yourself to breakfast?"

"She won't be eating hers, so I'll do it for her."

A wave of heat washes over me. Its adrenaline and a smidge of caution. He seems dangerous.

"No you won't," I reply in a calm, unfriendly tone.

"Look sweetheart. It makes sense since she isn't here to eat, and she invited me in her place," he reasons, with a mean look.

"Go back to where you're staying and eat there. You aren't welcome here. Please leave NOW."

He leans forward, getting within an inch of my face. "Babe, you don't know who you're dealing with. You'll be sorry." He drops the plate on the wood floor, shattering it, then calmly walks out the open French doors.

I follow at a safe distance. I need to get his license plate. I have no idea who he is, but I intend to find out.

I whip out my cell phone and take a photo of him from the back and dash after him to the car. When he turns to get in, I get a few of his face.

Now that he out of the lounge, I feel better.

"See you soon," he shouts, while slowly driving past.

"I won't leave the light on for you," I stupidly reply.

He presses hard on the accelerator and peels out of the driveway.

When he's gone I notice I'm shaking with rage and adrenaline.

Quinn comes running up in shorts and bare feet, still wet from the shower. "What's going on?" He's all business, even in his state of undress.

"Mia's Italian. There's more to him than we know." I hate the sound of my voice. It's a little shaky.

"Why the hell did I take a shower?" he fumes.

"Because you wanted to be clean?" I force a smile, but I'm a raging inferno inside. "Don't worry."

16

───────

THE REVIEW

Quinn sprints inside. Where is he going? Seconds later he's charging back out with his drone. He sets it down, on solid ground for take-off. In a flash, it's in the air.

It buzzes its way to a high elevation. "I'm looking for a speeding car," he tells me.

Nothing grabs his eye.

"It's a black Audi."

"If it isn't speeding, I won't see anything. It's just a black sedan, and nothing stands out."

Quinn calls a friend to give him the license plate. He comes back with the answer about thirty seconds later. It isn't the best news.

"The jerk doesn't own the car and it isn't in his name. It comes back to a company by the name of Tre Amici. That's Three Friends, in Italian."

"How are we supposed to find out who he is? Is he an employee, a manager, or the owner?"

"It may take a while. I'll get it rolling." He's already thinking a step ahead.

"I'll get the police involved by making a vandalism report. At least that will start a paper-trail."

I hurry back to the lounge for damage control. As I step through the open door, I see Janet cleaning up the broken plate shards.

I go with the truth as the best remedy. "That was Mia's 'friend' he just left and won't be returning." I adjust the lampshade that is a bit tilted and continue. "I apologize for his tantrum."

"It isn't your fault. You don't need to apologize for him," the man says.

He sets the tone for everyone in the room. They murmur their agreement and keep talking about it among themselves. It wasn't my fault and all is forgiven.

"Thank you. You're very kind," I reply.

I return to the kitchen with Janet to slice a loaf of banana bread. At least I can feed them more than they expected. I smile, set out the sweet bread, answer a few questions, and then stroll out the door.

The second I close the door to my cottage I'm on the phone with the police, making a report. There isn't a lot to add, and I know there are a lot of loose ends. It's interesting that Mia picks up this guy at the same hotel as hers, Axel shows up then gets his car stolen. There are a lot of coincidences on this short stretch of road.

Q comes in with his drone. "I'm sorry. I had no luck finding him." He sets it down by the door, ready for quick use.

"He ran to ground pretty fast."

"Is that a foxhunting term?" He looks puzzled.

"I think so. I haven't used it before." I head to the security desk and start replaying the latest of Mandy's office conversations.

Twenty minutes later, I shout to Q, "Listen to this. She's really a nasty woman. I gave her a chance, but she's showing her real self."

He leaves the table where he's working to stand behind my chair. "Oh?"

I click Play and hear the manager: "I wrote a scathing review she promised to post about Greenstone Cottage."

"You played up to her just right. That rich girl is such a fool," Mandy replies.

"It's especially funny since *stupid Jessica* sent her to us." She says my name with a nasty tone.

"No good deed goes unpunished," Mandy sounds happy.

Quinn reaches over my shoulder to press stop. "Jess." He squats down, below my level. "Now we know for sure."

"We'll know when I see what they posted." I click a few links and pull it up.

This is what the resort manager wrote and Mia posted: *"I couldn't be more impressed by the service I received at the Cambria Seaside (world class) resort. The guest accommodations are spotless and the breakfast is to die for. I'm shocked that Greenstone Cottage, down the road, is even in business. I couldn't get out of there fast enough after I saw three rats while I was eating a tasteless breakfast in their dilapidated room. One was carrying a piece of toast in its mouth. Can you imagine my horror?"*

"I have witnesses that didn't happen. She was eating with the other guests!" I'm breathless with my own horror.

"Get a screen shot and an attorney." He sounds cold. "She will be sorry."

I glance up at his face—one that looks deadly serious. Not that he'll kill Mandy, but she isn't on his list of friends. She has become an enemy.

He clicks PLAY and we hear more.

After Mandy hears the manager repeat the same post I read, she comments. "This is the most fun I've had all day. Three rats and a piece of toast in its mouth. That's perfect."

"Thanks, I thought so too!"

"Any time now, I will be posting my new sign, Under New Management."

"You'll have her on the run." The manager laughs.

"I'll start with the health inspector next." Mandy laughs.

"You go, girl!"

I stop the tape.

My face is burning hot over what they're saying.

"Do you want to join me for a run?" Quinn asks, seeing I'm flaming angry.

"Yes, I need to get out of the house!" I put on my running clothes and together we step into the clear beach air and I immediately break into a run.

"Hang on, keep it slow for a bit," he advises.

So I jog until we get to the curve in the road, then Q urges, "Kick it into gear." He takes off.

It's a struggle following him, the guy is an athlete, but I'm full of anger. That fuels me.

An hour later, I hobble back down the road, with heaving lungs and sore thighs. The man ran me into the ground, and he still looks good.

"Aren't you even tired?" I gasp.

"A little." He puts his palm on my butt to help push me up the rise. "I have to be fit, it keeps me alive."

"The same probably goes for me too."

"Knowing what you get into, yes, you're right."

We're walking on the narrow dirt shoulder the last quarter mile to the cottage. A red Porsche is speeding towards us on Moonstone —and I mean really speeding. It has to be going at least 60 mph in the other lane of traffic. Quinn and I automatically move over even further. He takes my hand.

As it gets closer, I see a strange-looking male driver. Quinn's hand tightens around mine.

It veers toward us, crossing the broken yellow line, toward us.

"Jump," Q shouts and throws me over the small retaining wall. He lands beside me.

The car scatters loose gravel in the air, slides a little, then regains control and accelerates away with a whine.

"That was close," I pant as I get to my feet, smashing the ice plant.

"The driver had a nylon stocking over his head," he snarls.

"So that's why he looked strange. I could tell he's a white guy with dark hair, but that's it."

"Tall and not fat," he replies, then jumps over the wall and runs into the road to see the Porsche disappear around the bend.

I scramble out of the bushes and we run home. Quinn takes the lead and reaches the door first, flies inside, and grabs his phone. He'll call the police; his breathing is heavy, but mine is worse.

He starts dialing, then disconnects and spins around to grab his drone. He'll be using it as his eyes, as he attaches his phone to the controller. He runs out front and sets it on the hard stone.

I call the police and manage to regulate my breathing while speaking with the dispatcher.

While waiting, I'm pacing in circles at the front. Quinn is pretty much doing the same, while scanning for the fast red car with his cell phone. The deputy can be here in five minutes; he is in town, just across the highway. Since they already have the information, he's checking the escape routes. They've put out a broadcast to the highway patrol and the other jurisdictions. Maybe we'll get lucky. There is only one highway that runs north/south.

"Where the hell is it?" Quinn sounds pissed off.

I guess his self-control is slipping a bit. I'm glad to see he is human. I was beginning to think he is as calm as James Bond.

About twenty minutes later, the black and white police car comes fast down the road. I raise my hand and give a quick wave. The deputy pulls onto my driveway and gets out.

"I guess he got away?" I shrug.

"Yeah, but I don't know how. We had the main roads covered. He didn't get out. He's in here somewhere."

"He got away in under five minutes. I had this bird in the air in that time," Quinn grumbles, while continuing to search. "Maybe he's in a garage or under a tree."

"I bet its Mia's car. You may be getting a report of a stolen Porsche as soon as she figures it out. It came from somewhere around the Cambria Seaside Resort." I point down the road.

"Is that where the owner is staying?" The deputy asks.

"Yes. She was staying here until she got irritated and left. Her name is Mia Huntington, if you want to call her. I'll get her number." I hurry to my office.

When I return he calls her, but it goes to voicemail. "I'll phone the hotel and have them call her room." He gets the correct number and calls. "Good afternoon, this is Deputy Packard with the San Luis Obispo County Sheriff's office. We've had a report of a possible stolen red Porsche. The possible owner, Mia Huntington is registered in your hotel. Please send someone to check the parking lot, and call her room to see if she's in."

"We cannot release any confidential information. We pride ourselves in protecting the identity of our guests." I hear her voice over the speaker. It's the day manager; the one who set up the rat review.

"Yes ma'am, but I'm not asking for information. I know she's staying there. Please send someone to see if she is in her room and if the car is in your lot. This could be a matter of her personal safety," the deputy isn't backing down.

"Oh. I see." She puts him on hold. The music is an ear-piercing violin.

The deputy gets his report book and begins getting the basic story.

She comes back on the line. "Hello, officer? I had a housekeeper check the room. She found Miss Huntington in bed. She is drunk and unresponsive, so I've called an ambulance for her safety." She doesn't even sound stressed. She is a well-seasoned employee.

"Thank you. Is the car there?"

"No it doesn't seem to be. I heard it race down the driveway a little while ago. That's a dangerous driver. We don't tolerate them here."

"Good to know. I'll be over in a few minutes."

"Well—" I look at Quinn without finishing my sentence. He's still searching, keeping his attention on the screen.

"What's the range on that thing," Deputy Packard asks.

"Nine kilometers."

"Nice. That's a good one." He's impressed.

Some male bonding goes on while I listen quietly. In the distance I hear a siren. The ambulance is coming for Mia.

Maybe I should call her mother. I'll see what shape she's in before I stick my nose into her business. Plus it's at Mandy's. What's the manager going to do, kick me off the property? I don't think so, I'll be with the police.

The ambulance pulls into the resort with the siren wailing. Oh, they'll hate that! Hahahaha.

The deputy lets me drive with him, but Quinn elects to stay home. No, I doubt the manger will have the guts to try anything while I'm with the authorities.

He parks beside the ambulance, making their serene resort look disturbingly like they have an unpleasant problem. They'll have some explaining to do.

The paramedics are the same ones who took Mr. Crown to the hospital when he fell over the bluff. They come out with Mia strapped to the gurney, covered up to the chin with a white sheet. At least it isn't covering her face. She's still alive and groaning.

They stop at the open back doors to let the deputy ask a few questions. I stand by while hearing that she drank herself into a stupor with her new boyfriend.

"Where is your Porsche?" asks the deputy.

"Where I parked it," she slurs.

"And where is that?" He doesn't find her amusing.

"Outside the room in my designated space." Even while dangerously drunk, she uses a condescending tone.

He gives her a little grin. "If you say so." He flicks a look to the numbered empty parking space. "Do you have the keys?"

"I don't know." It's a good thing she's strapped down, because she tries to crane her neck around to look, and would have fallen off. "Where's my car?" She slurs loudly.

"Did you notice the keys?" he asks a paramedic.

"No. Here's her purse with ID." He hands it over.

"No keys here." Deputy Packard gives it a quick search.

"What? Where's my car? Mom's going to kill me." She settles down a little. "Oh phooey."

The manager steps up to our little group. "We'd like to clean the room. Will that be a problem?"

The deputy raises his eyebrows at the paramedics, silently asking if she's going to die. She'll be fine. "I'll look inside. You can have the room tomorrow by check-out," Packard replies to her.

He heads over and I follow. I glance at the manager and she glares at me. Inside, I ask if he'll take the water glass for prints. "There's only one glass. I bet he wiped them off," he replies.

I find it in the bathroom and hold it up to the light with a tissue. Damn, it's washed and clean.

The car key has gone, he probably used it to start the car instead of some another way thieves use these on high-end vehicles.

"The fact that he vanished so quickly makes me think it's been planned. Especially since the black one was stolen just the other day," the deputy comments.

"A ring. I wonder if they followed her and Axel from L.A. or if they were already here."

"Good question." He considers the possibilities.

"We have a friend at DMV who checked on the Audi. It comes back to a corporation called Tre Amici." I pause. "She keeps saying the guy is Italian, and the Audi he drives is registered to an Italian-sounding company. Maybe they can track him down by his car."

"Let me have the info. I'll include it in the report and have the lab techs print the room."

"Is Detective Taylor around?"

"Yes, as far as I know. He had me looking for a suspect a few days ago."

"I know he's in homicide, but he might be interested in this."

"I'll send him a copy if you'd like."

"Thanks. That would be great."

I like to keep Josh Taylor in the loop. It's good to have as many authorities aware of my situation as possible.

* * *

BACK AT MY COTTAGE, Quinn is inside, having given up with his drone. I can tell because it's sitting on the table by the door.

"Hi sweetie," I sink into a kitchen chair with a glass of cool water.

He comes to the table and sits opposite. "You'll be interested to know I looked over the surveillance feed from where we placed a device at the resort. It shows Mia's man leaving her room, getting in her car and driving out. He turns left and puts on the speed. The time stamp shows it's the same as when we were being run down."

"Was he wearing a nylon over his face?"

"He sure was, it's probably hers," he replies. "I bet there's one missing from her suitcase."

"We can partially identify the driver and the video puts him in the car." I'm smiling again. The day has turned cheery.

"We'll have to testify to setting the camera in the trees. It will be embarrassing. The defense attorney will try to get it kicked out. You will have to take the heat and explain that you were trying to protect Phil Crowne."

"But it didn't protect him," I grumble.

"No, and his killer is still walking free."

"Whoever he may be. Though we're sure it's the roofer, there isn't enough proof." I take a gulp of water. "At least he's going to jail for receiving stolen property, hiding it in my roof, then cutting it open to take it back."

17

SPICES

The day returns to normal. No more cars are trying to run us down. Q works on his own plans and I catch up on my hotel duties. I even wrap a parting gift for two guests and request a nice review, if they can spare the time. It looks like I will need to be proactive for a while. Decades of an excellent reputation could go down the drain with a smear campaign powered by Mandy.

That's what I'll do—get inexpensive local gifts. I need to get out of the office anyhow, so I grab my keys and head to town. Quinn declined coming with me. He's in the middle of computing something and doesn't want to walk through a bunch of gift shops. There's a tracking device on my car, in my phone, and in my jacket. I don't want him wasting his time tagging along as my body guard since it's only a few blocks to town.

My first stop is to visit Kate at the Mysterious Chef kitchen store. She began making her own chai teas a few weeks ago. I have an idea that she can make small packs of hot chocolate/chai spice combinations for me. I'd do it myself, but I don't want to fiddle with packaging. I'd like them to look professional rather than home made in a zip-lock baggie.

While she's helping a customer I take a look around. The scent in here is a delightful mix of coffee and spices. Last time, I bought a chocolate and fennel blend. This time, I'll try something different, something I haven't had before.

Kate finishes with her customer and comes up to me.

"Does this really taste like streusel: cinnamon, nutmeg, cloves and brown sugar? How about if I use stevia instead?" I know I like it already.

She sounds apologetic, "If you want the nuance, it's best to use the brown sugar. Stevia is sweet, but it can be bitter and doesn't have any flavor. Brown sugar has hints of molasses and tastes great."

"So, to be slender, I have to sacrifice taste?" I look up with a frown.

"Sorry, I don't make the rules," she chuckles.

"All right, I'll get this and try to limit my intake." I look at the rest of the display. She has them in beautiful wooden boxes. "Do you have mini packs, or can you make some for parting gifts?"

"That's a great idea. No, I don't have any that small, but I could put some together."

"That's what I hoped you'd say. There's no way I want to mess around with containers of spices and then put them into lovely packages when you already have the equipment."

"I appreciate you thinking of me! I'd be happy to work up a few samples."

"Perfect. I love the Indian flair you have going. The colors made me feel like I'm walking through the Kasbah—is that the right country?"

"Not really. The Kasbah is a fortress in Morocco, but they have spices and exotic ingredients in their markets too. Maybe a bazaar, or a spice market in India would be more correct. Most people wouldn't know, but anyone who does may think you don't know what you're talking about."

"I don't. That's why I'm coming to you."

"Thanks, I appreciate that. When I was young and adventurous, I backpacked through Europe and down into North Africa, India and Tibet. I had the time of my life, and met the most interesting, life changing people."

"I'd be afraid to leave Europe."

"I met up with a group my age and made friends. I never walked alone at night and stayed safe. It was different back then."

"I don't think it's ever been different. There are always bad-actors out there looking for someone to prey upon. I like being armed," I think back on my experiences.

"I have a different state of mind, I see the best in people," she picks up the end of the colorful scarf that's tied around her waist, admiring the workmanship and beauty from a distant land.

"That's nice. I guess I've seen too much of the streets of L.A., and think the bad ones are waiting to pounce on me."

"I've never been pounced on."

"I have." A single laugh breaks out of me. "In fact, just this morning, I was finishing a run with my boyfriend when a red Porsche aimed for us. We had to dive over the wall to avoid getting run down."

"Really—in Cambria?" She's shocked. "Maybe the driver was inattentive."

"Well, there's more to it. He had just stolen the car."

"In Cambria?"

"It's some creep from L.A." I go with the easiest explanation.

"Oh, that makes sense."

"So, what would you suggest in the hot chocolate category? I think it may appeal to men as well as women."

"Tea is lower calorie," she points out.

"Will you give me a quote for a chocolate spice blend, a coffee, and a tea? That'll be a nice selection."

"Sure I'd love to. I assume you'd like them in paper, rather than a wooden box?"

"Yes, unfortunately. I'd like to keep the costs low enough that I can hand them out like business cards."

"That's a great idea."

"I think so too. I just thought of it right now. That wasn't my original plan." I have to laugh. Sometimes good ideas just pop out.

"You think well on the fly."

"I hope so." For many reasons.

"I'll put together a price sheet of spice blends."

"Oh, and maybe only one packet for the business card. No need to do three—I'll save those for my guests."

"Got it."

I spend a little more time in the shop, select a few spiced chocolate mixes to bring home, and then head on my way. I'm feeling pleased with my progress.

When I get back to the car, I'm sniffing each spice packet when my phone buzzes with a text: It's from Georgina. I'd forgotten about foxhunting with the drama over Mia.

"Be ready to ride Wednesday at 10 AM. The ground is firm enough. Make L. chase you. I want him in your pants, and get proof. I'm paying for results. Get them."

Darn. I slump down in the seat.

"Georgina, you are paying me for my investigation. NOT to sleep with your husband. If he is innocent, you can't force him into my bed. That is proof he isn't cheating on you."

"If he isn't cheating, make him."

This is an interesting change. She wants him to cheat on her? As I recall, she said they are divorcing. If he cheats, she won't have to split the assets.

"I'll be there. But I will not, under ANY circumstances sleep with your husband. And please send the additional money to cover my lessons from last time, for the hireling, and the work coming up."

"My accountant will handle it."

18

HUNTING AGAIN

Wednesday morning I'm in my diesel-guzzling truck, heading toward the vineyard in Los Alamos. It's a great central California day. There are only a few clouds, and the temperature in the low 70s is perfect for riding. My friend tells me they're having an ice storm in Missouri today. They have lower property taxes, so perhaps that makes it balance out with our great weather.

I pull alongside David's truck and park. Ryan is already saddled, but David is riding around somewhere. His horse's halter is dangling from the trailer, evidence that he's been and gone.

When I get the bridle from the tack room, I step into a beautifully arranged horse trailer. He pays attention to detail. The saddle racks, bridle hooks, and wall units are built in. He made a small section into sleeping quarters with a bed in the gooseneck part; that's the part of the trailer that rises over the truck. In many trailers, it's just a mattress, but his has a bedspread and throw pillows to make it more inviting for a quick nap between classes. There's a tiny cabinet, and a wash basin with mirror to make sure you look tidy before going in the show ring. Nice.

I grab the right bridle and step out closing the door to keep flies and inquisitive eyes away.

The group with Lyle and Roxy is milling around by the stack of wine barrels. I'd better get some photos to prove I'm conducting a thorough investigation. It will only show they're riding close together, but maybe it will help if they deny it. Then I head over to join the group. I'd prefer to ride with the slow crowd, but I'm stuck shoving my worries away and hoping Ryan keeps jumping well. I smeared sticky resin on the saddle again. I'm pleased to report it works great keeping me in the seat instead of on the ground.

I say hello to many people I recognize from the Christmas lunch. I especially remember the people from the dessert table, because we had such a nice chat. On Saturday, didn't have anything to say to the meat and sausage people and I still feel the same way.

Lyle nods at me and grins with a thumbs up signal. I take this as an invitation to be friendly. It looks like Roxy doesn't care for the idea. "Hi Lyle, hi Roxy." I'm friendly to one and all.

She nods and nudges her horse closer to Lyle's.

He gazes at me longer than necessary.

So I look back with, what I hope is a secretive smirk, rather than a bitchy smirk. "How's your horse today?" What else can I ask— how's your wife, your divorce, your affair?

"He's good. How's yours?" He keeps his eye contact.

Roxy scowls and moves her horse between us. Well, that's obvious, don't you think? She believes I'm moving in on her territory, but Lyle isn't hers, he's Georgina's.

"How was your Christmas?" I move Ryan a step forward so I can see Lyle's smiling face.

"Great. I spent it with my wife." His smile turns into a grin for a brief moment. "How about you?"

"Very nice thanks. I spent it with my boyfriend."

"Good, good." He nods, with little else to say.

"Nice day for a hunt," I try again.

"Sure is. I need to get out and work off some steam. Business has been very good over the holidays. Everyone wants their heaters working."

"That sounds familiar. It's like people waiting for the rain before they repair their roof."

"But you don't know you have a leak until it rains." Roxy cuts in.

"Sure, but you can see if your roof is missing shingles, or the tiles are loose." I refuse to give in.

She doesn't reply, though I have to admit, she has a point.

The huntsman shouts, "Tally-Ho," and the riders surge forward.

"See you around," Lyle shouts as he takes off with Roxy on his tail.

Well, that didn't go anywhere. He seems less interested in conversation than last time.

I let Ryan break into a trot, there's no need to gallop after the nuts ahead of us. David flies up, "Hey Jess, nice seeing you. Come join me!"

I have little choice but to canter along with him. After a few minutes of the clean air in my face, and the rhythm of the horse under me, I begin to loosen up and enjoy the ride. Until I see the horses flowing over a looming fence. From a distance, they look like lemmings moving as one, up and over, and continuing on. I hope I flow like a lemming. My confidence needs a little work today.

Today, the riders seem more competitive. No one wants to give way to let another horse go ahead of him. Ryan has his nose in his stablemate's tail and is ignoring my hands trying to pull him back. He fully intends to jump immediately behind David on Harry.

I see them swarm up and over while Ryan is beginning the take off part of his jump. There's the part in the air, that's the easy part, then the landing comes with a nice thud of his shock absorbing front legs. He gallops on with nary a hesitation. Whew. The horse is in good form today.

The dirt road winds up a gentle hill, then levels off before going down the other side. I don't gallop downhill. He has burned off some of his energy during the past ten minutes. The other horses have spread out a bit, slightly less intent on being first over the jump. I shorten the reins and slow Ryan to a trot going downhill. Some of the hot-shots on super athletes are cantering, but not me. Most everyone else is sane as well.

More jumps pass underneath us. I think I have the hang of it now. This horse is amazing.

I manage to let David go on ahead. He's riding up with Lyle and Roxy now, while I slow down with the rest.

Here comes a downed hundred-year-old oak. I'd like to go around it, but it's being used as part of a fence line to keep the range cattle out of the vineyard. Everyone goes over, but the far side seems to be a problem. Two horses ahead of us stumble on the landing. Oh dear.

And here we go, up and over. And down.

Down.

I'm flying through the air, separated from my horse.

He tripped and regained his footing. But I lost my seat similar to being thrown from a slingshot. Then I meet the ground and feel gravity re-exerting its control.

My fear isn't just the hard landing, it's getting mowed down by the others. I roll into a ball and hope for the best. Hooves thud around me, but the majestic equines manage to dance their way around my head, arms and legs. It has nothing to do with the riders steering clear. It's entirely up to the horse, trying to avoid stepping on me. The flood of riders has passed, so I roll out of the landing zone before the next batch arrive. They should be able to stop, since they'd have time to see a dismounted rider and a loose horse.

Ryan hasn't waited for me. He's galloping with the leaders in the distance. I quickly move clear of the jump, adjust my helmet, and keep walking. After a few strides I break into a jog. My hip hurts; that's where I landed. I always seem to land on my right hip. Yes, I've come off a few times in my life.

"Are you all right?" A lady pulls up next to me.

"Thanks, I'm fine. That jump has a sucky landing."

"Yeah, it needs fixing!"

"I'll see if I can catch up with David. That's where the horse is going—to be with his friend."

She looks in the distance. "They're stopping now, I'll go get him." She canters off.

I'm a bit embarrassed, but hey, the horse stumbled.

A few minutes later David canters back, leading Ryan. "That landing was a bad one. It needs fixing," he informs me.

"Right, so I discovered. I'm glad Ryan is fine." I look at his front legs. "Maybe he should take the rest of the day off to see if he pulled a tendon."

"He seems fine, but I appreciate your understanding. Do you want to ride with the gate keepers?"

"Yes. These boots aren't good for hiking."

I get on and ride with the slow pokes who go around the jumps and monitor the gates. An hour later, we circle back to the trailers and I dismount. I examine his lower legs again. They're nice and tight, the way they should be. The tendons and ligaments should look prominent, without soft spots or puffy swellings.

I take off the bridle, saddle, and pad. He's now standing quietly in the shade while I put it in the tack room. When they're neatly in place, I step over to the mirror. Not a pretty sight. I twist around to see my right side with a large patch of smeared dirt that can only mean one thing—I fell off.

Now that I've stopped, my hip hurts like crazy. I wonder if he has aspirin in the cabinet. I feel uncomfortable going in someone else's medicine cabinet. I've done it plenty of times on the department, when looking for drugs of overdose victims, or evidence.

Oh my.

Here's the aspirin, along with a box of condoms. It looks like David likes to have fun as well as ride. I'm quite certain he and Roxy were having fun in here the other day. I wonder if I can get a look in Lyle's trailer. Although, his doesn't have a mattress, it isn't a gooseneck/ fifth wheel trailer.

Should I go look? I am an investigator.

I hobble to Ryan's side, and look around with obvious guilt for what I'm about to do. No one is here, so I step it into gear toward Lyle's rig. His dressing room is unlocked. I pull open the door and glance around. There's nothing special except a trunk on the floor at the far side. I jump in and whip open the lid. Nothing, except leg wraps and veterinary things for minor accidents.

I get the hell out, close the door, and head back to Ryan. Whew. I hate that kind of thing. If this were a movie and the heroine did that, I'd be shouting, "Hurry up, hurry up!"

I make sure the horse is comfortable with his bucket of water and hay net, and has the dried sweat brushed off. Then I head to my truck to change into comfortable running shoes. Now what?

David likes to play around. That's fine, he's a single man, nice looking, and charismatic. For a girl looking for a nice guy in the horse business, he's a catch. I admit, I've taken a second looks at farriers, veterinarians, and any straight man on a horse. I'd prefer not to have a cowboy, but they tend to be straight, so I made an exception for them. Thankfully, I found Quinn, so I don't have to investigate the sound of a deep voice coming from the other side of a horse, truck, or stall door.

With time to kill before lunch, I wander around the bins that just three months ago each held a thousand pounds of Pinot Noir grapes. The destemmer is a giant stainless bin, shaped like a V, with a spinning auger at the bottom. The grapes are beaten, which can cause some to break open, but other machines don't do that. Regardless, they fall through the correctly-sized holes, but the stems don't. It looks like a painful process for the grape.

A huge, torturous-looking wooden barrel, held together with steel bands is the actual crusher. Hydraulics force the top, stabilized with steel beams, down onto the grapes, pressing out the juice.

There are other stainless machines with a German manufacturer's name on the side. It looks like they must be the high-end makers, but I've heard other vintners swear by the Italian ones.

That's about all there is to see. The buildings are empty and drafty in the winter. At harvest time, it must be busy, with the pickers picking, the crushers crushing, and the juice flowing.

The first riders are arriving back at the trailers, so I head over to see how it went. There's David riding with Roxy. She's looking vibrant and energetic—a sign that she is turning on the charm. She may be preparing him for a 'nooner' in the trailer.

I'll stay clear to let them have their privacy. I'll get the evidence later, to prove that Lyle isn't involved.

Lyle is riding up alone. He isn't schmoozing with the huntsman or whippers-in. Maybe he discovered they don't need his heating and air-conditioning services.

I brought fruit salad with a vanilla yogurt sauce. It's a sweet sauce, otherwise it would be too tart with the slightly unripe fruit. I have a shaker of cinnamon, and another with fennel sitting beside the bowl. This way, the riders can add a little spice if they want.

The same people made the desserts as last time. They are setting out brownies, fudge, and cake. We still have plenty to talk about as we sample each other's treats. A few minutes later, the riders line up, beginning at the plates and utensils.

"How are you doing after your fall?" Because of where I put myself, Lyle is in line behind me.

"I'm fine, thanks to my padded hips," I reply and grin.

"And they're nicely padded too." His eyes flick down and back up.

"You're so complimentary, it's good for my ego. Especially after embarrassing myself."

"We've all taken a spill. Don't worry."

We hear giggling from the end of the line. I glance back. Its Roxy being overtly responsive to something David said.

There's a gap in the line so we have a chance to talk softly without being overheard.

"I thought she was with you. Not that it's any of my business, but now she seems taken with him." It would be a catty thing to say if I was trying to separate her and Lyle, but I'm digging for information, and I don't care if it's catty. Whatever catty is.

"She's a little hussy," is all he says.

"Oh does that mean you're available now?" I softly ask, and put on a sweet, but not sexy expression.

He looks at me sadly. "You can do better than an over-the-hill married man with a struggling business."

I wait a second to respond, "I'm sorry about your business, and you're a handsome man."

"Thanks," he sighs, looking dejected.

Wow, he really wears his heart on his sleeve. Maybe he isn't such a schmoozer after all. Maybe he's trying to save his business.

At the end of the row, I let him go with a kind word. "You're a nice man. I wish you the best."

"Thank you. If things were different, I would have liked to know you better."

We part ways. I head for the table with the slow riders, and he goes to the big-wig tables to drum up business.

While chatting with the gals, I'm keeping an eye on Lyle, who is indeed with the men. David and Roxy are drinking from the same flask, and laughing with another couple who looks like they're having a lot of fun.

I get a woman to take a video of me, as I strategically position myself with Lyle at the table on one side, and David and Roxy in the background at the other side; she pans the whole scene.

I definitely chose the right table. These women are a bundle of fun. I relax and enjoy seconds of dessert as we have a good natured argument about fudge. An hour later, the hunt master is rising from the table. Everyone sees that as their cue to finish up. They dump their empty plates in the garbage and hurry to their trailers.

Lyle is explaining something to two men at the serving table.

David is already at his trailer, adjusting the saddle on his horse.

Oh look, there's Roxy, walking the long way around the trees. What is she doing back there? I keep an eye on her. She's making her way to David's trailer parked at the far end of the lot. Huh. Those condoms may come in handy this afternoon.

I record him leaving the horse and going to the tack room on the far side—and she's following him.

I go to the trailer—with my phone in hand. I go straight there, supposedly to check on Ryan. When I arrive, I can already hear whispers and moans coming from inside. I flip on the recorder and clearly get, "You feel so good," uttered by Roxy. And "Oh babe," by David.

If this isn't evidence, I don't know what is. I walk away knowing I've completed my assignment. Complete with Lyle having absolutely no interest in having an affair with me or Roxy.

I wait until she has gone, and he's back to tending to his horse. Only then do I walk up, friendly and innocent.

"Hey David. Do you want me to stay with Ryan, or is he okay alone?"

"He'll be fine. Go ahead and take off. Will you be riding Saturday?" He acts so normal.

"I'll let you know, if that's okay."

"Sure thing."

* * *

WHILE I'M on the road I begin to wrap up the case. "Hi Georgina. Please call me. I have good news." I don't mention my name, but I leave my number.

She gets back to me within ten minutes. "Tell me," she sounds eager.

"Again today, I did my best to entice and flirt with Lyle. He said his business is struggling, and he's over-the-hill. He again told me he's married, and if he weren't *then* maybe things would be different. He didn't take me up on my offers. He seems dejected and not at all looking to start an affair."

"That's great." She makes it sound anything but great. "So what's your good news?"

"The girl you thought Lyle was having an affair with, Roxy. Well, she had a nooner in David Reynold's trailer with him."

"With who?"

"With David Reynolds." Maybe I was unclear.

"No!"

"Yep. I have it on tape. She was chasing Lyle, but he didn't take her up on it; David did."

"You're wrong," she shouts into the phone.

"I couldn't find any evidence that Lyle even likes Roxy. The first day, he was responding to her attention, but she left him for David."

"Send me the proof," her voice is shaking.

"Ok. When I get home I'll email it." I hesitate, hating to ask, "But I haven't received your check for the two rides or renting the horse."

She hangs up without saying bye.

Well, that's strange for sure. Strange, as in she's livid about the idea of David Reynolds having a nooner with Roxy. I think she wants Lyle out of her father's business, but her anger with David is interesting. I wonder if she'd lose half the business if she was caught cheating on Lyle.

When I arrive home, I email a photo of Roxy stepping from David Reynold's trailer. I'll send the rest when she pays me.

She replies a few minutes later with this: "Immediately delete this from all your devices." That's it. There's no mention of getting more proof of her husband's infidelity, or paying me.

* * *

No, I won't delete it from all my devices. Something is going on, and I'll keep the evidence for my own records. "Maybe I should see if she is cheating on Lyle."

"Jess, it's not your problem." Quinn begins his lecture.

"You're right, it technically isn't my problem." I reply with one of those whole body shrugs. "It seems to me that she's up to something, and it isn't right."

"Yes, I think she is, but do you really want to put yourself in the middle of a nasty divorce and a possible lawsuit?"

"How will I be sued?"

"She hired you, and you'd be turning the information over to the husband"

"Well, I wouldn't be turning over any evidence. Nothing incriminates him. I didn't sign any paperwork. She asked me to look into her husband cheating on her."

"And did she pay you?"

"Only for the first ride and the hireling rental, but she hadn't paid me since. Are you saying that makes it a contract?"

"I would think so."

I do an internet search on private investigator's contracts.

"It looks like the only time I would be able to discuss the case would be by a court order, or if she agreed to it. Which she won't. But I'm only a person looking into a cheating spouse. She paid for the horse, and will pay for my lessons to learn to jump, diesel to get to the hunt, and my time. I'm not bound by any law. It says if there is criminal activity I can call the police since I'm not an attorney."

"You could be right."

"I'm sure I am, but maybe you're right too. I'll stay out of it."

19

INSPECTION

Quinn and I wake to another clear day. December is being kind to us again. I open the shutters and pull the curtains aside to let in the morning sun.

One of my not very feral cats is outside, howling. I guess she's hungry.

I open the door to a gift: An almost dead, white rat on my welcome mat. Kitty is proudly sitting next to it, batting the poor thing with her kitty paw.

"Oh great. Can't you just eat it?" I moan.

She makes a cute noise and continues to bat. I've heard that rodents and birds are the natural prey of cats. The commercial food companies do their best to mimic the cat's wild diet. So maybe they should include rats in their feeding plan, not just free-range chicken and wild-caught salmon. But who would pay top dollar for white lab rat and pigeon?

I close the door and let her finish the job. She can eat what nature intended.

Half an hour later, the rat is half eaten, and the kitty has gone. I know from experience, she'll return for the rest, but I can't leave it on my doorstep. I pick it up by the tail and transport it to my backyard, where it will be out of sight of guests. One of the three sisters can finish it for a noon snack.

The morning progresses fine. The guests have a quiet breakfast, courtesy of Janet. Quinn and I join them for a nice conversation, then return to my cottage. In a few minutes, he will be heading back to his place to work on his upcoming assignment.

"Adam will be checking in as soon as you have a vacancy. He's at the campground down the road. I don't want you alone. There's still that missing car thief who tried to run us down, and the SUV that tried to run you off the highway. Something is going on. They're slow about it, but they could be waiting for me to leave."

"I'll be armed *every* time I leave home."

"I've fine-tuned the security system. It's so sensitive you'll be able to count the feathers on a dove."

As Quinn is leaving with his heavy canvas bag he steps into the kitchen and lets it slide to the floor. "I don't want to go. I already miss you!" He wraps his arms around me.

"Are they sending you off to parts unknown now, or in a few weeks?" I ask while running my fingers through his shiny long hair.

"It will be soon. I'm sorry it's vague."

"Let me know what you can, and I'd like to see you before you go!" I gaze into his emotional eyes.

"I will. I'll get word to you, no matter what." He kisses me gently but it turns passionate. When he finally pulls back, his eyes look mistier than when he came in. "I love you," he whispers.

"I love you too." I grab hold of him. "Damn it, I don't want you to go. It's been wonderful having you here."

"I agree. It gives me something to think about. Maybe I should be your permanent body guard."

"That would be great."

He steps back and picks up his bag. "Adam is down the road. He'll be keeping a low profile, but he has access to the security system—in all but your bedroom!"

"And bathroom?"

"Of course! I forgot to mention that, but I don't usually put surveillance in bathrooms," he smiles.

"Ok, that's good to know."

He leaves on an upbeat note.

* * *

AND THEN IT HAPPENS. She walks through the open French doors into the office.

"Good morning, welcome to Greenstones." I look up from my computer and see a short, stout woman wearing a dark blue windbreaker. It's the type that government workers often wear.

"I'm Inspector Patricia Morris, San Luis Obispo County Health Department." Her tone is dry and unfriendly.

"Hello. How can I help you?"

"I'm responding to a complaint of rodents on your premises."

"Oh." Yikes, I had one on my welcome mat a few hours ago!

"I'll be conducting an investigation. Your permission is requested but not necessary."

"I'll be happy to comply. I have rodent control on site." Yeah, kitty was at work this morning.

"Where is the kitchen—it's usually the vilest place?" She lets her opinion show.

"Okay, it's around here." I move around to the front of the counter. "May I see your identification?"

That sets her off. Her attitude worsens. She flips open her jacket to reveal the laminated plastic ID card on a lanyard around her neck. "There, see?" She lets her jacket flop back.

"I'm sorry, but I didn't see it. Will you remove it? And perhaps a business card?"

If this is a scam, she isn't going to frighten me into compliance. I plan on phoning the county for verification.

"I was told you'd cause trouble. I can see they were correct."

"Who told you I was a problem?"

"That's confidential. We don't reveal our sources," she sniffs.

"Do I have the right to know who complained?"

"No. You don't." That's all she says as she passes me her business card and ID.

I study both. They seem real, but I go back to the computer and tap in Dept. of Health, San Luis Obispo County. It shows the same phone number. I pull out my cell and make the call. After two transferred calls, I reach the right person who advises me that yes, Inspector Patricia Morris is inspecting Greenstone Cottage today at 10 AM.

"Well then, I guess we'll go to the kitchen," I begin.

"Your delaying tactics won't help your case," she informs me.

"I was merely verifying your identity, not using tactics."

"If I wasn't forced to follow protocol, I'd shut your filthy hotel down immediately. You're a public health hazard," she snaps as she marches out the door.

I'm following behind, thankful the guests have eaten and gone sightseeing for the day.

"Janet," I shout, "The health department is here!" I want to give her a heads-up, just because.

"Your warning is too little, too late," the inspector declares as she pushes open the door to the kitchen.

Janet is doing the dishes. Her gloves hands are in immersed in hot, sudsy water.

"Please leave so I may conduct my investigation. This small space makes me feel cramped," she demands.

Janet quickly looks at me. I nod okay, please comply with the inspector. She removes her thick, yellow gloves, places them on the counter, and leans back against the sink. "Where is Inspector Vasquez?" She inquires.

"It was felt this case needed someone more experienced than Inspector Vasquez."

"She has been inspecting the hotel since I began working here, years ago."

"Exactly. We want to make sure you don't get her to overlook your violations."

"She would never do that, she's highly professional!" Janet exclaims.

"Of course she is, just as I am. Now, please stand aside so I may conduct my examination."

"Wait a minute, what violations?" She reacts to the rest of the sentence.

"Among other things, rodents." She opens a cabinet, gets down on her knees and starts moving everything onto the kitchen floor. She tilts the pots and pans over, expecting something to fall out.

I step back with Janet and whisper, "Is she looking for droppings?"

"Yeah." She tugs me out of the doorway into the lounge. "There's something going on. This inspector lives to find the tiniest of infractions. They send her out on cases with horrible violations. We've always passed with only a recommendation to change one of our protocols."

"Hopefully that's what will happen today." I know Janet keeps the place scrupulously clean.

An hour later, the inspector is furious. She hasn't found rat droppings or evidence of them in the lounge.

She marches out the open French door with me following—when suddenly she shouts. "There! I knew you were hiding them!"

It's another white rat, and it just ran into my office!

"And in broad daylight, no less. This means you have a large infestation of brave rodents. I'm writing you up!"

I happen to know our rats are brown with white bellies and big black eyes. This one is white, with red eyes. This isn't a normal rat. It's like they were hit by a zapper that changed them into alien rats. Where did they come from and what happened to the normal rats?

"This is the first one to come in. You saw we don't have droppings!" I retort.

"I won't close you down—yet." She rips off a copy of her check list and gives it to me. "I'll return in one week for a recheck. Good day." She marches down the path to her county car in the parking lot.

And I scramble to find the rat in my office. First, I close the door to lock him in and then I begin my hunt. Maybe I'll go for the natural method. Cami likes fresh rat. I'll get her in here. I close up and see Janet leaving one of the cottages.

"A white rat ran in the office." I tell her.

"White?"

"Yes. I found a half-eaten one this morning. Of course, I didn't tell her."

"That's strange."

"I know."

She looks over my shoulder, "You have a guest," she whispers, then rolls her cleaning cart to the next cottage.

"Hello, may I help you?" He's an average guy in average clothes, and is wearing a leather satchel over his shoulder.

"I'm Greg Sloan. I'm a reporter and I'm writing a travel and leisure piece for the SLO Times. Do you have a few minutes to spare for free advertising?" He holds up his little recorder.

"It isn't a good time right now, I am on my way out." I need to get him off the property before he sees a white rat. You can hardly miss them.

"I understand. You must be very busy running the hotel. Perhaps I can just look around on my own?" He steps back and begins scanning the place.

Hell.

All kinds of stories are crossing my mind. Everything from, "You need to leave because we're fumigating." Or, "You need to leave because a celebrity guest is arriving and wants her privacy." Neither one will work.

"Sure. This is the Rosemary cottage. Someone is staying here, so I can't let you in. But you can see each cottage has a plaque and is unique. Follow me." I start walking toward the front of the property.

He's snapping photos as we pass the other three cottages, Lilac, Rose and Sage.

"I'll be putting in a hot tub here, overlooking the sea. It'll be a lovely place to relax at the end of a day of sightseeing." I rattle on a bit about how my grandmother developed the property and that I helped.

He isn't saying much. Fine with me.

"I'd like to see your community room." He points back to the Garden cottage.

"Oh. Yes certainly." I open the French doors and make sure to close them again. "The fireplace is always going. I have cookies, and port wine in the evening."

"Do you serve a hot breakfast?" He snaps a few photos of the hearth, the conversation pit, and the breakfast area. He keeps loitering and looking at the floor.

"Thank you. Do you have anything you'd like to add?" He finally asks.

"No. Nothing. Thanks for coming by." I lead him to the door and look outside before I open it. All clear.

As he's right by the future hot tub, on his way to the front where he parked his car. He pulls out his phone and snaps a few pictures of the ground. "You have rats," he announces.

"What?" I look around the bush.

Three white rats are eating a cookie. They don't have a care in the world and they certainly aren't afraid of us.

"That will be a nice touch to the article." Thanks for your time. He snaps one of me, then walks down the steps to his little car parked in the dirt.

20

EVIDENCE

I burst through the door of my cottage. "Quinn!" I shriek to the surveillance system in the living room.

"What is it?" Adam's voice immediately replies with concern.

"There's something going on with rats."

"Please explain."

I go on about the health department, and haven't even arrived at the part about the reporter, when I hear clicks coming from his end. He's replaying and checking the video feeds.

"Jess. I have something," he cuts in, then pauses for a few seconds. "Last night at 9:04, a car is shown driving slowly. When it gets just past your driveway, the driver threw handfuls of something into your bushes on the rise above the street. She was there for twenty seconds. I can see her quickly reaching into something in her lap, then flinging her hand out the window. She does that three times, then continues driving south."

"Can you see the person?"

"There's a clear shot of the woman. She's middle aged, white, driving a dark Jag. I captured the license plate."

"A Jag?" I race out the door, closing it behind me to keep Cami in and the rats out.

"I've sent my contact a request for information on the plate."

"I'm looking in the bushes right now. I'll film it if I find something." I stoop down, moving the plants aside. "Oh, here is a chocolate. It's one of those single rectangles, like you get at Halloween."

Adam phones me. He was watching on our live-feed surveillance, but to speak, he needs to call. "Or from a hotel? I just received confirmation. The driver is Mandy Crawford, and the car is registered to her."

"I'll get a plastic bag. Maybe these are the chocolates they put on the pillow at night, minus the wrapper. I'll find out from the distributer."

"I see you looking for them. Make sure to stand back and point before you pick up anything. It's all on camera, but you will block it at certain angles."

"Right, so you can show it has been there since last night."

"Now, the good part. Prepare yourself," he advises.

I stand up and take a breath. "Okay, go."

"At 2:00 a.m. a pickup truck stops out of range of the camera. A man walks up carrying a cage full of white lab rats. He goes up to your retaining wall and opens the trap. I can see a few run across the road toward the beach, but the rest run into your bushes."

"So that's where my two white rats came from!"

"The man walks back to his vehicle, which I can tell is his, because he pulls forward on the dirt in camera range. The cage is clearly seen in the bed. I have the license plate."

"I'm sold on surveillance cameras"

"You can thank your man for this," he acknowledges.

"And you for finding it. Thanks for the fast help."

"You're welcome. Oh, and here is the info on the guy with the rats: Tony Atwood from Santa Maria. Does his name ring a bell?"

"No. But it may to Mandy or her team."

"Your evidence is in a cloud backup, ready for when you need it."

"I'll find an attorney, and see about getting even, financially."

If I were Mandy, I wouldn't have used white rats. And I wouldn't have been seen releasing them, or throwing food for them. But she doesn't know I have Quinn on my side.

I bet that reporter works for her as well. It's way too convenient that he, the inspector, and Mia's review came out all in the past few days. I'll see what Mandy's office recording says.

At my kitchen table, with a snack, I hear some good information after fast-forwarding through the usual patter.

"It's a shame to use our good chocolate as bait," Mandy complains.

"It's only milk chocolate. That's okay, everyone asks for the dark."

"How about some of this snack mix that went stale?" There's a crinkling sound of a bag.

"Sure. What else do they eat?"

"I don't know. I'll stay as far away as possible. They give me the creeps." Mandy sounds emotional.

A few minutes later, "That's it for tonight. Tomorrow will be fun. The inspector is a warrior, she finds the smallest infractions. Just wait until she finds rat turds," the manager chuckles.

"The little princess will be screwed by night fall, tomorrow." Mandy breaks into outrageous laughter.

* * *

"Adam, I heard great evidence from the Seaside Resort's transmitter, but I can't legally use it. Do you have any suggestions?"

"I could put up a street sign with a device aimed at the office. It wouldn't be on private property."

"Maybe like one of those unobtrusive white ones to stop people hitting a curb?"

"Yeah. I'll go find one no one will miss."

It's check-in, so I head to the office. Adam will be moving his RV to the back of my lot. We decided it will be just as safe for me with him in the parking lot as in a cottage. Plus he has expensive surveillance equipment at arm's reach from his bed if he stays in the RV.

I check the Cambria review sites, prepared for the worst, and I'm not surprised. The second of the rat reviews was posted this morning by JM Traveler. His name is new on the site. He posted his first one for a restaurant in town, and the second is for my place. He has no history beyond that, which is suspicious for sure. And now says he saw rats run through his cottage, which I haven't even rented to him.

I'm actually not getting upset. The more evidence I get that is false and documented, the more Mandy and her team are going to fry. So I keep searching.

"Do you want to go for a run? I'm tired from being antsy all day?" I text Adam.

"Sure. How about twenty minutes? I'll trail you by a hundred feet." And he'll be armed.

"Thanks. See you out there."

Adam has on a baggy t-shirt and running shorts. I wouldn't recognize him in a crowd. His brown hair is sticking out from under his baseball cap, looking messy and unremarkable. He went to the same CIA school of invisibility as Quinn did.

I'm carrying my phone and I am also armed. It doesn't make sense to be a target without being able to protect myself.

The run is just over three miles. The day is beautiful and safe, and nothing happens. I guess I should be happy, but I'd like to get it over with. Who else is out to get me, besides Mandy?

21

PREPARATIONS

I have two Have-a-Heart traps arriving tomorrow. I'll entice the rats inside with chocolate. That's what my mother used when she had a rat in her house. I'm not sure what I'll do with a bunch of the rodents after I catch them. Maybe find a pet store? Or I could release them on Mandy's property.

I get a text from Mom: "At some point, the rats get smart and refuse to go in the cages. You may have to resort to killing them."

Hmm. I'm not happy about that. Maybe my cats will catch them. I'll cut back a tiny bit more on their food. I'm okay with cats eating fresh rat.

Adam is looking official in a glow-in-the-dark yellow workman's vest and a white helmet. He's driving my truck with a printed plastic banner stuck on the door: Cambria Public Works Department.

I'm sitting at the front of my property soaking up the winter sun and watching him dig the hole. Then he props up the short sign, fills around it with cement, and pours in a bucket of water. That's it. He didn't even premix the cement with water before adding it. That's a fast way to get in and out without being noticed.

It's on the beach side of the road, because the property line on the resort side is on the dirt shoulder, and a sign wouldn't work there. The listening device is hidden in a drilled hole in the wood. It won't work well during the day, because of cars blocking it, but later at night, when Mandy usually has her conversations, it should be fine. It's one of the best, military-grade.

*   *   *

I CAN'T SLEEP—THERE'S too much static zinging around in my mind. The sleep sounds phone app is too distracting, I'm not hungry, and I'm afraid to have alcohol because I need to be prepared for war.

But war doesn't come to my house tonight.

The sun wakes me. Or is it another cat howling?

I drag myself out of bed and open the front door. "Good girl," I praise the tabby kitty as I carry dead rat number 2, by the tail, to the back yard. I decide not to let her finish eating it. That way she'll kill another. I go look for something to hide it in on the way to the garbage.

Cami was locked in the office all night. She isn't happy when I open up. "Didn't you find it?" I guess not. There are no bodies left for me. It may have escaped.

Janet arrives while I'm carrying her back to my cottage. "How is everything this morning?"

"There's a lot in the works. Mandy is fully behind this," I announce, but refrain about telling her about the surveillance evidence. I trust her, but it isn't safe to divulge too much information. It usually gets passed on by saying, "Don't tell anyone, but..." And then, everyone knows.

I check the night cameras and see skittering white rats everywhere. Holy cow, there must be thirty or more. Unless they're running in circles and I'm seeing the same ones. The video shows a ton of them.

I may resort to traps because two days from now is New Year's Day. I have a full house of guests coming to Greenstone Cottage's first annual liqueur-making workshop. I collected $80 each and have twenty people coming to the lounge to learn how to mix alcohol with the right amount of sugar and special flavors to make something tasty. Monica taught me how to make limoncello, coffee, Irish Cream, and almond. They taste good enough to invite your friends over.

Today I'll be cleaning the Garden cottage, known as the lounge, and I'm keeping the doors closed.

I invited Adam for an early meal so he doesn't have to rely on his own cooking in the RV. He eats a massive amount, so I had warned Janet to make double what she normally does. I hang out with him, chatting about nothing special. Later, when my not so early-rising guests arrive, I stay to keep up the friendly atmosphere. By the end of the serving time, I've eaten with two groups of guests, and had more than I should. But now the room is clear for me to give it a major cleaning. Janet has duties in kitchen and cottages, and I'm doing this.

It takes a full four hours to move the furniture, sweep, mop, dust and do the windows. Due to the number of people in and out, and dining here, I make sure to use a mild bleach solution to kill germs. I don't want anyone getting sick from here. Gram was always fastidious, and I'm carrying that through. There won't be any corner cutting on my watch.

Later, I speak to Mom about an attorney. "You can find an attorney, spend a bundle and have Mandy out-pay you. You might consider looking into the ownership of the resort. If she doesn't own it you could get her tossed out since she is bringing discredit to the company."

"What happens if she owns it?"

"If she owned it, I doubt she'd be as involved in running it. I know you are, but you have five cottages, not a one-hundred room resort."

"Okay, thanks."

She updates me on her vacation, then swings the conversation back to my worries, like a good mother does.

I begin with the resort's website, scrolling through news and information. The City will know more than they have posted, and I don't think I care if she hears I'm asking who owns it. She may think I'm finally considering selling.

They have a sister property in Carmel, CA. That's a nice place, very pricey. I'll come up with a quick story to ask the manager.

Because of their surveillance I have to go to my cottage to make the call. This is getting old.

"Resort at Carmel-by-the-Sea." A pleasant voice answers the phone.

"Hello. I'm conducting research for a client who is looking to invest in hotels. Can you direct me to someone who can tell me the ownership of your lovely property?"

She transfers me to the manager, Ms McCoy.

"I can certainly help you. We're corporate owned by Meadow-brook Hotels."

"I see. Is that an individual, or a group of investors?"

"I can't answer that. Would you like the number to our head-quarters?"

"Yes thank you. Do you know if Cambria Seaside Resort is owned by the same corporation?"

"Yes. It's our beautiful sister property in Cambria." She gives me the number for their headquarters.

"Do you know Mandy Crawford? Before I ask about investing, I'd like to know if she's a decision maker."

"Ms. Crawford runs the Cambria resort. She has been with the company for many years. Your best bet would be to phone corporate directly." The number is in the San Francisco area. That isn't where Mandy lives, but she could still be an owner, or silent partner.

"I'll do that, thank you for your time."

That was somewhat productive. Now I can research the Mead-owbrook Hotels Corporation.

I click the name into the search bar and come up with something unexpected. This is a worldwide conglomerate. They even have a resort on the French Riviera. I can't find Mandy Crawford's name related to anything corporate. I breathe a little easier now. I click on the Cambria property and scroll for contacts. She isn't listed.

I google her name and find years of posts from the Chamber of Commerce. She has been busy promoting the resort. They won Grand Prize in the 2015 Scarecrow Festival. In October of every year, beginning in 2009, Cambria has this festival. Some of the scarecrows are traditional, while others are humorous, or whimsical. The Resort's entry was a dolphin ridden by a mermaid. It's gorgeous in bright blues and greens. The mermaid has flowing green hair made from a living succulent that looks like a string of pearls. Her tail is made of pink shells.

A publicity photo shows Mandy next to the mermaid, smiling as she accepts the ribbon on behalf of the resort. I wonder who designed and made the piece—certainly not her.

I scroll through many articles. She's very active in the community. A reporter writes a glowing article highlighting how Mandy worked her way up to resort manager. *"Ms. Crawford supervises all of the day-to-day activities. She promotes and markets the resort, hires and fires employees, and plans events to grow their client base. She is a powerful woman to emulate. 'You have to be tough in this business.' That's Ms. Crawford's motto."*

"When asked if she has higher aspirations, she again showed her fierce determination, 'As far as I am concerned, the sky is the limit.'"

It sounds like Mandy is trying to get rid of me, her competition. Is she trying to acquire Greenstones for the corporation, or for herself?

I need to replay their office feed, but I also have to prepare for my liqueur workshop.

22

MORNING BEFORE

Again this morning, I find a rat on my door mat. I'm not complaining. I need them gone before they give birth to hundreds of rat babies.

The delivery van drops off my no-kill traps. I also ordered three ultrasound devices. Hopefully the high pitched noise will send the rodents scurrying somewhere else when my lounge is full of guests. I'm taking the devices to my backyard to absorb the sun, where they will be safely out of sight.

I have a few minutes to listen to the play-back from Mandy's office. It takes so long to skim through hours and hours of talking at the front desk. If I were into computers, I'm make a program that listens for key words. I bet that's what the government has. I wonder why Quinn didn't suggest it. Maybe he doesn't have access to it.

I make myself comfortable at the kitchen table. The windows are open, the breeze is gently moving the sheer curtains, just like a perfect little seaside cottage. It's a bit chilly, but I like the mood—so I put on a soft jacket.

More than an hour later, I get to something. "The health department investigator called today. She went nuts when I told her you saw the rats running down the street like a flood. She's going to close the place down tomorrow!" The manager gleefully reports.

"Perfect. It doesn't get much better than this." Mandy sounds unusually giddy.

I press Stop, and begin to sweat. I mean real sweat, breaking out on my forehead like rain drops.

How can I put on a workshop tomorrow, New Year's Day, when she's going to shut me down today? Any appeal will take days to work through the system. She's getting her evidence from a lying, conniving witch, and she won't listen to me. She has pronounced me guilty without any hard evidence.

"Adam, I have a problem!" I phone him.

"I'm on it. I've been listening to our sign-surveillance system. I have something we can use. The quality isn't the best, but it's good enough."

He plays it for me. It's a bit garbled, but I can understand them.

"And you know what else, this will shut down her little class. Can you imagine all those people, looking forward to making liqueur, suddenly left with nowhere to go on New Year's Day?" Mandy snickers.

"How about we put up signs on cars parked along the street, directing them to us for festivities, alcohol, and live music. What else can we have?"

"If they want a class, how about if we give them one? I'll get the vodka and make it a mix-ology class. I'll get a friend of mine to be the bartender and teacher," Mandy sounds exuberant.

"You're brilliant," the manager gushes.

"Yes, that's why I'm the boss," she sighs with self-confidence.

Adam turns off the recording. "So you see, I have something."

"I have a few hours to set this right before I lose twenty clients and my reputation."

"You have the option of a lawsuit if she succeeds in her plans. Or you step in before it happens and have it quietly go away without the public made aware."

"While I'd love to have it publically blow up in her face, she'll still be embarrassed when her boss finds out. I need to get on this right now, before everywhere closes for the afternoon."

My next phone call is to the County Health Department. I get through to Inspector Morris' supervisor and explain the situation. I'm very careful to paint the inspector in a good light, as someone who is dedicated to her job and seeking to do the best for the public. However, the situation is that I am the victim of a smear campaign so that someone can run me into the ground and buy my hotel at a reduced price. I play the recording for him after stating my case, and have Adam send an excerpt of the video of the rats being released.

When he receives the email, he watches it while I'm on the line. "This will require further investigation. I'll speak with Inspector Morris. However, rest assured, she won't be closing down your facility today. May I place you on hold? I'll call her now and have her return to the office."

"Thank you very much! I so appreciate your time and willingness to listen."

"We're not the bad guys. We're here to keep the public safe. With the evidence you have, there is cause for concern that Ms. Crawford is manipulating the system," he explains.

When we finish the call, I immediately speak to Adam as if he's in the room. "Oh my goodness, thank you for sending him that video!"

"You're welcome. I'm angry with that P.O.S Mandy Crawford, so I'd be happy to exact revenge."

"I know what you mean. However, we'd better do it the lawful way, since I plan on remaining in business, not spending a few decades in prison," I'm serious. He isn't someone to joke with about this. I've heard that Special Ops guys are sometimes known to be loose cannons. Not that I'd object in this case. But still, it's my battle, not his.

So the workshop is on—or back on!

I leave an appreciative message for Quinn. There's too much to text, plus it will be more personal for him to hear my voice. He can listen at his convenience, after he rids the world of—um, people our government doesn't like. He did a great thing by leaving Adam to help me. I'm not complaining that Q is saving our country, or something.

I have a few minutes to see if Meadowbrook is still open, but I think I'll wait. The emergency over my shut down is over. I'd rather have time to prepare with masses of evidence for a discussion with someone in charge, rather than have them wanting to get out of the office, and get me off the phone, so they can leave early before the holiday.

My next four hours are spent filling little bottles with tasty flavors. I ordered ten gallons of good vodka through Caleb at the Red Horse Saloon. He has a friend who makes it at a distillery in Paso Robles. I'm supporting local vendors, like we should—if possible.

Each person gets three pint-jars to fill with good vodka, simple-syrup, and a special flavor that goes in each one. The vodka and syrup water are in equal-ish parts. I had to play with the math, which told me I need eight gallons of vodka. I bought ten to be safe, in case of more students, or mishaps.

I move all the bottles to my locked office. That way it's only a few steps to the lounge after breakfast. I still have to pick up the vodka tonight after 6:00. It's so new, the distiller bottled this batch yesterday.

* * *

"Adam," I raise my voice instead of phoning. "I'm running to town to pick up the special vodka for tomorrow. Shall I drive your Mustang, or take my Subaru?" His car is about as hot as they come. It has an extra-special engine under the hood.

"Be smart, take my car. Q will be pissed if anything happens when you're off the property."

"You're right, and I'm being monitored, right?"

"Darn right."

"Perfect. I'll try to keep it unscratched." Or I'll be carefully buffing it out.

"Thank you. I appreciate that," he quietly says.

I'm sure he does. I've driven it once before, and it has more horses under the hood than I'm comfortable controlling. But let's face it, if he didn't want me driving it, I would be in another car.

It's 6:00 p.m. when I enter the open door of the Red Horse Saloon. The band hasn't started, so they are playing a CD of light country music. Caleb is behind the bar, chatting with two guys I've seen here before. They're regulars and don't make trouble.

"Hey Jess." He waves me over to an open stool. "You have to try this. I got it from Darryl Margolis. He bottled it last week." He reaches under the counter and pulls out a specialty bottle with a picture of a fruit on the label.

I hadn't planned on having anything to drink since I'm supposed to be on alert for that Italian maniac of Mia's, and the guy who tried to run me off the road.

"Just a sip, Caleb. I've had some trouble lately and need to be ready to—." I shrug. I need to be ready to do something, anything.

"I gotcha, I'll make it one sip." He pours just a drop.

"Thank you for understanding."

"The last time you had trouble, the whole town was reeling from a Russian invasion," he chuckles good naturedly.

"Yeah, I'm sorry about that. It all happened in your bar."

"Oddly enough," he lowers his voice, "It's been great for business. Every few days, I get someone asking about it."

"Good, so I'm still welcome here."

"You always will be." He gives me a wink. It's a nice wink, and I don't take it any other way. He's married to a beautiful lady whom he loves and works with in the business.

I take a minuscule sip. "Huh, this is interesting. It has spicy, fruity notes. But it's strange. What on earth is it?"

"Persimmon brandy. They make it from a local orchard."

I have the last of the clear liquid. "It's potent. I bet it would go well poured over persimmon bread."

"That sounds really good. I'll ask Faith to make one."

"Does she like baking?"

"On a cold winter's day. Otherwise, no," he laughs. "Let me help you with your order." He moves toward the office.

Faith has gone home for the day. Her job is to keep them stocked and find new drinks for customers to fall in love with. Caleb carries two cardboard boxes, and I take one, and we head to the black Mustang a few cars down.

"This is a hot car. I didn't take you for a muscle car aficionado."

"It belongs to a friend of Quinn's. It has more power than mine, should I need it."

"I see." He nods and gives me a look.

"You have something going on, something bad, don't you?"

"Well – I hope it's not that bad. But let's get the other box and I'll get out of your hair."

"Is your man around?"

"No, but he left his second in command, and he is pretty impressive."

"Alright. But if you need help, don't hesitate to call me."

"Thanks."

I'd never deliberately get him involved in my situation. It wouldn't be fair.

I stand guard at the car, and he returns for two more boxes.

"Happy New Year's," he wishes me, as he puts the last in the trunk.

"Thanks, you too, and Faith."

I back away from the angle parking and head for the short cut through the alley. I bet I shouldn't be doing this. So I reverse and go back to the main street. It's dark now, and I feel like a little bird— aware that I'd be a tasty morsel for an owl.

23

NEW YEAR'S EVE

"Adam, I'm on my way back. Are you there?" He can see me by GPS and by the two cameras mounted in the car.

"I sure am. I don't see a problem," his voice comes through, reassuringly.

"Thanks. I'm coming through town. It sure is pretty with the Christmas lights." I'm acting like a tour guide. He can see what I see, but I know many of the stories.

"See the jewelers on the left? They were broken into ten years ago. The crook came back for the gold he'd hidden in my roof."

"So that was the place?"

"Uh huh."

I turn onto the 101 north, and carefully press on the accelerator. The car easily moves faster. "This thing sure likes to go!"

"Yes she does," he says with pride.

I ease off the gas, since I only have a quarter-mile before my turn on Weymouth.

"You just passed a black Chevy Suburban stopped at the light. Did you see it?" Adam asks.

"Yes. Back at Windsor Blvd."

I begin to slow for my turn. The headlights from the Chevy are coming fast on my tail. The highway doesn't have a traffic light or left turn lane for this street. This is why I never turn here during the day, because the traffic is going 65 mph and will run right up my tail.

"Step on it, girl," Adam tells me.

I speed up and make the turn. The headlights follow me. I'm not sure if I should be worried. There have to be millions of black Chevy SUVs—right?

"Jess. Come straight home, I'll be in the parking lot," he sounds concerned.

So that concerns me.

"I can't bring him home. There are innocent people there."

I speed past my cottage where Adam is waiting to save me. I don't want it becoming another Shootout at the OK Corral.

"What the hell are you doing?" he shouts.

"I'll go in circles. Call the police. He can't catch me in your car."

"Roger. I'm calling now."

For a top-heavy Suburban, the thing is right on my tail. He's a better driver than I am.

It feels like a forever, but Adam comes back on. "You're driving like an old woman. Step on the gas!"

"Your car is too powerful, I'll outdrive the headlights."

"You need lessons," he growls.

"Great, but what about now—I don't want to crash!"

"Keep going around Moonstone Drive, take the highway, turn left and go around again. Try to get some distance. The ETA for the police is ten minutes."

"Holy cow. Ten minutes is a lifetime!" My voice just went up an octave.

"I'll talk you through it, unless you want me to try to catch you in your dually."

"No, let's try this."

"Cut across the lane," he calmly instructs. "Let the car slide." "Cross over to the other side, and let it slide to the right!" He says with authority. It's as if he's in the passenger seat. I had pursuit training ten years ago, but it's been a while since I've driven like this. I've only been making short runs in my big Ford truck.

I can tell he's a good instructor, because I'm finally pulling away from the Chevy. It would be fun if it weren't so dangerous. There's still a bit of traffic out. Most of it was on Main Street in town. At least people are hunkered down for the next few hours, partying, and waiting for the ball in Times Square to fall.

And I'm spending my New Year's Eve running from someone. He doesn't have a front license plate, so Adam can't find out who it is.

"He's giving up. Go get him!" Adam actually shouts.

I slow the car, letting precious seconds escape as I do a small U-turn. I know there is a way to do a bootleg turn, but I forgot how.

"Don't let him get away. Catch him!"

I carefully step on the gas. The highway is straight for a few miles. I see his tail lights in the distance. He's speeding north. But north is scary because it's away from town, the police, and help.

"I'm not sure this is a good idea. If he stops, I'm screwed."

"He won't stop. He peeled off the chase," he sounds certain.

"He'll reevaluate his tactics, since I'm following him."

"Do you want to know who he is?"

"Yeah," I don't say it with much conviction. "If he stops, or if I follow him into a dead-end, I'll be in trouble."

"First, keep him in sight. Then reevaluate. There is a State Parks K-9 officer at Hearst Castle. He's waiting until they pass then he'll stop them.

"In LAPD-speak that means he's Code 5." The thought pops into my agitated mind.

"I'm sure that's what they mean," he replies with a laugh.

I feel better knowing in about 3 miles I'll have a friend.

"The car that passed you going the opposite direction just did a U-turn. It might be another enemy. Watch your tail."

"Great. Not great, bad."

In fact, the Chevy is slowing from over 70 mph to 60, and I doubt it's because we're entering the town of San Simeon that consists of a cluster of hotels, and a Friends of the Elephant Seal visitor center. The Chevy brakes hard. His tail slides out as he moves through the left turn lane on the highway. He ends up on the frontage road, going back the way we came.

"He's a good driver," Adam comments dryly.

"No kidding."

I brake hard and turn across the lanes to the frontage road. The car behind me, that made the U-turn, comes in fast and makes the same sliding turn as the SUV. He's behind me.

"They're definitely together," Adam muses.

"I don't like a guy in front and one behind. It's a bad situation."

"I'm on the line with the State Parks officer. He's coming to help."

"Can you patch him thru to me?" This car does everything else, it should allow someone else on the phone.

"Will do. Give me a second."

"Hello, Jessica? This is Keith Hilton. I'm in a 4x4, coming up to the town now."

"That's him, Jess, behind the Beemer."

"Thanks, I'm somewhat boxed in. The Chevy is slowing down, and the Beemer is crawling up my tail."

"You want me to light them both up?"

"Both at once? I guess so. The CHP does it." The California Highway Patrol. But that's with traffic offenders, not potential killers.

In my rear view mirror I see the flashing red and blue lights—but nothing seems to be happening. The bad guys know he's a park ranger, and won't shoot or ram them. He doesn't have any backup. There aren't other law enforcement cars for miles around.

"They're refusing to pull over," Hilton's voice comes through the phone system.

I pull closer, voluntarily closing the gap to the slow driving SUV, and the Beemer moves in for the kill as I become boxed in.

"You're too close!" Adam shouts, losing some of his control. There's nothing he can do besides watch me get caught.

"Plan B." I confidently growl as I wrench the wheel to the right, darting into the driveway of the Morgan Hotel parking lot. The BMW doesn't react in time to follow me. The Chevy slams on the brakes, but that's all I see as I navigate toward the empty hotel portico. There aren't any cars blocking my way.

Just as one pulls up, facing me.

I jerk the steering wheel to the right, to the side of the building leading to the parking lot in the back. It zigs and zags around the buildings. I sure hope there's an exit, otherwise I'll be doing a little off-roading.

"Good move. They're both trying to follow you." Adam sees them through the 180 degree camera on my rear view mirror.

I hear Ranger Hilton on the loudspeaker "Pull over. This is the police."

They ignore him and turn into the parking area as I speed through.

I'm speeding down the driveway with two-story hotel complexes on both sides. I still don't see their headlights.

Thank goodness there's a street at the end. I turn left since I'm trying to get back to Cambria which has law enforcement able to stop these two.

Adam comes through again, "Turn left at the street. It will curve and take you out to the highway." He has been looking at Google maps.

With renewed confidence. I step on the gas, then brake hard at the dip at the street. This car is low to the ground and would bottom-out.

I make it through the turns and hit the 101 going south. Soon I'm at 77 mph and still pressing down on the accelerator. There are head-lights behind me, but I have breathing room!

As I get to a rise, I see the red and blue lights of the ranger, about a quarter of a mile back. This Mustang has a throaty growl and likes speed. But since this isn't a divided highway, I'd better watch what's coming up in front of me, instead of behind.

"Good move back there," Adam sounds calm and complimentary.

"Thanks. But now where do I go?"

"We got the license plates from both cars, so you may as well come home. Just in case they don't know where you live, make sure to out-drive them. The Beemer's plate comes back to a VW, so that's a dead end unless the police can get him stopped. The Chevy is the one registered to the Tre Amici. They know where you live anyhow. They were hoping to get you alone."

"Ok. Thanks." I don't say anything more, as I'm concentrating on driving fast.

Ten minutes later, I pull into my driveway, and tuck the Mustang out of sight beside Adam's RV. I open the door, and sit there for a moment, recovering.

He walks up with purposeful strides. "You're more impressive than I gave you credit for. You really think on your feet."

"I could have told you—I'm not just a cute face," I lighten the mood, like one does to show their confidence.

"Yeah." He looks impressed.

I stand up and give him a hug. "Thanks for being there. And thank you for this car."

He doesn't let go immediately. When he does, he looks thoughtful, then covers it quickly. "Did you scratch the paint?" He glances at it.

There isn't anything to see in the dark. The engine is making clicking noises as it cools down.

"Come on, let's get you a jacket. Quinn will kill me if you catch a cold," he jokes.

He phones the police to update that I'm home, safe. They keep the officers looking for the suspects, who have vanished, and send a unit to take a report from me. The ranger returns to Hearst Castle, since his older, Parks Department 4x4 couldn't keep up with the fast crooks on asphalt. Maybe if they went off road...

A few firecrackers go off at midnight and the New Year quietly arrives a minute later.

I get a text from Quinn at 0001 hours: "Happy New Year sweetie!"

"Thanks love. You too."

There isn't a reply because he's somewhere unpleasant. He may not even have typed it right now. He could have scheduled it in advance. But he remembered and sent it sometime, and that's what counts.

24

LIQUEUR WORKSHOP

I just checked the time. I have plenty before the class starts. Will there be a dead rat on my mat to greet me? I guess I'd better go see what the morning has brought to my little cottage.

I head to the door in my silky lavender pajamas. They look classy for a boutique hotel owner who may need to help someone in the middle of the night. In the past, a comfy old t-shirt was sufficient.

There isn't a rat on the mat. What a shame. Maybe that's because I have those sonic zappers pointed around the lounge like laser beams. I'd better go check.

It occurs to me, I'll look through the surveillance feed. It's all quiet, there aren't any rodents scurrying or dying now. I quickly go through the past few hours, looking for darting white rodents. There's one in the street, squashed.

At 10:30, I'm in the lounge making last minute adjustments, like turning up the fireplace to counter the cool air coming through the open window. Claire has finished the breakfast dishes and comes up to talk.

"Jess, before anyone comes I wanted to let you know I spoke to my friend who was fired from the Seaside Resort."

"Really?" I look around then move closer to the informant.

"She is still upset. She found a job at another hotel in town, and said she'd be willing to talk to you."

"Did she tell you anything we can use? I only have a few minutes before the first guests will be arriving."

"She wants to make it right because you're a nice lady, and your grandmother was always nice to her. Since she has a job, she's feeling financially safe enough to talk about it."

"That would be great, because I'm planning on contacting the company Mandy Crawford works for and seeing what they will do about her."

"That sounds good to me." She stops when the first guest opens the French door.

* * *

THERE IS one less person here than enrolled, but I have nineteen eager new friends who want to partake in the liqueur making and tasting process.

I begin when everyone has taken a seat at the breakfast tables and is giving me their attention.

"I'm Jessica Wilcox, the new owner of Greenstone Cottages. Some of you may have known my grandmother Lucy—she passed away in October. It was her wish that I continue the business she began more than three decades ago. Thank you for joining me on New Year's Day for what I hope will be a fun and tasty few hours."

I reach down for the bright yellow bottle of lemon rind soaking in vodka. "This elixir will turn plain alcohol into an Italian treat."

The door opens, stealing the attention of my audience. A guy who looks like he could be the brother of Mia's man strides in, looking tall, dark, and incredibly handsome—I mean Italian.

"I'm sorry to disturb the class. I was unavoidably delayed in traffic." His gaze smoothly moves over the room, then stops at me with a challenging smile. "Where would you like me to sit?"

My blood pressure spikes. I want him arrested, except that I'm not even 10% sure he was chasing me last night. There's a lot of circumstantial evidence about the theft of Mia's and Axel's Porsches. He's a problem who needs to be removed from my lounge. I can either wait for him to cause a scene, or hope he doesn't. Should I have Adam drag his ass out? It will disturb the class and he knows that.

"The empty chair right here will be fine." I indicate with a sweep of my hand.

While he's making his way through the room, and has the attention of my students, I click the button in my pocket. It sends an alert to Adam. The room is under surveillance, but he may have missed this guy coming in with the other guests moving around. He won't know if I want him removed, or watched. He'll have to follow my lead. I don't want to cause a fuss if it isn't necessary. The guy may be trying to scare me. That's fine, he doesn't know I have one of Quinn's guns hidden in the office paneling, but that isn't close enough if this turns ugly.

"We'll be making limoncello because it's my favorite, and I'm sure you'll love it too." I smile, like I revealed a sweet nugget of information.

"Now I'll introduce you to the collection of goodies you'll be taking home." I'll hold up each item to engage the audience. "In front of you are two mixing jars and three twelve-ounce canning jars half full of top quality vodka. They will hold your freshly made liqueur, plus you have a vegetable peeler to peel your lemons, and a pamphlet of the recipes you'll learn today." I pick up the coupons to use as a visual aid. "My friends with local businesses gave me valuable coupons to hand out."

"The Red Horse Saloon, just off Main St., donated a shot glass with their logo. Darryl Margolis of Paso Distillery in Paso Robles made the vodka. In fact, he bottled it yesterday. He also generously printed the labels for your new creations. Kate at the Majestic Chef donated two envelopes of chia tea. After class, if you want to continue your tasting adventure, be sure to stop by and have a sip of their special drinks."

I change my tone and return the coupons to the table. Then I pick up the twig of rosemary and give it a sniff.

"I tried a fun experiment last week. I picked a sprig of rosemary and scraped the leaves into a jar of alcohol. Ten minutes later, I could see the liquid was turning faintly green. I took a sip—and it tasted like rosemary. It had infused that fast. It works with rosemary, because it is an aromatic, oily plant, so the result was much quicker than with lemon, which takes several days."

I turn to the table behind me and select one of the interesting looking bottles. "I made this infusion yesterday. So if you're someone who can't wait to taste a sweet liqueur, you don't have to. I'll start you off with a little sip. If you don't like the flavor, I won't feel hurt. I'm not usually a fan of rosemary, though I like it sweet and in alcohol." I smile and proceed forward to the closest student on my right.

There's some shifting around as people get their expectations and glasses ready. One lady speaks first, "I love the rectangular bottle. It looks so fancy. It makes it look special."

"It's funny—everything seems to taste better when it's nicely plated, or poured from a pretty bottle. This shape isn't just for whiskey, though it's what we've come to expect."

I pour about an ounce in their glasses. Those who don't care for rosemary give it to their friend or spouse.

There are appreciative murmurs before I've finished dolling out the last sample—to the handsome jerk. I make sure to serve him last. He is seated at the front on the left, and could have come first—but nope, not in my class. I give him a humorous smile, like I'm confident enough to play his game which, in fact, I am. Because I have Adam, the surveillance cameras to provide proof of whatever he does, and a 9mm in the office—which is a bit far away, but I'll make do.

"Rosemary is easy to find. It's a bushy, sturdy Mediterranean plant that grows well in Southern California. I use it as part of my landscaping because it's low maintenance and has low water requirements. I'll point it out if you'd like."

I walk around again, placing sprigs of the newly cut herb in front of each person. "Place your thumb and forefinger around the tip and gently run them toward the cut end. The leaves, like pine needles, will peel off easily."

The Italian leans back to give me room, but I drop the twig onto his placemat from a distance, almost like he has the plague.

Back at my "lectern," which is only a table, I continue my happy speech, as I watch everyone marvel at how easy it is to remove the leaves from the sprig. The room smells like a kitchen. Even the Italian is sniffing his fingers. The resin is quite pungent.

"In Italy, it grows wild. The scent reminds me of my grandmother. She uses it in olive oil," The Italian sounds like he's reminiscing.

"I love it tossed with salt and olive oil on oven-roasted vegetables. It keeps its flavor and makes everything taste delicious," says a woman who takes the time to roast vegetables, not just microwave them—like I do.

The Italian breaks into conversation about roasting vegetables. "Si, it's so easy to do. Have you tried lemon, rosemary and garlic on chicken?" He smacks his fingers with delight.

"Oh, you're making my mouth water," the lady's voice goes throaty.

I need to get my class back under control, in case this is his devious plan.

"It sounds like Anthony has a culinary background. Maybe he'll stay after the workshop to give us recipe ideas." I smile and seem pleased to have such a wonderful student in our midst.

For the next few minutes everyone is pushing rosemary leaves into one of their bottles of vodka. Then pouring in the sugar syrup to taste.

"If you like more sweetness, add more syrup. If you like more of a kick, use less," I explain. "This is the nice part of making it yourself, you aren't stuck with an insanely sweet liqueur."

Everyone is tasting their product to see how sweet they want it. At this rate they'll be tipsy soon.

After a few more minutes, I move the class to the limoncello section. "You have to admit, its bright yellow color makes you feel like you're soaking up the Italian sun."

Anthony the Italian, and a few ladies begin chatting about the delights of Italian cooking. I rein them in and continue.

I can't help it, but I look at the darned Italian and raise my eyebrow. I'm not falling for him, I'm playing with him. It doesn't change the fact that he could be one of the men who was chasing me. It doesn't change the fact that I know he could be dangerous. I'm willing to take appropriate action should he do something radical.

Think of a cat, playing with her mouse. She plays...then she eats it. Unless the mouse fights back. I've seen one stand on his hind legs and wave his front legs at my cat. Figaro backed up and looked horrified that the little thing hadn't given up or run away.

One of the male students who has had enough of the suave Italian speaks up. "It's not only the Italians who like limoncello."

"Quite right. There is a local company that makes it with lemons grown in Ventura County. California grows millions of pounds of citrus a year." I know the industry well. "In fact, we're going to peel five lemons from Santa Paula, where they have a packing house called Limoneria."

I have everyone get up and select five washed and wiped lemons from the buckets. I'm doing this to get them moving around. I've heard it keeps the interest level up. Then back at their seats, they get to use their new peeler to make a pile of rinds on their plate.

There's a bit of laughter as the pieces flip across the table; it's hard to control them.

"You won't be adding the syrup to your lemon until you soak them in the vodka. It takes at least three days to extract the color and flavor. You can add it at home this weekend, but if you get busy, don't worry, it will keep until you're ready."

With my own rinds that I've already soaked, I show them how to strain off the peels and pour the golden liquid through a funnel. "This works if you have a narrow bottle you want to fill with your new limoncello."

"I'm sure you'd like to taste it now, so I have a treat for you." I hold up my forefinger and smile broadly as I step into the kitchen and produce a large platter. "Ta-da! Limoncello pound cake."

I put it down on my table and return for paper plates and forks.

"Maybe our Italian would like to help me serve?" I give him a quirky look. He's been good in class, engaging both the ladies and the few men. It will also show I'm confronting him head-on—with grace.

"I'd be honored," he jumps up, acting happy to be asked, rather than surly.

I cut generous slices, as he delivers a plate to each person, quietly saying something in Italian to each. He has the ladies almost passing out in his arms as he serves them.

He also handles the coffee and cups while I place sugar packages in the center of the tables.

For a few minutes we feast and have seconds. Yes, I made enough for more. The conversation is fun. With dessert and a little alcohol, good cheer is flowing.

Twenty minutes later, I move on to the segment on coffee liqueur. "I'm going to show you how to personalize your own version of Kahlua. Your choice of coffee ranges from instant, to brewing your favorite varietal."

I slowly sweep my hand across the two pots of coffee beside my table.

"Here, I have excellent quality coffee. The decaf has the orange spout and the other is regular. I chose this blend specifically because of its robust flavor, which I think will have punch, plus it's a dark roast."

The pots get passed around and poured into their jars.

"This coffee is different from what we drank, right?" One of the men asks.

"Yes. The one we had with the cake is milder. I made these extremely strong. This way you can dilute it with the sugar water and it won't become watery.

"This is more Italian," the lady closest to Anthony says with a sexy smile.

He preens, leans back and crosses his legs. My eyes rest on his shoes. Oh my... they are amazing. I'm not an expert on men's shoes, but I know good bridle leather when I see it. They have a deep color that means a tanner took the best hide and used quality dyes. And the shine would pass inspection by a military drill sergeant.

I have to chuckle at the exchange. He is still being exemplary. He may ruin the class later, but he hasn't yet. In the past, when I arrested someone, I would try to stay cordial because it wasn't personal. Usually I was responding to a radio call from the victim of a crime, and the person I handcuffed was the suspect who did it. I basically arrived to sweep up the mess and write the report. The rest of the investigation went to the detectives and the district attorney. Well, it's the same here. I will be polite and even friendly, but if he steps over the line, he'll reap the consequences.

I head to the kitchen to heat up the next ingredients. It gives the students a few moments to themselves.

"Since this is mixology, it doesn't need to extract the flavor, so we can drink it right away," a lady says before she takes a sip of her coffee. "Wow, that's strong!"

"Right. Instant happiness," says another.

I return with two jugs of hot simple-syrup. "If you'd like to add powdered bakers chocolate, which is dark chocolate without the sugar, you'll need to heat your syrup so it will blend. That's what I have here. I also have an assortment of spices: vanilla, ginger, allspice, fennel, and others." I place the jugs on the tables, and return with two trays of spices.

"Pour the hot syrup into your jar, then add the dry spices and chocolate. Make sure to blend well and keep tasting. When you get it where you like the spice and coffee-chocolate ratio, pour in the vodka. You may need more syrup if you want it thick and luscious, or less if you don't have a sugar-tooth.

I stand back to let them play. They are mixing and tasting their concoctions in a separate jar so they don't ruin the whole batch with the wrong spice mix.

I walk around looking over individual shoulders and offering advice. I start on the right, across from the Italian, and make my way around the room. I plan to avoid him completely.

"Miss Jessica—will you taste mine and tell me if you like it?" his voice reaches my ears.

"Mr. Anthony, I'm sure you have a well-developed palate and know what you like." I raise one eyebrow.

"Yes I do," he lowers his tone.

"All right now, it looks like we're ready to move on," I announce loudly as I take three strides to get behind my table. "For those of you who haven't already combined the alcohol with your spice/coffee mixture, go ahead and do it. Then see what you've made."

The class is on their own for a few minutes, tasting, talking and laughing. While they're having fun, I take a breather and a few sips of water.

"Now we're ready to apply your beautiful labels. I'll again thank Darryl at Paso Distillery for creating them. He has a friend who is an artist and creates the watercolors for him."

The class pulls off the backings and applies pictures of coffee, lemons, and rosemary to their concoctions. Some are a little crooked, and others are precisely measured from the top of the jar to make sure the label is perfect. This adds a lovely end to their work.

I head to the kitchen for the pound cake with coffee liqueur poured over it.

"This is the last of our sweet desserts. I hope you aren't tired of it yet."

As I slice it, the Italian appears at my side. It's a bit close for comfort. He should be on the other side of the table.

"Please let me. You've worked so hard today." He goes to take the serrated bread knife out of my hand. I smile and quickly jump back, still holding it.

"Signorina," he drawls, "I won't hurt you." He holds out his hand for me to place my knife in his.

I smile. "Signore, thank you, but I'll slice." I say it in a sing-song accent, but stay out of reach.

He returns to his seat muttering something about how I don't trust him.

I finish the process, return the knife to the kitchen, and *then* ask if he'll help me serve.

He looks reproachful, but gets up to help.

The cake is a hit. Of course.

They go on to sample their own coffee liqueur against mine. I pass around more coffee to keep them a bit more sober. Not that it actually does.

They slowly pack their bottles in the Greenstone Cottage reusable bag I'm providing.

"This was a great class. Thank you very much!" Someone comments.

"I'm going home to try these other recipes." He holds the packet in his hand.

"I'm going to get more cake and douse it with Kahlua."

The room empties, but the Italian, who I doubt is from Italy, remains.

Then it's just the two of us.

"You've changed my opinion." He studies me carefully. "You're not what I thought you were."

"Oh?"

"You're okay. I won't bother you again." He smiles, then carefully packs his liqueurs and vegetable peeler in the Greenstone bag. He's about to leave his place, when he turns back and drops the coupons in.

"Arrivederci." An honest smile changes his already handsome face to a thing of beauty. He turns and walks through the open door with his gift bag.

He said I'm okay, and that he won't bother me again—implying he has bothered me in the past. Who is he associated with—the SUVs and stolen cars?

25

EVERYDAY STUFF

My heart is thumping. All afternoon, I didn't know if I'd be running for my office, or discovering what he was doing here. It turns out to be neither one.

I hurry to the door and watch as he confidently walks down the path to the street. He gets into a black BMW and swings a U-turn. I'm at the rise where the hot tub will one day be. He sees me and waves. I catch the license plate—and run back to my office with it fresh in my mind to get it down on paper.

I lock the office door and close the lounge to a potential invasion of white rats, then I hurry to the parking lot to chat with Adam in his RV.

He meets me before I get there.

"That was something." He looks like he needs a break too. After all, he was on guard the entire time.

"Yeah. Did you also get the feeling his opinion of me changed? It felt like he's no longer going to do whatever he had planned."

"Uh huh, but I wouldn't put much faith in it. He still has a friend."

"I know, but at least he didn't do anything horrible today, at least in class. Here's the license plate." I go to hand him the paper.

"I already have it." He smiles. "I got it when he arrived."

"I should have known you'd be watching."

"Jess, I'm not an amateur." He gives me a look and shakes his head like I'm an amateur.

"Sorry. No you certainly aren't."

"That's okay. And hey, your class was interesting. Do you have any cake left?" He smiles like a little boy.

"Sure, come on. You'd better eat it before I do."

He comes in the lounge and surveys it from a different perspective. "You're a good speaker, you held the attention of your audience."

"It helps that they had alcohol in their system," I laugh.

"Of course," he agrees with me. "But I'd come to your next one," he says in an off-hand way.

I relish the compliment from the military man.

I begin cleaning up. The lounge must be inviting for our overnight guests. One couple is staying here, but my other four cottages are spending New Year's Day at the beach, or hiking, or something. I'm glad I used paper plates. Yes, there is a lot of waste, but since we have water problems it also saves on washing up.

Adam moves the tables and chairs back to their usual places so it will be tidy for the afternoon. I cart everything else to the kitchen.

"That went well. I can't believe he didn't try anything." I'm still thinking about that. "I'm sure I'm not mistaken about him."

"I'll check the plate right now if you want."

"Please do. I've been trying to be patient for the last hour. It's driving me nuts."

"All right. I'll do it now and put you out of your misery," he chuckles and heads out. "Oh, you have a rat that wants to come in." He stamps his foot and something white runs.

"Darn it. I still have that problem."

I've made a decision. I'll face it head on and tell my guests that someone released a bunch of lab rats in front of my property. The cats are eating them, the cages have yet to catch them, and I hate to put out the traps. The owls that live in the area will have a feast with these bright little bodies running around. They certainly can't hide...

Until they interbreed with the native ones and become beige. No, that can't happen. I must catch them before the town is overrun with white-ish rodents.

With this, I'm no longer having a panic attack over my guests seeing a white rat, or two, or three. I head into the office and type up a flier with the info. I even ask them to tell me if they've seen any. I'll get everyone on board with my problem, and let them know the rats will disperse to other neighborhoods because I've made life miserable for them with cats, ultrasonic devices, and owls.

I even say a few words for Mandy to hear and comment about, thus incriminating herself. "What the hell, I just saw a white rat." I'll see how she runs with the news tonight. Oh and I just had another idea. I'll call Mandy and confidentially ask her about the rats. In fact, I'll do it right now.

"Cambria Seaside Resort. How may I help you?" asks the woman at the desk.

"Hi. May I speak with Mandy Crawford? This is Jess Wilcox from Greenstones."

"Just a moment please. I'll see if she's available." She puts me on hold. "I'm sorry, but Ms. Crawford is in a meeting. May I put you through to her voicemail?"

I think for a second and decide not to leave a message that can be replayed. If she plays the recording from her hidden device, that's illegal. "Will you ask her to phone me when she gets a chance?"

She gets my number. Darn it. It occurs to me, even if I tell her, she will still have heard about my rats via a legal method. I need to come up with something else to tell her.

My phone buzzes with a text from Kate at the Majestic Chef. "I just had two people redeem the coupons I gave you. Thanks! They bought a lot of tea."

"I'm glad!"

I just made friendly points for sending her customers. This went so well I think I'll keep doing these classes. Maybe every six months? I should also try other things. Cheese making? Or perfume making with essential oils? Yes, I think perfume is better than making cheese. Maybe a class on natural medicine. Just the basics, like how to use arnica, and some medicinal home garden seedlings, and a bag of compost for each student.

I start catching up on the bookkeeping and updating the supply list. Then my cell phone rings with the number from the resort. It has to be "her."

"Hello, Jessica. This is Mandy Crawford. You phoned?" She sounds abrupt.

I put her on speaker, so she can later hear the playback on her transmitter, AND I'll also get it on our surveillance. This is so complicated!

"I had a liqueur making workshop today and it went well. I wondered if we could do a joint one next month. It would bring attention to both our businesses."

She loudly exhales, then waits for a moment to make sure I know she thinks this is a stupid idea. "Jessica. I have more than enough business. Why would I be interested in your little bungalows?"

"They're cottages!" I snap. "But aside from that, I thought it would be a nice gesture to bring in good will and tourists to Cambria."

"Cambria has plenty of goodwill and tourists. We don't need your help. I have more important things to do than consider your amateur suggestions." She flings that nastiness at me, then hangs up.

Oh. Wow. I'm glad this was only a ruse, not that I was serious about a joint workshop between Greenstones and that witch. I would have been devastated if I were serious. Just wait until the corporate owners hear this.

I lock up and dash to the RV to see Adam in person.

He comes to the door. "She's a real pig, isn't she?" he asks without needing an answer. "And you're here to rant about her?"

"If you want to listen, I'll rant. Otherwise, I'm aware your time is precious, so I've come to see if you can put together the surveillance so I can go on the offense."

"So you can annihilate her?" He has a strange look.

"Yes. That."

"I'll put all the recordings on a file and email it to you. If you aren't in a rush, will tomorrow night be okay?"

I hadn't realized it would take that long. I guess he's busy doing other work in there. "Perfect, thanks."

He goes to close the door, when I speak up. "Have you heard from Quinn?"

He nods. "I know he'd like to be here, but he's engaged in something."

I hope it doesn't mean he's acting like James Bond, wearing a tuxedo at a gambling table in Monte Carlo. A slinky woman with long hair, wearing a clingy black dress, is standing behind him. Don't scoff—Jack Courtland had the lovely Jacqueline-Noelle, so I know it happens when a man is "saving his country or engaged in something."

But I don't say anything like that to Adam. I simply smile and say thank you.

Back in my cottage I stand in front of the closed refrigerator door. What can I eat? I guess I should plan ahead. I have dried beans and lentils that need soaking overnight if I want to get rid of those horrible lectins... whatever they are. Instead, I open the freezer and pull out a frozen pizza, which I'm sure is much worse than a few lectins. Oh well.

I made $1250 profit from the workshop. It doesn't take into account my three hours teaching. There was prep time to get everything together, visiting local stores to see about coupons. And ordering the glass jars and such. But it was fun, and I would have spent my time doing something if not this.

The sun has gone down, the night is turning cold and damp. I've tucked my rat-notes into the doors of my guests. I'm sitting in front of my gas fireplace, reading a romance—of all things.

A business call comes through, routed from my office. "Greenstone Cottage. May I help you?"

"This is Mrs. Huntington. My daughter Mia was staying with you for a few days. Now she's missing!"

"Oh dear." I reply, and let her explain.

"She had her car stolen, and I haven't heard from her for three days."

"Yeah, she was seeing a sketchy man."

"She's such wild-child. I don't know what to do. I phoned the resort where she was staying, but they said the last they saw here was being loaded into the ambulance. I've phoned the hospital and was told she wasn't admitted. I don't know what to do."

"I guess you could hire a private investigator."

"Will you look for her?"

"I'm sorry, I have a hotel to run."

"I googled you and see you're good at finding people and capturing criminals," she tries to get me to agree.

"I'm sorry, but that was several months ago. Those investigations landed in my lap. I didn't have a choice."

"Can you suggest anyone?"

Mom is seeing a P.I. who hired me to look for a stolen agility dog. I give her his number and feel relieved to be finished with it.

I pick up my iPad and continue with the romance set here in Cambria. I reach over for another piece of pizza and relax.

A while later, my phone rings. It's my personal line. I recognize the number: it's Mom's P.I. boyfriend, Rick Newman. He used to be a detective with LAPD.

"Hi Rick."

"Jessica. It's great hearing your voice, and thanks for the referral. I'm working another case—would you be interested in finding the missing young woman?" he chuckles.

"No. I don't have any idea where to begin."

"Her mother told me her credit card was used last night at a hotel in Paso Robles and today at a restaurant. Do you want to check into it?"

"If she's using her Visa then she isn't missing. She just doesn't want to go home yet."

"I tend to agree, but if you're willing to be ready to run over to the next place the card is used, I'd appreciate it."

"Uh. Why are you pressuring me? Can't you get someone else to find her?"

"You're good at it, and her mother likes you. Plus I don't want to turn down the job."

"Are you finding it expensive taking my mother out to wine dinners?" I laugh.

"I'd never admit that. It's just that I hate turning down work."

"Fine. When she checks into a hotel, or is somewhere she may stay for a while, call me."

"Thank you."

"Wait a sec. She wrote a bad review about me that was a complete lie! I take that back. Let her stay lost."

"You're not doing it for her. You're doing it for me. And you know I pay well."

"I made $1250 today. I don't need the work."

"But I do. Come on, help out a fellow copper."

"I will consider it when you call. If it's midnight and pouring rain, and the little idiot is in a remote area, the answer will be no," I give in.

"Thank you."

I turn my phone to Do Not Disturb. I don't want any more calls tonight.

26

BACK TO WORK

It's the morning after New Year's Day. I open the door to find another rat on my mat. Good kitty. I nudge it into the bushes with my running shoe to be picked up later. I'm deliberately staying away from my phone for the first few minutes. I don't want to be asked to do anything.

Finally I turn it on and get the barrage: The first is from Rick Newman, "Answer your phone! Mia is at a B&B in Paso. Here's the address..."

Another is from the foxhunting, cheating husband: "Hello, this is Lyle Stamford. I have a situation. Will you please phone me?" He leaves his number.

Adam has sent an attachment in his email. It'll be the surveillance videos and proof of Mandy's dirty deeds. I can't wait to go through it. I'll need to give the dates and times, with a brief summary of each occurrence in chronological order. My email and letter will need to be perfect; I'm sending them by both methods. I intend for this to reach the top of the food chain at Meadowbrook Hotels Corporation.

I'm already feeling overwhelmed by things to do just to catch up with my day. I don't want to drive to Paso to track down that lying little brat. I skip my run. It's one thing I don't want to do, so it's a good excuse. I head into the lounge for breakfast. It's already crowded at 8:00 a.m.

"Why is everyone up so early?" I enter with a smile and friendly greeting.

The responses vary from one couple to another. The sweetest reason is because they miss their dog.

Janet will get a jump on cleaning the rooms. I sit and chat with those still eating while starting my own breakfast. It'll be a fast one for me, since I have to leave for Paso, and I'll call Lyle on the way.

An hour later, I'm in Adam's Mustang, after having a discussion with him that he doesn't have to come with me. I have my .45, the car has surveillance, and Adam can talk me through performance driving. Anyhow, I have a gut feeling that one of the Italians isn't angry, but I still don't know why the other is. This car will outrun a lot of my problems.

As soon as I get a breath, I place the call to Lyle. After his greeting he gets to the point. "Will you do a fellow horseman a favor?" He a waits for my reply.

"What favor do you want?" I'm not falling for it by blindly saying yes.

"My wife doesn't ride to hounds much these days. When we first met, she was always out here with me. It was an activity we enjoyed together. Well, she's been distant for the past six months or so. I think she may be having an affair with David Reynolds."

"Oh, that's a shame." And very interesting! She had me investigating her husband, but she could be the one cheating. I wonder if she loses her share in the divorce if she is having an affair.

"You've seen Reynolds, he's a ladies man. I need someone to follow her during the ride on Wednesday. It's the first ride of the year. I don't know any private investigators who can ride to hounds."

"I'm not sure how good I am, I fell off last time."

"No you didn't. The horse stumbled and launched you over his head. There's a difference," he reassures me.

"It's nice of you to put it that way."

"Roxy came after me like a fly to manure, but I'm not interested. Reynolds will probably take her up on her offer if she asks. Georgie, my wife, has known him for years. I think I saw them together two weeks ago, but can't prove it."

"Do you think they'll have a fling in his trailer?"

"Probably not, but I'd like to see if you can find anything."

"What horse will I ride?"

"See if Reynolds will let you ride his hireling. I'll pay for it, of course."

"I'm not fond of foxhunting. I'm more of a trail and dressage rider. I was only doing it on a dare." I kind of lie.

"I'll be happy to make it worth your while."

"Worth my while to break my neck?" I snort.

"A thousand dollars to ride the horse, come to the potluck, and tail them."

I don't need a $1000 that badly. Especially when his wife pays me, I have the proceeds from the workshop, and a fully booked hotel. But, if she's cheating on him and trying to weasel out of a prenup, that isn't right.

"I'll try it." I'm such a sucker.

"Thank you. See you on Wednesday, and Happy New Year!" He already sounds happier.

* * *

I PULL up to the B&B which is actually a private residence where Mia is staying. It's just before 10:00 a.m., so I won't be disturbing anyone when I knock.

A normal looking woman answers the door.

"Hi. My name is Jessica Wilcox. I was asked by the mother of Mia Huntington to ask her to come home." I get to the point, and don't bother asking if she is staying there, which could cause her to balk.

"She is still in bed. It isn't my place to wake her."

"I understand. Will you leave a message with her breakfast to call her mother?"

"Certainly." She agrees, since I haven't asked anything wrong.

"Thank you." I turn to go.

"Oh, and will you ask her why she wrote that awful review about my cottage when it wasn't true?"

Her expression changes. "Okay." She looks confused.

I lower my voice, like I'm divulging a secret. "Mia's mother made a reservation at my place in Cambria for several weeks. She stayed for a few days, then got involved with a man she found in a bar. He is a troublemaker and the three of us had words. She left my place and went to a competitor of mine who got her to write a review about seeing a rat in the breakfast room. There were other guests dining at the same time, and I was there; there wasn't a rat. If there had been, she wouldn't have been mute about it."

"Interesting." She says, but like me, doesn't say anything about her guest when she doesn't know my agenda.

"Anyhow, her mother wants to know she's safe."

"I'll make sure she gets the message." She smiles thoughtfully.

"Here." I hand her my glossy business card. It's a photo taken at my window, with the sheer curtains blowing in the breeze, and the ocean in the background; most definitely a great vacation spot.

"This is lovely." She inspects it. It isn't a homemade card that someone uses to imply they have a legitimate business.

"Thank you." I turn to go.

"Jessica?" She softly asks.

"Yes?"

"She has a man with her. He's a bit strange. Will it be a problem?" She looks concerned for the first time.

"Do you know his name—is it Axel?"

"No, I think it's something like Damien, or Diesel."

"Wow, it sounds like she picked up another one." I show her a photo on my phone. "This is her, right?" Since she's already giving me the information, she should be able to answer a few questions.

"Yes, when she looked like a student."

"Her mother wouldn't have any other type." I doubt she has any showing cleavage at a party.

"Could this be dangerous? I'm a single woman alone."

"I don't think she will be a problem. Hopefully this guy just has a curious name, but is actually nice."

"I'll call my brother. He's on the other side of town." She makes a decision.

"That sounds safest. See how they are at breakfast."

"I'm trying to make a little money renting out the room. This isn't what I expected."

I nod in sympathy.

When I get back to the car, I phone Mrs. Huntington to let her know Mia spent the night. I leave out the part about a man; I don't want them to give the homeowner a bad review.

"I'm calling the police right now. They have to take her in for safekeeping."

"She's over twenty-one. There isn't a crime, nor is she unable to care for herself. The police can't do anything."

"What is this world coming to? She's my daughter. She has to come home when I say," she steams.

"You could cut off her Visa card. That might bring her running, or at least it would get you a nasty phone call." She may find other ways to make money, but I don't say that.

"I'm sending two strong men to bring her home. Will you stay there until they arrive, or follow her if she leaves?"

"Oh dear. If you force her home, that's kidnapping."

"I'm her mother!" She rages through the phone.

"I think it's a bit late for that. Perhaps when she was younger, you could have reeled her in." And not given her a $100,000 Porsche when she turned twenty-one.

"I'm sending one of my employees. He'll bring her home. You stay there," she insists.

"If I help him take her, I'd be aiding and abetting a felony kidnapping. I think your best bet is to find out what she's up to. Use her Visa card as leverage."

She gives a tormented sigh.

"Okay. Maybe you're right," she moans. "My baby has grown up."

I head back to Greenstones with an eye on the rear view mirror, actually an eye everywhere. This Mustang is one heck of a powerful car. No one is following me—maybe they know they'd have a fight on their hands.

27

HUNTING AGAIN

Wednesday arrives sooner than I want. I'm not looking forward to jumping again. I'd put it behind me as an interesting experience, but now it's looming in front of me again. My first question is which vehicle to drive. My big truck is safe, but if the SUV rammed it just right, I'd spin off the road. The Mustang won't like being driven into a dusty vineyard full of horse trailers and the fresh deposits from fifty horses.

Adam and I get into a heated discussion. He doesn't really want me taking the car, but he's afraid Quinn will be furious if I don't.

"Why don't you come with me, be my lay-off car, but don't come into the vineyard. You can find a shady spot for four long, boring hours."

"That may be the best answer. I can protect you, and save my baby from goodness knows what you'd do to her."

"And I'm sure my clothes and boots would smell like leather and sweaty horses."

"I like the other uses for leather," he jokingly suggests.

"Oh brother." I shake my head.

He shrugs.

So here we are, I'm in the lead in my big truck. He's following several cars behind and squirming at the speed I'm driving.

"Can you press your foot a little harder on the accelerator?" His prompt comes through the radio speaker system.

"I'm going 67 mph. Get over it." I laugh at him, but increase it to 72. My gas mileage will suck.

We make it to the highway exit in record time. He follows me until I swing into the dusty driveway. "I'll wait until you're on the horse, then I'll head to town to try out the eateries on Los Alamos." It's only four miles back.

"And I'll be galloping across the hilltops with the wind in my hair." I make it sound wonderful.

"Don't land in a ditch." He injects a touch of reality.

"I'll try."

There's Reynold's trailer under the large oak, with the horses tied in the same places. David is consistent, I'll say that much. And there's Lyle's rig. Except he said he won't be here, Georgie will be. I have to chuckle at calling her Georgie. She doesn't act that cute.

I've already thought this through. I don't want to park next to his rig. I need to give him and Georgina space to have a fling. But if they're having an affair, why would they have sex in his dressing room? That doesn't make sense. I'll see what I can find out. This could be a dangerous quest if my seat becomes separated from my steed.

Georgina sees me striding across the lot. Her expression changes to puzzlement, and her hands turn upward, meaning "why are you here?"

I nod and try to look like I'll tell her later. The only thing I could come up with was that I'm writing an article for submission to a wine country travel magazine. Which doesn't make sense because tourists can't go foxhunting without knowing a club member.

"Hi David," I stride up with a perky expression.

"Hey Jess." He looks at me a bit longer than is necessary. "You look refreshed. Did you have a good holiday?"

"It was very nice, thanks." Let's see, I was in a car chase, taught a slightly stressful workshop, and had a pack of rats set loose on my property. I smile invitingly.

Maybe I can start a spark that Georgina can ignite. I think men are like that. If they're thinking about sex, but can't get it from the woman they desire, they'll look to someone they can get it from. That's what I've heard, or maybe I made it up—I'm not sure which. It's a wonder I have a boyfriend with the lack of trust I have in the human male.

We riders mill around while the hounds search for scent. The poor coyote is about to have a crummy day. Already, David pulls out his flask. He's riding through the throng, chatting and moving on. Until he conveniently rides up to Georgina and stops. I don't look, but I'm aware he's been there for a lot longer than with everyone else.

The shout goes up, "Tally-Ho." And we take off at a canter.

It's the same route as last time. The coyote has a favorite trail through the trees at the bottom of the canyon. I follow behind the second group, letting David and the leaders fly ahead. Georgina is only slightly ahead of me on a nice horse who jumps steady and safe. I would hope so, since she hasn't ridden for months.

So far, I'm glad I'm staying on and in one piece. I need to get into a better frame of mind—one where life can't get better than this, seeing the countryside on the back of a flawless horse at a gallop. Soon, worries about my expanding rat population, car chases, and Hector swoosh from my mind as the breeze carries them into the ether.

Georgina meets up with me at one stop. "Why are you here?" She doesn't sound suspicious yet.

"I'm writing an article on the hunt. I'm making it from the perspective of a new foxhunter enjoying galloping and cama-raderie." I go on excitedly about the things I'll be writing until I see her lose interest. I say a little more, for good measure.

"Good for you. Have you spoken with the hunt master?"

"Yes. Thanks for the advice."

"Great. Well, I'm going to check in with my friends, glad you're still hunting with us." She rides off.

I passed that test, but I didn't ask her when she was going to pay me. I'll do it later. I don't want to take her out of the mood.

By the lunch break, I've spoken with other riders, flirted with David a few times at drinking stops, and am more than ready to take a breather.

I sit in my truck for a few minutes to chat with Adam. "I feel guilty about you waiting for me as I frolic with my horse peeps."

"Don't worry about it. I'm used to being on surveillance for days and weeks on end. I have plenty to do, I'm connected to my work."

"Okay, thanks for saying that."

I lean back and relax for a few minutes. Then I unzip my hot dish from the insulation bag. It's a twice baked potato casserole with cheddar and bacon. Before leaving home, I even gave a tiny slice to Adam. He claims to like it, though I know he's into protein, just like Quinn. I guess when you rely on your body to keep you alive, you give it the best food you can find. I don't rely on my body that much, so I get to eat for fun, too.

I rejoin the others and set my dish on the table, along with a card listing the ingredients saying that Jessica Wilcox made it. Almost everyone has theirs already set out, so the line forms, and the hungry riders queue up to load their plates. I'm trying to let Georgina and David go ahead of me, but he looks up and his eyes lock on mine—and he walks back to stand with me. Oh No!

"Great riding today, don't you think?" He begins with in a smooth tone.

"Yes. Ryan is going great. He's such a nice horse, it's a privilege riding him," I reply, honestly.

"You're welcome." The line has stopped, so he takes a swig from that darned flask. "You're a natural in the saddle." He smiles. "Ryan is a lucky horse," his tone drops a smidge and he holds a smirk and eye contact.

"David, there's a lot of innuendo flowing from your lips." I smile and tilt my head. I make sure Georgina can't see me. That would piss her off and prevent anything from happening later.

"What?" He acts innocent. "You know you ride well."

"Um hum, put it back on me." I smile again. "David, you're a flirt." But I say it with an invitation.

I remember he schtupped Roxy only two weeks ago in his horse trailer. I refuse to be next.

"Jess, you're a lovely woman." He takes another sip.

"Is that brandy?" I ask, for something to say.

"Yeah, with coffee."

"Sounds like a delicious Kahlua."

"Here." He hands me the silver flask, still attached to his waist.

I hesitate. Should I, or shouldn't I? I go for it, to prove my theory.

I take a tiny sip. Tiny, because Ryan doesn't need a tipsy rider. "Mmm, tasty." I flash a smile again.

His face turns tomato red. I know he's thinking about sex.

The line begins moving, so I turn my attention to what interests me: food. I add a small piece of roast chicken, then move past all the other dead meat, to the side dishes. My potato casserole looks tasty, and everyone ahead of me thinks so too. A spoonful will give me the energy needed to continue the hunt in good form.

He's close at my side. "You made the casserole?" He sounds impressed.

"Yeah, I make things taste good." It isn't really an answer and it crosses into the suggestive.

He doesn't answer right away.

"Should I take two?" he asks.

What?

I recover and try to say something, anything. It almost doesn't matter what it is, just as long as I say it with a smile. "Two would be great." I nod. "So much better than one."

Oh hell, this is getting a bit much. I take a breath and look at the next dish to bring myself back to normal. I help myself to a small scoop of pasta salad, even though I don't like cold pasta.

There's a break in conversation for a few dishes. He begins again at the dessert. "What, no limoncello cake—I like the flavor of sweet lemon and satisfying cake."

How do I turn this into something? What word goes with limoncello? Acid. That won't work.

So I change the ingredients. "Sweet and salty?" It isn't salty, but what the heck.

"Yum." He doesn't know or care.

I swear, without looking down, I see his pants stretch.

There aren't any more tables. Now what?

"Why don't you sit with Georgina—she's looking at you hungrily?" I suggest with a quirked eyebrow, and very gently place my hand on his shoulder. She's about five people back, and looking at him.

I'm not looking at her, I don't want her sensing guilty interaction between David and me.

I bet he thinks she can be the second woman to our... No I'm not going there. I don't know what he thinks. I just need to end this before I have to literally run away.

"Go talk to her," I whisper, then make my escape while he looks at Georgina.

I sit with the trail riders and relax for half an hour.

The hunt master has had his fill and is itching for a kill. He's on his feet, sending his whippers-in to hunt for a wild canine victim. I need to get my evidence before the hounds get the scent. The hunters glory in it, but I find it disgusting and vile. I'm a city girl. I don't even like my meat to look like meat. I don't even like it in cellophane. I hate the smell at a meat counter. Give me lentils and beans with onions, celery, and spices. I like cows—they're friendly and innocent. What makes it acceptable to eat them, but not a horse? What makes it terrible to kill one animal, but another is taken without a thought? It has to do with their usefulness to man: Cows, chickens, sheep. A problem for man: *Rats*, coyotes, boars.

This David Reynolds flirtation is sending me over the edge.

"How do I get out of here?" I whisper to myself.

A voice in my earbud replies, "You're talking yourself into a corner. You'd better figure it out, fast."

Adam.

"I'm trying to get him ramped up so he goes for Georgina when I'm not available. Was it that enticing?"

"That and more," he reveals.

"Oh." I stop, embarrassed. "He needs to make a move for her."

"If you're not careful, he'll be dragging you into the woods."

"Hell."

"You don't have any sense about men, do you?"

"Uhh-what?"

"You can turn a normal man into a hunter."

"Oh dear," I gulp.

"I'm just warning you."

"Ok. I'm warned."

And getting panicky. I need to steer this in the right direction.

Plates are being thrown in garbage bins, and riders are running for their horses. The hounds have found the scent. Damn it. I barely move out of a walk toward my horse.

"Come on, babe, the hounds are..." His words are lost as David sprints past me to the trailer.

Run, coyote, run.

I feel like crying. This is sick. How can someone who likes the outdoors, horses, and friends accept this as okay? I'm reaching a tipping point. My so called article on foxhunting will be turned into an exposé on the grossness of coyote hunting.

David canters past, waving, "Come on! We're off!"

I untie Ryan, mount from the trailer wheel-well, and walk after the others. Georgina, trots up. "David isn't interested in you."

"What?"

"He isn't interested in you," she expands her sentence.

"No he isn't." I agree.

She looks surprised.

I repeat, "He isn't interested in me. He was next to me in line, but he wants you," I proclaim.

She looks relieved—I think. Unless I'm projecting.

"Why don't you go get him?" I suggest.

She studies me for a second, then gallops after the group.

"Well that was something." It's Adam in my ear again. "Sometimes you're good at reading people."

"Thanks."

I sure don't feel alone. It's like I have an audience.

"Sorry Ryan." I turn him around, heading back to the trailer where I jump off and tie him up. I'm done for now.

I mooch around the food tables. The platters and dishes are still there, forgotten in the quest to kill the coyote. I take another paper plate and go through the empty line once again. This time, without a man panting behind me. A few small scoops, and a square of fudge, that will satisfy me. I take a seat under the oak and prop my booted feet up on the chair next to mine and nibble in peace.

I cover the trays of food, then wander around for nearly an hour when the first riders return.

"What a great hunt." They look excited as their horses walk with loose reins to the trailer.

I don't ask if they got the coyote. It would ruin my day if they did.

I'm scanning the distance, and there I see Georgina and David riding, side by side. So I watch and wait.

Riders are hosing off their horses, sponging cooling liniment on them, and heading home. David is taking his time, hanging around. Georgina is at her trailer, and I'm sitting in my truck. Very soon, it will be obvious that I'm still here. It had better not look like I'm waiting for him. She keeps looking at his trailer, and at my truck. It's clear nothing will be happening with me acting as a guard to her passion.

"Hey Adam, I'm moving the truck, then going back to the hunt club for surveillance."

"Roger."

28

MUSCADINE'S

I drive down the road, around the bend, and turn in the small driveway with a sign on the open chain-link gate: Muscadine's Wine Barrel Storage. The posted hours are 9-5; I have lots of time. I park by the steel building with a big stack of wine barrels at the side. My truck will fit in nicely next to the other trucks parked in the dirt.

A forklift passes by. It's moving three barrels to the bed of a white pickup. I should buy a few. It might give more ambience to my new hot tub and Bellini bar.

I change my tight riding boots for running shoes, grab my jacket with the compact .45 zipped in the pocket, and go look at the barrels stacked outside. I can tell by the seared markings they're French oak. It has the maker's name, the forest it's grown in, plus the amount of toast. This is M+, which I know means a medium plus they use for Pinot Noir grown in this region, closer to the ocean. I don't recognize the other markings. I'll ask if they want to sell two when I return.

I push through the weeds growing beside the tall hedge along the road.

But I don't get far.

"Hey. What are you doing?" A gruff voice demands an answer.

I jerk around and see a bearded man in a camouflage shirt and pants. He's standing behind a tree across the muddy ditch.

"I'm—going back to the hunt club." I edge backward.

"You left your truck in my lot."

"Yeah. That's because I don't want to be seen." It comes out in a rush.

I back further away. The left side of his body is hidden. He's big, not particularly friendly, and I think I am somewhere I shouldn't be.

"You're not leaving 'till I find out who you're working for."

"I'd rather not say."

"It would be best if you do." He steps from behind cover, revealing what I feared. Well, almost what I feared. I thought he'd have a shotgun, but it's an assault rifle.

"Okay, fine. I'm working for Lyle Stamford. He hired me to get evidence of his wife cheating." There, I revealed my employer, though I don't think he means that.

"Not the right answer," he snaps, and brings the barrel of the weapon up. It isn't pointed at me, but more like at the ground an inch from my feet.

"I—well. I was working for his wife two weeks ago to prove he was cheating on her. But he wasn't."

"Aren't you cute, pretending to be stupid—what are you doing here?" He steps forward.

"I'm only using your property to get back and catch them in the act. As you can see, my truck doesn't hide well. I'll leave now, and find another way to sneak over." I make sure to keep sounding young.

"You're working for Dennison," he growls his conclusion. "Put your hands up, or I'll take you out, right here."

I half raise my hands. My elbows are bent, looking like an "L."

He allows it, but it's an incomplete position. I was trained that when you tell a suspect to raise his hands, you also command "Lock out your elbows." My hands are closer to my gun than if they were straight up in the air. It may give me a half-second to unzip my pocket—but I doubt it.

"I can prove that I was riding to hounds. See, I'm wearing riding britches." I look down. "My boots are in the truck, and the riders at the hunt club will verify who I am."

"There's a small problem."

I don't need to reply. He'll tell me his small problem without it.

"You were reading the barrels." He points the rifle in the direction of the warehouse, telling me to move along.

"I'd like to buy two of them." I reply, though I think we're past the innocent part. He thinks I'm working for Dennison. I have to get my gun before he thinks to search me.

Once with the other men, I'll be in trouble. I need to act now. So I cross the ditch, but stumble a few steps—which makes my hands drop. I land in the mud, flailing around trying to get my feet underneath me. It could be an episode of I Love Lucy. "Help me up."

While he turns away with disdain, I get my pocket unzipped and pull out the .45 while looking like a spaz in the mud.

"Lay down the gun, or die," I growl.

He glares at me without moving. He can shoot me faster than I can react, even with the barrel pointing at the ground. He can swing it up on target and fire with one hand before I know what his intentions.

My option is to shoot him right now, before he shoots me.

I hear shouts and running feet. Oh hell. His friends are coming. Either I shoot him, or die in a few seconds by their guns. "Tracy, what've you got?" one yells.

"Drop it now." I whisper. Good, my voice sounds stressed. Stressed women are likely to shoot.

He raises one hand, the other carefully lowers the rifle to the ground.

"Step back."

He does.

"Tracy, what's up?" Another shout.

"Say something smart," I hiss.

"It's all good, nothing here," he shouts back.

"Where'd she go?"

"To the horse club."

"Dumb broad," the other guy says. We hear his steps moving away.

"I want to leave here alive. You could have let me sneak over the street and I wouldn't have known you were up to something. But no, you had to make a fuss over nothing." I talk too much.

"You won't shoot me." He smiles, trying to be friendly.

"You were going to take me prisoner. Now, back up."

He moves a few feet away from the rifle. "Back more. I'm not leaving this for you to shoot me."

"You won't shoot now we've had a nice conversation." He slowly lowers his hands. "You're not a killer."

Hell. If I shoot him, it'll alert a bunch of criminals that I'm here. I will have a little time, but what a mess.

"I don't care if I shoot you, but I'd rather not. I want to leave, safely."

"I give you my word—you can leave safely," he says what he thinks I want to hear.

"Back away from the gun. If you go for it, I'll dump you." I can do that easily enough. It would be clear self-defense in my mind. Not like a nebulous line he shouldn't cross.

"You won't shoot me. You're a nice girl. You ride horses and love animals. You care for the environment, and want to help people." He is using a tactic he thinks will wear me down. "You love Jesus and your mother too."

That last line distracts me. It sounds like a Tom Petty song. My brows are pinched. I'm sure he won't back away and let me take the gun. I bet he'll slowly move for it. If he dives for it, he knows I'd react. But the slow, stealthy way makes it hard to know when to shoot.

He inches his foot forward, causing a little twig to snap. He stops.

I'd shoot him in the leg if I thought the others wouldn't come running.

"Jess, it's me. I'm on the other side of the bushes. Don't move." It's Adam, whispering in my ear bud. "Clear your throat if you hear me."

"Um mm," I reply with a throat clearing.

His deep voice barks from inside the hedge, "Step away from the rifle."

The guy jumps back. It's amazing what a commanding, male voice coming out of a bush can do.

He tells me to get the rifle, which I do, then I back up to the bushes with the gun. It feels like we're a special operation, and the suspect is complying perfectly.

"Pass me the rifle. Go get your truck and come pick me up."

I pass it through and hurry back the way I came. I'm not worried about that guy anymore. Now I have to get to the truck without being grabbed. My gun is in my hand, hidden in my pocket. I reach the truck, get in, and drive out without being stopped.

Three men beside the pickup with the wine barrels stop talking, but they don't move toward me. I keep them in my peripheral vision, but drive out of the lot in a smooth sweep.

I turn right and go slowly enough to let Adam come out of the bushes when he hears my diesel engine. I idle close by until I see him back out of the hedge. I pull forward with the passenger door open. He leaps in and whispers. "GO, GO!"

I apply as much pressure as I can while maintaining consistent acceleration. Spinning the tires would be a waste, since they aren't going anywhere, and only make a lot of noise.

It's quiet for a minute until he compliments me, "Good job back there."

"Thanks." There's nothing else to say—he's the one who got us out.

"What possessed you to pull into the warehouse of an arms dealer?"

"What?"

"That's right. I just heard. The Feds are taking them down. You may have blown the whole operation."

"Damn. How was I supposed to know? I was only looking for somewhere to park."

"I know, I heard you." He looks at the weapon in his hands, removes the magazine, and clears the chamber. "It's fully automatic."

"Yikes."

"How do you do this? How do you land in a can of worms every time you turn around?" he asks with awe. "I've heard Quinn explain it, but I just saw it with my own eyes, and it doesn't even make sense."

"I guess I drive into places I shouldn't and talk to people I shouldn't. Maybe I should stay home and cook."

"I think your man likes you the way you are. You certainly aren't boring," he chuckles.

"I'm glad to hear that." I could elaborate how my ex-husband used to think I was dull, but it doesn't matter anymore.

We're quiet as I drive, watching my rear view mirror.

"Just so you know, I was about to shoot him in the leg. It was a hard decision because he was inching toward the rifle, instead of diving at it. I'm glad you shouted. It stopped him cold."

"You'd have killed him if you'd hit the femoral artery," he quietly says.

"It would have been an accident."

"It's like you're drawn to this stuff," he brings it up again.

"If you'd told me about the place, I wouldn't have gone in," I counter.

"It was need-to-know. I only found out when I saw the agents staging where I parked the Mustang. We were talking for a while. I didn't know you were at the same place they're raiding. Oh, and get this, your truck fit in with the others. The team thought you were another buyer. They're selling stolen military weapons in those wine barrels."

"Wow, I had no idea. I was standing right there, inspecting them. No wonder he freaked out." I glance at Adam. He's looking out the side mirror to make sure we aren't being followed. "It's like an action movie. I thought that only happens in South America, with the CIA."

"It happens everywhere."

"What about that guy—won't he go shouting about the security breech?"

"It may not matter, they're taking it down any minute now. I came in fast to get you out, just before they got word to go, but the crooks could still chase us before the ATF gets there."

"It's strange they told you about the raid and let you leave." I slow down, since no one is following.

"I have my military ID, I talk the talk—and I've worked with their boss." He smiles.

"You have good contacts."

"Yeah.

"Those arms dealers aren't too bright—the gate was open, and the sign said it was business hours."

"I'm not saying you did anything wrong. In fact, you always do the right thing, but it turns out crazy."

His phone rings. He listens while pointing in a circle. It's okay turn around. A minute later he hangs up.

"The agents from the Santa Maria office are taking it down now. They'll let us know when we can meet. They want the M-16 back." He taps the barrel.

"I figured we couldn't keep it."

"Apparently they aren't pleased. The captain said they're using their contingency plan." he says dryly. "They were concerned that you might have spooked the dealer. He might have taken his weapons and cleared out, or thought you were the raid, and met them with heavy firepower when the agents arrived."

"It isn't my fault. They can point their finger at someone else."

"Be sure to tell them." He cracks a smile as he looks out the window. "In case I wasn't clear, you did a good job keeping your cool. And you follow directions well."

"Thank you." That's a high compliment. I'd better savor it, because the ATF guys aren't happy.

* * *

THE ATF RAID GOES DOWN, but I don't need to be there for a while. There is something I can do in the meantime.

I slow just before the vineyard and pull to the side. "I'm dropping myself off here. You can take the truck."

"You're kidding me."

"No. I need to wrap up this foxhunting fiasco."

"You're diligent." His expression is unreadable. Either it's a compliment or he thinks I'm an idiot.

"I have my phone, gun, and the ear bud. I want this wrapped up today. If not, I'll be back Saturday, jumping fences and hoping a coyote doesn't get killed." I get out, then lean in the door. "If I need you, I'll yell."

"Fine," he laughs. "I'll return the machine gun."

Five minutes later, I'm running through the vineyard toward the only two horse trailers parked in the lot: Georgina's has her horse tied to the side, and David's, with the two geldings standing there munching hay.

I have my phone ready as I watch from behind a giant oak. I take a video of their two rigs, showing they're the only two left. I don't see them talking anywhere, so I begin my stealthy approach to his trailer. Nothing terrible will happen if I'm caught, but still, I don't want to be. I turn on the video to capture everything I can.

Ryan whinnies when he sees me creeping up. Darn it.

I hear them moving around through the aluminum walls.

"The horse is upset," Georgina speaks softly with a hint of concern.

"He's tied up. He's fine."

"I should be going."

"Yeah," he quickly agrees.

"You don't need to kick me out so fast," she gets defensive.

"I'm not, but it's time to go, don't you think?"

"You didn't miss me at all, did you?"

"Of course I did. You're my Georgie-girl."

"I hope so. I heard a blond girl was chasing you."

"There are women who find me attractive, but you're the only one for me," he lies.

"Are you sure?"

"Yes."

"I have it from a reliable source she was seen leaving your trailer."

"She was returning a piece of equipment."

"Really?"

"Yes. I told you. You're the only one for me."

"Okay, I believe you. It made me uncertain for a while, but I can tell you love me."

"Always," he says with passion.

"Sweet Dave, you're so handsome. I don't know what you see in me," she sounds shy.

"A beautiful woman in the prime of her life," his voice goes soft.

There are a few minutes of silence, then he says, "Well, we should probably get moving..."

"I could stay here all day." Georgina laughs.

"Right. Me too." He gets off the mattress, landing on the floor. "Here I'll help you down."

"David, don't rush me!" She scolds.

"Never!"

As soon as they start moving around, I know I can sneak away without being heard. It would be harder if they were lying in each other's arms. Then they might hear the sound of my tip-toeing feet stepping on sticks.

Behind my tree, I wait for them to emerge. She steps from the trailer as if nothing happened. He comes out, adjusting his pants.

"Adam. I'm stuck here until they leave," I whisper.

"Roger."

It only takes a few minutes before her rig pulls out, and a few minutes later, his follows.

Adam parked my truck down the road from Muscadine's. He's waiting there, out of the way. I arrive, lower the tailgate, and take a seat. He stays in the cab.

Our vantage point allows us to see above the hedge. I see men dressed in black with nylon equipment belts, and armored ATF vehicles. It's too far away to hear anything, but it's been at least twenty minutes since it went down. The suspects have been taken into custody. Now is the time they'll need to account for each of the firearms.

The patrol car blocking traffic moves aside to let it flow again.

Adam gets a call. I hear his side, "I see. Thank you."

"It's a good thing we didn't shoot that guy. He's one of theirs, undercover."

"Oh hell!"

"Do you want to meet him? He'll come out in a few minutes."

"I guess." I feel sick with the thought of what could have happened.

Ten minutes later, here comes that guy. The crooks called him Tracy. He looks the same, but the hostility has gone, now that he doesn't have to pretend to be one of them.

I hop off the tailgate to meet him in the street. "I don't work for Dennison," I hold out my hand to shake his. Adam comes up and shakes, all manly-like, then steps back to let me talk. We move out of the road to let a car pass.

"And I don't work for them," he gives a slight nod to the place behind him. "Care to tell me what you were doing?"

"I was doing exactly what I said—trying to catch a cheating wife."

"No kidding? I thought the story was too lame to be true. Who walks into the biggest arms shipment they've ever had?"

"Jess does." Adam gives a laugh. "She's known for that."

I nod, "Yeah, but it teaches you guys to have a Plan B. Anyhow, were the weapons in the wine barrels?"

"Yes, and ready to be put into trucks and taken away. The forklift had just loaded three in a truck when you walked right up to them and began reading what was inside."

"I was reading that they're French oak, with a medium toast. I didn't know what the rest meant."

"It gives the number of M-16s, along with the code name for the buyers."

"Great." I'd roll my eyes, but I don't do that.

"Yeah, you showed up at the wrong time, with a weird story, and started sneaking through the place."

"Do you know how close I came to shooting you in the leg? I had a mental line in the ground. If you crossed it, I was going to shoot."

"I was going for the rifle," he admits.

"That would have been a disaster all around!" The others would have come, shooting.

Adam is standing by with his arms crossed. The agent is still thinking of being shot. "Thanks for not taking me out."

"I prefer not to on American soil." He's doing the testosterone thing.

"What's your real name?" I ask Tracy. "And who is Dennison?"

"The name's Joe Croft. Dennison is a competitor in the arms business."

After he gets our contact information, Adam hands over the M-16 and ammo.

He gets called back to the compound a few minutes later. "It was interesting meeting you. Thanks again for not plugging me. It would have been a bad ending to a good day." He quickly smiles at me, nods to Adam, then jogs back across the street.

"Who'd have thought we have arms dealers right here between the vines and the foxhunters. What a strange world." I grumble.

I drop Adam off at his car, half a mile down the road.

"I think I owe you a car wash," I apologize.

"Try a detailing." He glares at me.

I'm sure he's kidding, after all we've been through today.

But maybe not. That Mustang is his baby.

Just to see if he's serious, I ask, "Should I wash it in a bikini?"

29

THE NEWS

Friday morning, after an easy three-mile run and a shower, I step into the lounge. I'm hungry and ready to chow down. Janet is hurrying into the kitchen holding several newspapers. She's been clearing tables after the guests left.

"Good morning, how's everything going?" I sound cheerful after resting all day yesterday.

"Don't read the paper," she advises, as she steps in front of them on the counter.

"Oh?" I try to look around her.

"That reporter from last week—he wrote something," she hedges.

I instantly feel sick.

"I'd better see it," I whisper.

"Consider it this way, it can't get any worse." She moves aside.

The headline on the front page reads: "Rats, Rodents, and Lies at Greenstone Cottage." I've heard that any advertising is good advertising, but they don't mean this. "As part of an ongoing investigation, this reporter uncovered hundreds of rats at what used to be a lovely place to stay for the night. We know nothing remains the same, and that includes hotels. The beloved woman who used to own Greenstone Cottage passed away last October. Her granddaughter, Jessica Wilcox, took over and the hotel hasn't been the same since."

I look up, and see Janet watching me. "I'm sorry Jess."

"This reporter was alerted to the horrific facts by an informant who recently stayed in one of the cottages. She confided in me, under the promise of anonymity, that the cottage was filthy and rat infested. I read many posted reviews and found them to be accurate. I cannot understand how Ms. Wilcox can stay in business with this dangerous situation. I contacted the Health Department and was advised there is an ongoing investigation into the public health hazard this hotel poses to guests and other businesses on this truly spectacular section of California's central coast."

"That's a lie. It isn't true!"

"Many hotels, including the Cambria Seaside Resort have been impacted by this. The resort has increased its rodent control, as well as doubling their hotel security for the safety of their beloved guests. The general manager of the Cambria hotel, Mrs. Mandy Crawford, has made this her mission. She will personally guarantee every guest who leaves the vermin infested Greenstone Cottages will receive special attention at her resort."

"Hell." I lean on the counter and brace against the wave of sea sickness.

It goes on a bit more, but this is the worst of it.

"Jessica," Janet's voice has a disciplined tone. "This is libel. It's a smear campaign. I read it several times and picked out the lies. Did you see how he brought in Mandy's hotel? He's giving her a plug while knocking you down. I can see he's in bed with her."

"Maybe so, but no one else can see it through the lies."

"An attorney will," she hisses. "And if you can connect him to Mandy, she'll go down as well."

This awful article may give me a lot to use against her. I'm collecting everything in print that attacks me.

"I wonder how the editor could put this on the front page. Is he involved too?" I'm starting to question everything.

"Or the journalist has a good reputation. Or the paper wants an eye-catching headline for its advertisers."

"That would make them as bad as the tabloids." I pause as a flood of anger replacing the nausea. I gather up the papers to take to the office. "Thank you for your support. I can't run the place without you."

"You're very welcome. Both you and your grandmother have been good to me, and I'm happy working here."

I give her a thankful smile, because I plan on keeping it that way.

I slowly walk into the office, full of thought. I'm planning on saying something that can be overheard by the nasty women. In the office, I sit in front of my computer and fire it up. Another awful review about rats came in yesterday. The reviewer hadn't even stayed here. I print it out and investigate who he is. This is his only review. That's typical of a scam. They don't have a long history that I can check, though it still comes up first since it was posted yesterday.

I'll get a bunch of friends to post good reviews to counterbalance that one, until I can get it removed.

It takes a few minutes to get into character, then I pretend to call Mom, and here goes, "Mom, this is terrible. I just saw the newspaper. They're crucifying Greenstones!" I wait a second. "It's the local paper. Listen to the headline, Rats, Rodents, and Lies at Greenstone Cottage. What am I going to do?" I wail.

I'm deliberately acting young. I want Mandy to underestimate me. Yes, she'll think I'm a fool, but I want her to make sloppy mistakes, rather than being on guard.

"I wish I'd never moved here. The rats are taking over. I saw three today." I pause. "I also have a septic leak. The tank is leaking. It smells like well, you know." Another pause. "There are baby frogs in the puddle. The frogs are everywhere. It's like one of the plagues!" I add a wail and then pretend to listen.

"I'd sell this place in a heartbeat. I hate it here!"

"I'd take anything, but who'd want it with all these problems? I don't think it's worth anything, being overrun by vermin. It's just a bunch of dumpy old cottages with leaky roofs." The roofs certainly don't leak. I know that because we've just had days of rain, and Evan the killer reroofed them only a few years ago. He may be a killer, but he does good work.

"Do you really think I can get a million? That much?" I sound surprised. "Yes, please tell her. If she wants it for a million, she can have it." I just presented a fake buyer. This should get Mandy to make her move. There's nothing like having someone else want what you want.

"Thanks. I'll wait for her call tomorrow. I want to go back to the wine country and ride my horses. This is too much for me. Bye Mom."

Then I head for my own cottage to listen to Adam's tapes and line up the times and events in a proper letter addressed to the head corporate honcho. To find who that it, I make a few phone calls. It's quite easy to find out who the boss is.

It takes until after the 4:00 check-in to finish the letter. After welcoming two guests, who haven't read the article, I come back to add a few links to the article, and the reviews. Then I call mom, for real, to explain what happened. She knows how professional letters should read. This one needs to be perfect for me to get what I want, so I send her the draft.

Later in the evening, she sends it back, marked up, with corrections and suggestions. By the time I've finished it's nearly 10:00. My body aches from sitting all day and night, but this has to be perfect.

Plus, it's time to listen to the replay. I'm not disappointed. Tonight, Mandy and the manager are both in the office. The time stamp is 8:33.

This is what she says, "She'll sell. She'll let it go for a million dollars." The manager rejoices.

"What else did she say?" Mandy sounds excited.

"She's sick of the rats. And she said there's a septic leak with frogs everywhere." She pauses. "Did you know about that?"

"No. It means replacing the tank, and the lines. That will cost a bundle, so I'll offer her less."

"Less than a million?" The manager is shocked.

"This will be a breeze. She's overwhelmed. By the time she find out what the value of the property is, the paperwork will be signed, and the money transferred. She'll be out in the cold. It will be a legal transaction."

"That article may scare away some of our future clients."

"Not a problem. I'll have Greg write another one announcing that I'm opening a boutique resort for the ultra-wealthy guests who want privacy and personal attention. I'm so excited, I won't be able to sleep until this is in my hands." Mandy sounds like an eager child— she probably hasn't allowed herself to act like that since she was ten.

"Play it back for me. I want to hear it with my own ears," she instructs.

And there it is. My voice wailing about the rat, frogs, and leaking septic tank.

"Perfect, just perfect. I'm going to pay her a visit tomorrow with my offer," Mandy announces.

I'll make sure the devices are working in my office and everywhere. I want every word captured.

30

MANDY'S OFFER

I'm in the office early, spending time on the computer while waiting for Mandy to arrive.

"Welcome to Greenstone Cottage, Mandy." I make sure to sound depressed as she opens the closed French door. I'm still trying to keep out the white rats.

"Happy New Year, Jessica," she replies in her business-like voice while leaving the door open. "Did you see the newspaper yesterday?" She lays it on the counter, with the headline facing my direction.

"Yes." I plan on keeping my answers short. I hurry around to close the door so I don't get any furry visitors, then return to my place behind the computer. I guess I'm keeping it between us.

"It's a shame this venture didn't work out for you." She looks at the counter and brushes her hand across it as if to say there's dirt on it.

"Yeah. We're having a few problems at the moment."

"My dear, I caught the scent of septic just outside your door. I think you have more problems than you know."

"Septic?" I add wide eyes to my expression.

"Yes, dear. Do you know what the county will do? They'll shut you down in an instant and fine you thousands of dollars."

"Oh no!"

"Oh yes!" She looks at the floor with raised eyebrows. "Is that a frog?" She jumps back.

"No. Not a frog. It's only a leaf," I reply nervously.

"My dear. You're out of your element. Your granny was too old to maintain the place. It's falling down, you know that, don't you?"

"Uh?"

"Yes dear. 'Granny' told me she wanted to sell me the place, but she didn't get to it before the poor dear passed away." She sighs. "I'd like to help with her last wish." She smiles, looking hopeful. "I know you would too. So I'd like to make a fair offer, taking into consideration the terrible state of disrepair."

She reaches into her purse and pulls out a stack of real estate forms. Putting them on the counter, she smiles and says, "This will solve all your problems. I feel it's only right for me to take the place off your hands because I promised 'Granny' I would." She puts an expensive silver pen on top.

"Thank you for your consideration. It's nice to meet someone who cares enough to stand by their word." I can't help but rub it in.

"I try," she demurely replies, then picks up the pen. "Sign here, and you will be free."

"Free," I repeat, and look at the papers. The sales price is $769,000. I almost choke. I've looked through the listings, and know that a three bedroom house, several blocks from the beach is listed at that.

"What do you think it's worth? My mother knows someone who will pay a million."

"I'm here, right now. This other person may be a figment of your mother's desire to help you. I scraped the cash together, so it won't even need an appraisal or a loan. You know, loans are hard to get, and require a lot of documentation. If you wait, I may have bought another piece of property." She looks sad. "You need to be smart, Jessica. I'd like to help you, really I would." She ends the lie with a smile.

"I promised my mom I would always sleep on big decisions. I

believe you have my best interests at heart, but I will need to honor my promise. I'll let you know tomorrow."

"When will you be hearing from the other person?"

"At noon."

"I tell you what. I'll match her offer." She smiles but looks nervous.

"Thank you. I appreciate that. You're very generous." I'm enjoying this because I'm not really negotiating a million dollar deal.

She picks up the pen again, lines out the paltry amount she offered, and writes in One Million Dollars and 00 cents. "There, I've met her price. Let's close the deal before something happens."

I slide the papers toward me and roll them up. "I am so happy. Thank you! I will look them over, just to make sure everything is accurate. You have to know the property disclosures, and if there are termites, or radon gas. I bet I have termites!" I walk around from behind the counter and go to the door. She needs to go. I have plenty of ammunition now. I hold it open for her, while looking for invading rats.

"Would you like me to call you when I've signed them tomorrow, or drop them off at your office?" I give her the only two options.

"Please call me. I'll be happy to save you the trip."

Two hotels away is a trip?

"You're too kind."

She nods and walks through the door with her head held high.

Whew. I draw a breath deep into my lungs and slowly let it out. That's the extent of my yoga breathing exercise, but it seems to work.

I lock up and head for my cottage. Just as soon as I close the door, Adam speaks. "That woman is a trip."

"Yeah, a bad trip."

I have another hour of work adding the video feed from the office. This time it's audio and visual. They will be able to see her with the papers. It may not matter, since I don't have to take her offer, but she listened in on my conversation and knew my bottom line.

I email a copy to Mom. I'd like to get away for the day. I'll make a trip down to Los Olivos to see my horses, grab something tasty at Monica's, and catch up with her and Nikki.

REMINISCING

"Adam?" I raise my voice.

"Yeah?"

"I'm going to Los Olivos. Are you staying here, following me, or driving with me?"

"I'm working on something. Can you go in a few days?"

"Not really. I want to get away for the day. I can stay home, but now I have the itch to go, and it's a quiet day here."

"Quinn wants me with you. I can't let you go that far alone."

I know, and I appreciate his concern.

"How about if I drive the RV, and you sit in the back, doing your work?" I think that's a great idea, but I stop talking to let him assimilate it.

"That could work. Fine. Let's do it." He seems happy to get out of this parking lot.

Twenty minutes later, I'm driving an RV I've never driven before. It feels like an 18-wheeler. I'm sorry, everyone in line behind me. Once, I pull over to let the stream of annoyed drivers speed by, but by the time I get the acceleration to get back into traffic, there are another half-dozen slowing down again.

"How do you drive this thing faster than 60 mph?"

"I drive 65, and don't worry about the angry people behind me," he grins.

"Alright, I'll coax more speed out of this thing." I press a bit harder on the gas.

I'm on the phone, legally through the vehicle's system, chatting with Nikki. I'm stopping there to see my horses, first. It's been nearly two months. Yikes. I know they're fine. Nikki is riding them once a day leading the easy rides. She texts pictures all the time. They're happy, and I don't really know if they care that I'm not around.

I pull up to the gate at the ranch and click it open. They keep it closed ever since the problems Quinn and I brought. I'm loved, but they're happy I don't live here anymore.

I park by the barn. It looks the same. I'm glad to see that, because I like stability.

Juliette is in the pasture, looking a bit fat. I squeeze between the bars and head over to say hello. She pricks her ears, but that's the extent of her greeting. Nothing like The Black Stallion, or those other wonderful horse books I read as a kid. This is reality, and I don't think she's impressed by my visit. I stroke her neck and tell her she's beautiful. She nudges me with her muzzle and looks happy. I guess.

After a few minutes of looking her over, examining her feet, legs, and body, there's nothing to do. Our conversation has ended. She's walking toward another horse. I guess she's done with family time.

I head over to Bunny in the corral. She's interested in establishing rapport. I run out of things to say. When I go to leave, she follows me to the fence. I feel bad about this. "I'm sorry, I have to leave. I don't know what else to tell you. I inherited a place on the coast, but I can't bring you. I'm sure you're happier here."

When I walk back to the RV, I turn to look. She isn't looking. She's watching the horses return from a trail ride. They're her friends now. I'm glad, it relieves my guilt.

Nikki is leading the ride. It's great to see her in the saddle. She loves the ranch and this life. While she's unsaddling the horses, I do the wine tasting for her. It's a nice change. It feels like old times.

After the customers drive away, it's quiet as Nikki feeds lunch to the herd. I replay some of the things I faced when I was here. The gunfight with Pickett in the stall. He shot 14 times but missed me. It was a fun week when the movie production company came to the ranch. I wonder what would have happened if I'd followed the cowboy to other movie locations. I wonder how he's doing. It hasn't been that long, about seven months, but it feels like a lifetime ago.

Nikki and I catch up inside the barn doors at the big table that also was where Jack and I had our first picnic. Nikki and I often had our girl talks here. We're here again, though I feel like a visitor.

"Does it feel strange to see me here?"

"No. Everything feels the same to me. Your horses are here, your horse trailer you insisted on sleeping in is parked in the same place. Nothing much has changed, I'm happy to say."

"So it's just me then. I feel like a guest, out of place."

"If you stay a few days, you'd get right back into the swing of things."

"I had a very low offer on the B&B this morning. I'm not taking it, but this got me thinking. I could put it on the market for real, and come back here."

"You were bored here. After leading hundreds of rides, it gets old. You were doing code enforcement work to keep busy. You're just feeling melancholy." She smiles, then takes a long gulp of water to rehydrate before the next ride.

"I guess you're right. I don't have any friends up there, but I have several enemies."

"You've been there for two months. Give it time. You're living in a beautiful place, have a career with your own boutique hotel. You'll be fine." She stops. "Maybe if Quinn would stay around longer." She looks at the RV.

"At least he left his guard dog to protect me."

"I heard that," Adam snickers.

"Thanks for keeping her safe," Nikki laughs.

I told her I'm being monitored, so she isn't surprised and doesn't say anything private about herself and Travis. Adam doesn't need to know that kind of information.

"How are Monica and Charlie?"

"They're fine. I don't think anything has changed with them since you left. She works till 8:00 PM, and he stops by the bakery after he's finished with his rounds. They come home together late and leave early. But he now has four Thoroughbreds here on lay-up. I'm taking care of them, and he does the doctoring, like ultrasounds and x-rays. They'll be here until they go back to the racetrack."

"I'm glad he got that going. That was one of the reasons they bought the place."

We talk more. I really don't want to leave. There's no rush to get home, and it's only a 90 minute drive. I can leave this evening. Janet will be there until 4:00 for any problems. Otherwise, the lounge is open, and I left cookies.

"I'm turning off your mic. You ladies can talk privately. I need to concentrate for a while," Adam lets us know.

"Do you believe him?" Nikki whispers.

"Yeah."

She tells me that she and Travis are doing great. He's with Quinn doing whatever they're doing.

"Has he told you anything they're doing, or where they are?" I wonder if he is as secretive as Quinn.

"He won't say a word. I've given up trying to pry it out of him."

"Ok. Quinn is the same. I'm fine with not knowing, as long as no one else knows."

Nikki has a ride to prepare for. I help her saddle six horses, and Bunny as her lead horse. Then I get in the RV and motor down the driveway.

"We're going to Monica's?" Adam asks from the kitchen table.

"Yes. She's expecting us. There'll be goodies, if you'll allow yourself to be tempted."

"I work out hard enough and run every night. I'll have a bite as long as it's too good to pass up."

"She uses the best ingredients. I'll get you something healthy."

I park in the back and walk in through the kitchen. The smells are delectable. We have an air hug, since she's rolling dough and wants to keep going.

We talk for a few minutes. I pull out the office stool and we catch up. She's doing great with the workshops I got her going with. I'm proud of that, but it's taking up one night a week.

"I'd like to hire someone else to teach them," she sighs.

"But the people come because of you," I point out.

On the way out, I bring Adam a cup of delicious coffee and a hazelnut biscotti. It amounts to four bites and he proclaims it isn't too sweet for a health conscious man. I've already had four cookies, but I won't tell him. He'd probably think I'm a glutton.

I drive past the new wine tasting room that had been the bakery Aquamarine, which always sounded like a boat repair shop to me. Heather and her stepmother are in prison for a few years, hopefully.

Soon I'm struggling to park at Mom's. He lets me deal with it. I guess it makes me a better driver.

"Come on in. I have lasagna for dinner." She's standing in the doorway to welcome us. Adam is coming along for the lasagna.

"Thank you, ma'am, for inviting me to dinner." He's very polite.

"Here are the papers from Mandy."

Mom looks through them and comments. "That no good creature is trying to take it for pennies on the dollar."

"What's it worth? I was wondering if I should sell and do something else."

"What are you planning on doing?"

"I have no idea."

"Then keep the property. It's a gold mine, paid off, and solidly booked."

"Except when the *Rats, Rodents and Lies* article gets out."

Adam finds a chair and pulls out his laptop to continue with his own work.

"Remember I said I have an attorney friend? Well, I actually have several. I've been busy today on your behalf." She heads for the kitchen with me following. "He said a corporation owns the hotel," she continues.

"Meadowbrook Hotels," I reply.

"Yes, them. They'll be scrambling to get Mandy Crawford out of there. They'll throw her off the property as soon as their board of directors and attorneys have a conference."

"How long will it take to put together that conference?"

"In this instance, only a few hours. They'll do it virtually. They would be on the hook for libel, slander, and millions of dollars in restitution if the rats do any damage. She is the general manager of their Cambria facility, and they don't want that kind of bad press."

"She has influenced the newspaper, the County Health Department, Cambria Public Works which tore up your driveway, Yelp, and other travel reviews which could amount to thousands of dollars in lost revenue." She pulls the steaming lasagna from the oven, puts it on the burner to cool and continues, "Jarod has been in corporate law for decades. He knows what he's talking about when he says she'll be out on her tail by the end of the month."

During dinner, we chat about what's going on in town, and the latest gossip from her favorite wineries. It's a nice change for me. It feels safe and light hearted compared to the insanity in my life. Maybe I need a vacation. That's an idea. Maybe Mom would like to run the hotel for a week while I hang around Solvang, wine taste, and catch up on my reading.

32

DETOUR

Our return trip to Cambria is slower than anticipated. The highway is being shut down due to an overturned tanker truck. Adam is diligently working at the table, while I'm behind the wheel, inching along with the hundreds of other drivers. A detour is being set up, but it will take a while to get up to that point.

They are running a traffic break so we can cut across the median, go back the way we came, then exit in the middle of nowhere to follow the hastily put up signs. I glide to a stop at the end of the off-ramp,

Adam raises his voice from the back, "Turn left at the intersection."

"But their detour sign points to the right."

"The app says turning left is the best way," he speaks with authority.

"I don't like apps."

"Are you going to argue the whole way home?" Apparently, he believes an app over the posted arrow sign placed by the police to direct hundreds of cars the correct way.

I'm not willing to start a fight, and I don't care enough to argue, so I turn left. I'm not the only one who turns, but 99% of the cars are going to the right. Will we be the smart ones?

The road winds around dark fields and empty vineyards. "Go left at the next road," he updates.

I'm driving along, when he shouts, "Why didn't you turn back there?"

"Where?"

"At the road."

"What road? There wasn't a road."

"I'm looking at a road on the app. You missed it."

"Can't we find another turn if I keep going—there's nowhere to do a U-turn around right now?" I'm navigating a two-lane farm road out in the boonies. This reminds me of the countryside where I meet Quinn when he was under cover as a drug dealer. Today sure has been a trip down memory lane.

"There's an intersection coming up. You can swing around there," he advises.

"Fine." I give up.

Here's the intersection, but it's hardly what you'd expect. The lanes are so narrow that trying to do a 3-point turn becomes more like 6 or 7-point. I can hear him in the back, clearing his throat, and grumbling.

"Do you have to jolt the rig each time you stop?"

"The road is too narrow. I can't just swing around smoothly like on a normal road," I shout back at him.

"You need to learn to drive."

"Then you come up here and do it!"

"I have work to do, which you are making impossible," another shout from the peanut gallery.

The only other car that was either smarter than the others, or as dumb as us, passes. A mile later, I slow for the turn. I'm tempted to ask if he's absolutely, positively sure this is the way, but I know it will lead to another lecture on the attributes of satellites. Yes, he told me the military uses satellite directed precision bombs. But the highway patrol knows these roads. A local officer put up the orange signs with a bold arrow pointing the way to go. Can't we accept that maybe he knows the best way to the highway?

Despite that, I follow Adam's directions to turn onto the dirt road. It's smooth for a while, then the pot holes seem to increase every few yards.

"Do you think you can avoid the ruts—it's hard to write?"

"Your stupid road has pot holes. It's not my driving." I shout back.

"You're going the right way. It's only a mile to the freeway."

"Alrighty." I almost hope it doesn't—that'll show him.

I'm keeping the speed slow, which makes the bumps less pronounced; but it's as dark as the back side of the moon. It seems to me, this will be my "I told you so" victory. I can't wait.

The engine complains as the road goes uphill. I press on the gas and struggle to the top.

"What a lovely view of the town about five miles away." I shout back to the kitchen as I stop the RV.

We're at something like a lookout point under a high power line. Beer cans are scattered all over the place.

He comes up to the front, ducking his head to look out the windshield. "Why didn't you tell me we were on a dirt road?"

"Couldn't you see when you looked out the window?"

"I was focused on my work, I didn't notice."

"Well, it looks like your precision satellite was incorrect. We should have followed the orange signs on the dumb traffic cones." I give him a totally fake smile.

"The app was probably hacked by the Chinese," he determines.

"Or the Russians, or a sixteen-year-old kid."

He ignores that. "Turn around if you think you can without running us into the tower."

Headlights light up the inside of the RV as someone else is coming up the hill just as we're going down. They're also on the wrong road.

"I bet it's a man driving. A woman would have followed the signs," I snip.

He doesn't reply. That's probably best, because what can he say?

The car flashes its high beams a few times, then leaves them on and stops in the middle of the road.

I stop and wait. The car isn't moving. I can't see what anyone is doing, but we aren't going anywhere with him blocking the way, which has been graded lower than the brushy sides.

I turn when I hear Adam jump up from the table.

There's a loud bang. A hole appears in the front windshield, and a yell, all at the same time.

Adam is shouting, "Get down. Get down!" There's blood spreading across the top of his chest. He's wobbling on his feet, and grabs for the couch.

He has been shot.

I dive for the floorboards. The inside is still lit up by the car's headlights. There aren't any dark places to hide, except directly behind the seats, where I am trying to become one with the floor.

The full sized door to the living compartment flies open, crashing against the wall and almost slamming shut. I look up to see a masked shape stop the door from closing. He leans in and takes aim at Adam. From behind the seat, I launch myself at the man, who is leaning in the door. He flies backward, as we both tumble to the ground, locked together.

I feel hands grabbing my arms and dragging me into the darkness. I'm trying to punch someone, anyone. I hear him growl in my ear, "Stop fighting."

Is this a friend I don't recognize in the darkness? I don't know what to do.

I can tell he is a big, strong man. He has his arm around my neck, forcing me toward the the bright headlights. I try to pull away, but I can't break free. He pulls open the passenger door of a black SUV, roughly shoves me in the back seat, and immediately jumps in behind.

"Go!" he shouts. I hear gunshots. Someone is shooting back from this car.

He's drags me off the seat onto the floor, flattening his body on mine, jamming me into the hump in the floor. My shoulder is getting crushed, but I keep quiet. Only my beating heart and ragged breathing give away my fear.

The driver reverses and whips the car around in something like a bootleg turn. I can tell we're flying down the dirt road. I'm still on the floor, but a minute later the weight gets off me.

"That went well," he sounds remarkably calm.

I'm not moving yet. His feet are down here, and I don't want to get violently kicked. I'm not sure I want to see their faces. If I do, they might kill me.

He nudges me with his boot. "You okay down there?"

"Yes." I immediately reply, without a pissy attitude, and without sounding cowed. Just a simple yes.

"Good."

Unfortunately, I left my cell phone on the center divider of the RV. I hate to keep it in my pocket all the time, as I don't want cancer. I could have used it now, for the GPS tracking at least.

I hope Adam isn't bleeding out—he was shot in the chest. I think for a few seconds and come to the conclusion that he wasn't shot in the heart because it's on the other side.

If he can make it to his phone, he can get help for both of us, which will include air support.

The driver is taking the turns fast. I can feel the centrifugal force and hear the tires sliding on the pavement. I can't tell which way we're going. There isn't anything I can do. I adjust my arms and legs into a more comfortable position, but most of all, I keep quiet. I don't plan on pissing them off.

33

PACOIMA, CA. 91331

The men aren't speaking. This strikes me as having been well planned, because they aren't arguing about where they're going, or fussing with details that have been worked out. I wonder if I should be counting the minutes so I'll know how far we are traveling. It may come in handy, or maybe not.

Usually, I'd be trying to get away, but there's no way I can get to the door, open it, and fling myself onto the road. Not with the man's legs squeezed against my back.

Who wants me badly enough to hatch this elaborate plot? The only ones I can think of are Mia's elegant one-night stand and his handsome cousin in my liqueur class. If they're the same ones who rammed me in the Subaru, and the same who chased me in Adam's Mustang, they want me something bad. The guy next to me isn't one of them, he's much too big. That means either they hired people, or there are a lot of angry men after me.

And there was also the guy who tried to run us down in Mia's stolen Porsche. Is the guy sitting next to me the one? Is he a killer as well as a kidnapper? I wouldn't put it past him. The driver shot Adam, and was going for the kill when I jumped on him.

He's been driving a while. I know we're on the freeway because we're passing tractor-trailers. Their engines have an unmistakable whine I hear even through the rolled-up windows.

My body hurts from being in a tweaked position. I roll over, put my butt on the floor, and inch my way up the door. At least I'm sitting. I'm keeping my head down, but my eyes flick up. Damn. He's watching me through the nylon stocking on his head.

In the movies, the heroine always demands, "Where are you taking me?" "You'll never get away with this. My boyfriend; father; husband (fill in the blank) will hunt you down and kill you." She gets slapped, or punched, and it doesn't accomplish anything. I'm not that dumb.

So what should I do—wait for him, without staring?

There! An illuminated highway sign flashed past. We're driving south, toward – what, and where?

I sit up a little straighter and see more. The SUV's interior is very dark and the windows are blacked out. I know by the names of the exits that we're racing through Santa Barbara.

I assume Adam will be in touch with law enforcement and an ambulance. The last I saw, he was mostly okay, shot, but okay. He'll be checking his cameras to get the license plate and ownership info on this Chevy. But let's be realistic, if I were doing this, I wouldn't use my own license plate; they're not that dumb.

More time passes, and I'm almost lulled to sleep. This is the aftermath of extreme adrenaline, as well as sitting on the floor with nothing to do to help myself.

He's taking the exit. Damn. Which one is it? I'd given up looking.

"Get down." The man on the seat kicks my leg. I jerk in pain and grunt, then slide down as I was told. My head is bowed down, but I'm looking for billboards, businesses, or hotels, apartments... anything to give me a clue as to where I am.

We pass a sign 'Mercado' in red, green, and white colors. That helps. "El Matador" with a bull. Ok, I get the picture. We're in a Hispanic neighborhood. It's in the L.A. area. If we're still in the Valley, which I think we are, I bet we're in Pacoima. I worked patrol at Foothill Division, before going to Hollywood. This feels reminiscent of Foothill, because it's right next to the freeway. I hope I'm right, because I still remember some of the streets and alleys.

"Put this on." He throws a bag at me. In the movies, they use something like a black pillowcase, but this is a paper bag from a market. At least it isn't a plastic bag.

We pull up to a light and stop. I hear the hoot of a train, and feel the ground shaking as the locomotive rumbles past. If this is the track I think it is, they tend to have a hundred cars or more. There's booming bass music coming from another car at the light. I'm not thrilled by the sound, but it means there are other cars on the road tonight.

Can I get out while I'm reaching for the bag? It will give me something allowable to do with my hands as I move for it. The door handle that I've been leaning on for the past 150 miles is encouraging me to do something.

I move my legs to make sure they still work. They do, but moving them is not the same as getting them to run fast. I twist more than I need to reach for the bag on the seat. Yes, I'm being dramatic, but I'm not complaining. Hopefully he won't be fast to react, because he won't see it coming. I've been good up until now.

Of course, the door may be have a child proof lock. I hope not.

Here goes. I reach for the bag with my right hand and throw it in his face, while my left hand claws at the handle. It opens!

The best exit is to roll backward, like scuba diving off a small boat. Included is a shoulder roll to hopefully stop me from hitting my head on the pavement. It works! I'm outside, struggling to my blood deprived legs and forcing them to stand.

I get them moving as soon as I can and dart away from the SUV. There is only one other car on the road, on the other side of the street, facing our direction. It's a vibrant yellow, lowered pickup truck. It's so low to the ground it resembles a couch without legs. It's perfect if I can get in the bed and have him drive away. The light has turned green and he's pulling away slow enough not to bottom out on the drainage dip. This isn't a fancy part of town, there are lots of dips here.

I'm running toward him waving my left hand. The man sees me, then I see his eyes look behind me. He presses on the gas. Oh no you don't. I literally dive into the bed as he increases speed. It's easy, super easy.

I have to hand it to him, he keeps driving. Maybe because he just saw a woman run from an SUV with a man in pursuit.

He continues on, though not as fast as I'd like. I sit up and see the SUV spin a U-turn and gun it to catch up. My escape vehicle stops in the middle of the street. Apparently he wants nothing to do with them, or helping me.

"Get out, lady," he shouts out the open window.

"No. Please, just drive. The police station is down the street."

He puts his hand out and points a stainless steel handgun, upside down, in my direction. "Out!"

"No. Can't you just drive?"

Damn. The SUV is on us. He doesn't have a good grip on the weapon. I seize the opportunity, and grab it with both hands, wrenching it out of his.

"Drive!" I shout, leaning over and looking at him. "I'll shoot your truck."

He steps on the gas, just in time. My heart is pounding as I see the two men getting out of the SUV and confidently stride toward the truck; they're still wearing stocking masks.

I slide across the slick bed toward the tail gate. The engine has loud, throaty engine, but it can't go as fast as you'd think, because I'm now sliding forward. He's breaking for another dip. Damn it.

He turns right on a dark street, then left down an even darker alley. "Get out!"

I won't be shooting him for not driving to the police station, so I jump over the side; it's only a short drop to the ground. "I'm keeping it. Get in touch with me at Greenstone Cottage, Cambria. I'll give it back. Call the police." Off I go as fast as my legs will carry me. I shout my last request as I sprint toward a fence. He's smart enough to step on the gas and get out of here.

I don't have the energy to spring up, so I run down to a lower wall and awkwardly over it. I land in a backyard prepared to run somewhere, but where? It's safer in a yard than it is on the street—provided they don't have a dog. I'm panting loud enough to attract one. Nothing yet.

I stand in the shadow of a large tree. There are few streetlights. I know from past experience, they've been shot out.

I need the police, but how do I call them? Maybe I can knock on the back door without being shot or hit with a baseball bat. I think that perhaps the front would be better, especially since I just noticed a large bowl of water by the hose. I make a quick dash to the side gate, which is locked, naturally, but it's easy enough to climb.

I land quietly on the other side, and creep close to the house until I come to an open window. This should work. "Hello? Hello? Can you help me?" I ask in just over a whisper.

No answer.

So I ask a little louder, with a tap on the window. "Hello. Hola?" I try bilingual.

The dog bowl from the back yard has an accompanying friend in the house. An open mouth with a big square head and canine fangs appears next to my face. Both paws scratch on the windowsill. He sees me standing here and starts a low, angry snarl that quickly turns into maniacal barking. He's lunging at the screen, fully invested in protecting the house and killing me.

I jump back, my heart racing again.

He's shoving his nose at the screen, and it's bulging. How long will it stay there before giving way and letting the beast out?

I race away from certain disaster.

Staying close to the house and fence, I make it next door. The barking dies down at about the same time I see headlights on the street two houses away. I drop to the ground, flattening myself next to the junipers and try to control my breathing. They have a flashlight. I see the beam flicking across the plants and then continue forward as the car moves on.

I'm lying here, still glued to the ground. It occurs to me it could have been the police, searching for me. Maybe the guy in the yellow truck called them. I scurry to the corner of the house and peer out. It was the police! I see the tail lights as they turn the corner. I all-out sprint down the sidewalk. By the time I reach the corner, I see it speeding away, faster than I can run. They did their token search, and are off to another call. NO!

It's back to square one. I need to find someone to call them back. Someone without a killer dog. I feel braver now I know they're in the area. I run toward the closest house, prepared to pound on the door.

I don't make it.

A big, dark shape lunges out of the bushes and grabs me in a bear hug. "Got you," he pants, as his hand clamps across my mouth. He wrenches my arm behind my back, clear up to my shoulder blades. The stainless steel six-shooter drops from my hand.

He turns me so I'm flat against him, my face is at his chest. Then he shuffles us toward the street. His angry voice speaks in my ear, "I'm going to release my hand. If you scream I'll break your arm." He tugs it up a little higher, making me groan and stand on my toes to escape the intense pain. "See what I mean?" He releases the pressure and takes his hand off my mouth.

"Got her. We're on the sidewalk. The cops just left." He's on the phone.

I hear a car coming, fast. He moves us into the street, so I know it's his partner, not the police. He opens the door, throws me in, and clambers in after me as I reach for the door handle on the opposite side. He drags me back by my ankles, then leans over to the cargo area. I hear the unmistakable sound of tape stripping off a roll.

The door shuts and we're speeding away.

34

THE WAREHOUSE

I'm bound with duct tape, hand and foot. He even put it across my mouth, running a strip around the back of my head to be sure. The last thing he does is to put the paper bag over my head. At least it is wide open at the bottom. He was good enough not to tape it shut.

I'm sitting upright, next to him. And still, no one has spoken.

It's only a few minutes until the car stops again. I hear a touch-pad making responding beeps as the driver taps in a code. The gate rolls open. It has a cheap, chain link rattle, rather than the smooth hum of something expensive. He drives over a little bump then swings around to the right and stops.

The driver exits, but my keeper stays next to me. A few minutes later, I hear several sets of feet approaching.

The back door opens, he gets out. I keep sitting here.

"Welcome, Officer Wilcox. I hear you were a problem this evening." His voice sounds familiar.

He said Officer Wilcox. That isn't a good start.

"Get out."

There's no reason to put up a fight until it will help me escape, so I swing my legs out and stand up.

Someone slices the tape from my ankles. It's probably best that I didn't see the knife coming.

"Walk." A hand grabs my elbow and we're walking. It's cold outside, with a light breeze. The sound of freeway traffic isn't too distant, and it's still busy, even at this hour. I figure it may be around 1:00 AM, give or take.

Someone pushes me inside a building with gray linoleum tiles that echoes the footsteps of four men. I'm watching their feet through the opening in the bag. The guy holding me has big shoes, I'm guessing size 11 or 12. We go through another door, where I'm shoved onto a hard, wooden chair. Someone wraps a rope around my waist, tying it to the chair, then the paper bag is pulled off my head.

But I can't see who is holding me captive, because there's a bright light shining in my face. I keep my head and eyes down.

"I've been waiting for this for a long time." Says the voice I know from somewhere.

I rule out several men, but I'm so scared my thinking isn't completely clear.

"I have to hand it to you. You're braver than I gave you credit for." His tone changes, "Take off the gag."

Whoever is behind me tries to pick at the end. "Use the knife." The voice tells him.

He pulls it away from my skin, then slides the blade under. I'm expecting a cut that hasn't come yet. Goose pumps are jumping up across my arms, and I'm starting to shiver. Damn it. I don't want to show fear.

The tape is stuck to my hair, he pulls it hard and it rips some. He uses the knife to cut the rest free.

"So, what do you think now, Officer?" His voice hardens from behind the light.

"I'm wondering why you went to this much trouble, wondering who you are."

"You changed my life. This is pay back."

"I didn't deliberately harm you. So I assume you're blaming me for more than what I did."

"Do you know how five years in prison changes a man? I'll give you a demonstration," the voice is hostile. "You have your cozy life, but you left me to rot."

I can't defend my actions because I don't know who he is, what he did, or what I supposedly did.

He begins shouting and walking around my chair. He crosses in front of the light, allowing me to briefly see his shoes; they're expensive loafers. The leather is shiny with a rich color. Just like Mia's one-night stand, the Italian who isn't from Italy. He circles me, ranting for several minutes, insisting I ruined his life.

He's in his early thirties, good looking, well-dressed, and had a sour attitude toward me from the first time we met. I thought it was because I was getting in the way of him and Mia, stealing her Porsche, stealing Axel's Porsche. But that man got away. He didn't go to prison.

Wait a minute. I arrested a wealthy man who stole high priced cars when I worked patrol in Hollywood. My testimony sent him to prison for four years. I was told he was released on parole. Well, here he is. He showed up at the cottage, aged and with a goatee. I'd forgotten what he looked like.

"Hector Adriani," I announce.

"It took you a while. I was strutting in front of your nose for weeks."

I nod a little. Looking back, I remembering seeing him strut, but I thought he was just full of himself.

"Your friends couldn't save you," he snickers.

"Did you ram my Subaru that day?"

"Yeah, but you got lucky. And you surprised me in that Mustang. Sometimes you have an angel looking after you, but tonight he took the night off. Speaking of that, your body guard didn't help much."

"You shot him."

"Not technically," he laughs.

"Your men were going to kill him. He didn't send you to prison. That wasn't right," I carefully reply.

"He's with you. That makes it right," he insists.

I hear a murmured question, "You shot him?" And the reply, "It was us or him."

"He was going for the kill when I dove at him. That wasn't self-defense, it was murder." I leave off an exclamation point, keeping it clear, but unemotional.

His shoes immediately leave my peripheral vision, striding behind the spot light.

A muffled conversation starts, with a raised voice, a whisper, and continued murmuring. What I said sends someone into a tizzy. I'll make sure to speak up about the worst of what has been done. I seems to bother someone on his team.

"Watch her," Adriani commands as he walks further away with the other person, their voices fading.

Time passes—a lot of time. I slouch down, cross and uncross my legs, arch my back, and finally, I try to get some rest by leaning my head on the back of the chair. I can still hear someone here. The shuffling of feet, an occasional throat clearing and cough tell me I'm not alone.

I must have dozed off, because I never heard his feet coming. What jerks me back to reality is the sting of my cheek as he slaps me, hard. I'm beginning to mentally crumble. The light is still on me. The man is back.

"Bring it over," he tells someone, then moves in front of the light and growls. "Look at me."

I work my way up his pant legs to his crotch. It occurs to me, while my gaze quickly flicks past it, that I don't see a pronounced lump, thank goodness for that. He isn't getting a sexual kick out of this. I continue upward, across his fine leather jacket, to his neck, then his stoic face.

"You're probably sorry you ever saw me," Hector Adriani begins.

"No kidding," I reply.

His eyes get hard. "Four years in prison. That was uncalled for. The cars I steal are insured. No one gets hurt. I'm a businessman."

"It was nothing personal. If you hadn't run the red light, I never would have singled you out."

"I'm not at fault!" He bellows, inflamed and angry, nose to nose.

I flinch. Squinting with reaction. Damned tears spring into my eyes.

"You're only tough hiding behind a badge."

What can I say? That isn't true.

"You never say much do you? Except to say I'm under arrest, or order me to leave your crappy hotel."

I'm breathing hard, trying to get oxygen to my brain, trying to focus on something besides his nose jammed against mine.

I twitch. The reaction races through my body. I want to jerk my head to the side. My mind is fighting that reflex, because I've always been a strong woman. I was strong when my horse would gallop toward home, and I couldn't stop him no matter how hard I pulled on the reins. When he'd throw me off, but I held one rein, making him drag me until he came to a stop. I got back on every time, every week. All that when I was between the ages of twelve and fifteen. Then I got bigger and stronger and we came to an agreement. Those were my formative years.

I try to blank this out and remember one of my most difficult horses. I survived, he survived, and he finally mellowed.

He stands up. "I have something for you." He walks away, the bright light again streams on me. I squeeze my eyes shut in time to avoid temporary blindness.

He returns, wheeling a cart. "Dreaming about pay-back kept me sane." He selects a sharp knife off the tray and tosses it in his hand like a gangster trying to scare his prey.

Oh hell. I've seen movie scenes like this. I always mute them and turn away, or change the channel.

He lays the cool steel on my cheek. "Maybe a little scar to remember me?" He smiles, and moves the blade across my skin.

My right cheek is pressed against the tall, wooden back of the chair. I can't go anywhere. If I shake my head, I'll get sliced more, or stuck in the eye.

It feels like a paper cut which everyone knows hurts like hell. All I do is grunt as he slices my skin. I'm keeping my jaw tightly clenched.

"You're braver than I thought." He puts the knife down.

I see bright red blood on the blade and feel it trickling down my cheek. It tickles, screwing with my mind because of the painful cut. I'm still not moving.

He stands aside. "Very pretty. I should let you see it." He reaches for a mirror hidden under the cloth. Then holds it up for me to see the damage.

Except that I refuse to look. I would probably pass out. I hate cutting and suturing with knives and needles. I also know if I don't see it, I will be able to overcome the pain better. I don't want the picture in my mind.

"Look," he commands.

I keep my eyes averted to the right.

"Look!" He moves the mirror in front to my turned head.

But I shut my eyes.

His hand grabs my jaw, forcing it up. "Open your eyes!" He's squeezing my face so strongly my teeth hurt.

There's no point fighting. I open my eyes, and see a bloody A on my cheek.

"Adriani." He laughs, stands back and looks. "It may not be deep enough," he muses. It needs to look like an A when it heals, not just a scratch. "How well do you heal?"

"Not well," I quickly answer.

"Let's make sure." He picks up the knife once more.

Running feet and shouting come from another man. He stands in front of me, blocking the light. "Have you lost your mind?" He reaches for Hector's wrist, knocking the knife to the floor.

The two scuffle over the knife. "Back off. Let me do this." Hector shouts, as he goes for the blade.

"No. This is sick." Anthony shouts at him.

That's Anthony from my liqueur workshop. He didn't cause a problem and seemed to enjoy the class. At first, he looked tense, but settled down, had fun, and even took home the liqueur he'd made.

"Your dad wouldn't approve of this," he growls.

"Dad? Don't bring him into this."

"We chose this career knowing we could get busted. It isn't her fault."

"Listen, little cousin." Hector puts him in his place. "You're either with me or against me. There's no middle ground. I'm doing this," he insists.

There's silence, as the cousin thinks about it. "Fine. Have it your way." He looks me in the eyes. Then walks away.

Oh no.

35

ANTHONY

"Now where were we?" Hector begins again, retrieving the knife from the floor.

My options have thinned to zero. The only place I can go is to the ground, but if the chair topples over, I'll land on my arms, breaking my shoulder, wrist—probably everything.

But my legs are free and I can kick—and that's what I'm about to do. I've thought about how to do this with my arms tied behind my back. I lean forward and hope for the best. I visualize the ball of my foot connecting with his kneecap. I play the sweep of my foot in my mind.

Before he moves the knife any closer to my face, I pull my right foot up and snap it out as hard as I can to the front of his knee. The power is intended to carry through his leg, causing damage. Here goes... My foot travels straight to his knee.

Seconds later, Hector is howling in pain.

I rock forward onto my feet with the chair still strapped to my back. I head for the exit which I think is on the other side of the light. There's a small window in the steel door. It's letting in just enough light to guide me. I can't open the door because I can't use my hands. I'm bent over with the wooden legs sticking out behind. I hear voices in another room, but I have a little time.

I hobble toward a room with an open door. It's a sparse office. Maybe I can find scissors in the desk. I use my head to nudge the door ajar. There isn't a phone—everyone uses a cell these days. I move around the room, lean back, and let the chair legs land on the floor. I shuffle backward to the drawer, and reach my hands through the uprights on the chair back.

It's pretty easy to get my hands on the drawer handle, but then I have to inch the chair forward while having my finger over the edge, thereby opening it.

Looking over my shoulder, I only see a few paperclips and pens. That's it. Come on! Nothing else?

I hear shouting coming from the storage area—they see I've gone. There has to be a sharp edge somewhere, otherwise this will have been in vain.

There is a stapler, which isn't sharp enough to cut myself loose. Anthony Adriani appears in the doorway.

"Shhhh," he softly says as he puts his finger to his lips. "I'm getting you out of here."

I have no choice but to believe him. If he were going to sound the alarm, all he'd have to do is yell. He quietly pulls the door closed, then hurries to me and begins picking at the rope bindings. When it's off, he goes for my duct taped hands.

"I can't find the end. Can you lean forward?" he whispers.

He finds it and starts pulling at the wrap. My arms hurt and my hands are numb from the compression, but I'm finally free.

"Come on. What he's doing is wrong. I'm getting you out of here." He hurries to the door with me hot on his tail. He opens it enough to look out. "It's clear." He pushes it open and sneaks down the hall to another door—with me on his heels.

He flips on the lights in a large warehouse with several expensive cars including a red Porsche. "Get in the black Porsche."

I hurry to the passenger side and get in. Anthony races to the steel rollup door and hits the OPEN button. It slowly clanks its way up as he sprints back to the car, jumps in and turns the key as he shifts into drive and carefully puts his foot on the gas. He won't spin the tires out of here, he's careful enough not to lose traction on the smooth concrete.

And here they come, shouting, behind us.

The front chain link gate that had been opening changes direction and begins slowly closing. "What a shame." He steps on the gas.

I duck, just in case it doesn't fly over our heads like in the movies.

No, it doesn't do that. Since it's a partway open rolling gate, it doesn't fly at all. It gets caught, as it valiantly tries to close. But the car is more powerful, and blows right through, bending the cheap frame and ripping it off the track.

And the Porsche? It sustained some nasty scrapes. Anthony speeds to the end of the street, goes a block then turns left on San Fernando Road. With our speed, everything becomes a blur.

"Dial." He commands the car and begins the slow process of calling the police. It gets routed through the highway patrol. By the time he tells them he's dropping me off at the Foothill Station, we're swinging to the curb, against the light flow of traffic.

As I step on the sidewalk, I realize the engine is still running, and he's still seated. "Aren't you coming?" I shout.

"No. I have to make amends with my family. The police will be in touch soon enough." As I stand back, he jams his foot down and speeds away in a cloud of expensive Porsche exhaust.

I dash around the block wall that protects the front of the station, and tug open the big glass door. I was told the watch commander and three officers would be ready for me, and yes they are.

"Jessica Wilcox," I pant, as I slide to a stop at the counter.

They're staring at my cheek.

"Hector Adriani did this."

"Do you need an ambulance?"

"No, I'll live. It doesn't go all the way through. We don't have time to worry about this. We have to catch him." I'd love to kill him for forcing me through this horror, but that's a matter for another time.

"I doubt they're still there, but there are some expensive cars, one of which was stolen from Cambria last week."

"Where is it?" Sergeant Moselle is ready to dispatch units to the scene.

"It's on Bradley, just south of the 118 freeway. I don't know exactly which building, but it has a broken gate."

"Come on." He waves me toward the security door which he clicks open with a button. I run though, following him down the hall, and out the back door to his patrol car. We speed out the driveway, followed by another unit, and are met by two more while en route. The dispatcher puts out a city-wide crime broadcast to be alert for an expensive imported sports car with a male, white driver. Also for the blacked out Chevy Suburban.

A train is moving alongside us at 55 mph. We are forced to wait until it passes to cross the tracks. While sitting, I look around the interior. It's about the same as when I worked here. The computer is still in the middle, and the shotgun. There's a new addition of an AR15 because of the firepower the suspects have these days, but only the sergeants carry them.

The long line of box cars finally passes, the crossing gates come up and we make the right turn.

"Hey, there's that yellow low rider." He was driving toward us, but puts on this turn signal, and makes a quick right turn to avoid the police. I wonder what he's doing out and about at this time of night. And he had a gun, which I took and lost.

"You know him?"

"We met when I dove into the bed of his truck."

"I bet that went over well."

"Yeah, especially because one of the suspects was chasing me, and the other was in an SUV speeding up on him. He waved his gun at me, which I relieved him of." I said he waved the gun, rather than pointed. It makes a difference.

"Let's discuss this later, in more detail." He makes a left on Bradley, and now I have to replay the escape scene to figure out which commercial building it is.

"There it is—right there!"

He advises the units, who slip in behind us on the street. The gate is broken and hanging, but the rollup door is closed. There's an expensive Mercedes in the parking lot. An officer touches the hood of the car, the engine is cool. It hasn't been driven for a while. I can tell because he shakes his head no.

The officers check the exterior doors, but they're locked. Sergeant Moselle explains that because there isn't an immediate threat to life, he can't enter without a warrant. But that doesn't mean Adriani gets away with it. The officers guard the perimeter and wait.

He gets in touch with the night detective working downtown, explains the situation, and starts the ball rolling.

"May I use your phone? My friend was shot. I'm sure he got help, but I have to know for sure." I hold out my hand.

I don't know Adam's number because it's in my phone in the RV. I call Nikki twice, so it rings through, waking her. I ask her to knock on the door of the mobile home to wake Dave, who knows the number.

Ten minutes later, I'm speaking with Adam.

"I thought that was the last of you," he sounds more emotional than I've ever heard him.

"It nearly was." I touch my cheek. "I'm alright for now—waiting with the police for a search warrant. It's like old times, like I never left the department." I'll probably fall apart when the chase is over.

"I'm coming to get you—be there as soon as I can."

"How is your shoulder?"

"I'll live," he mutters.

"You're so macho." I have to smile.

"Darlin' I've been through a lot worse than this." He pauses. "But thank you for saving my life."

He saw me dive at the man with the gun.

"You're welcome."

"Quinn is flying in. He got an emergency exception, he'll be landing at at 0800."

"Whoa, the government is letting him go, for me?"

"He told them he's leaving. He wasn't out of the country, so it was doable," he explains.

Once off the phone, I explain the full details to the officers. The follow up investigation will get complicated since I was kidnapped in Santa Barbara County. The stolen cars are recovered here, and I guess you'd have to say what happened to me is torture. I'm glad Anthony stopped that. I don't want to think about it, but I know I will later. Hector was just warming up with his knife.

* * *

TWENTY MINUTES LATER, the search warrant has just been approved by a sleepy judge. The sergeant isn't requesting SWAT because he was on the team before he promoted to sergeant, plus he doesn't believe this is a high-risk situation. He believes the suspects have fled. I'm wondering if they had enough manpower to get all their stolen cars out of here. They left the Mercedes, so perhaps they did.

The strongest officer rams the door and they flood in. I stay back so they can do their job. It's quiet inside. No shouting or shooting. Then the roll up door clanks open.

And there's Mia's red Porsche. With only a few drivers, they left it so they could escape with the best cars. She'll be happy about that. Maybe she'll remove her nasty hotel review when she finds out I played a hand in it.

"Jessica?" Sgt. Moselle comes out to get me. "We located the room where they held you. We're sealing it off to keep the evidence uncontaminated. If you go back in, the defense will say you left evidence after the fact—that you contaminated the scene."

"Yeah. That's okay, I have a permanent mental screen shot of it. But maybe it wouldn't look as bad in bright light."

"I'll get a picture for you."

The crime scene investigators arrive to photo, measure, take prints, and collect evidence. The remaining cars are towed on flatbeds, not by a hook. That includes the Mercedes registered to the Tre Amici. Hector Adriani and his family certainly get around.

Sgt. Moselle shows me a photo of the office where Anthony untied me from the chair. And the empty room where I was under the light. "We can't locate the knife or the spotlight, but here's some evidence you were there." He shows me the photos. One of the wooden chair with the rope dropped on the floor. "We know the suspects didn't go in the office because the rope was still there."

"And this." He enlarges a photo of the floor. "Blood. Hopefully yours."

"Once the techs collect their evidence, I'll walk you through the place." I cross my arms and hug myself. "If you want." He looks closely at me. "You're cold." He gets on the radio, asking if anyone has a jacket in their trunk they aren't using.

A blond female officer comes up, with a coat in her hands. "I don't need this." She smiles with compassion as she passes it to me.

"Thank you! It's a bit chilly tonight." I slide it on and immediately notice it's warm from her body heat. She was wearing it. It hadn't been in the trunk of her patrol car.

"You're welcome. I think you need it more than me." She returns to her job.

I turn to Sgt. Moselle, "Just so you know, she was wearing this and she'll be cold because she gave it to me." I give credit when it's due.

He agrees it was generous, but he isn't as impressed as I am. He isn't even wearing a jacket. He is muscular from hours of working out. Many of the other officers have long sleeves, but aren't wearing jackets. I know it's dumb, but it's a macho thing to be able to go without if it isn't freezing outside.

I finally sit in the front seat of the sergeant's car with the engine running, letting the heat pour on me. I make sure to get the jacket back to the generous officer. A while later, as the eastern sky lightens, two Foothill detectives arrive, bundled in coats. They're working today and they came in early because of this case.

I have a long story, from the stolen car in Hollywood, the trial and conviction of Hector Adriani. To Mia and her one night stand with Hector who I hadn't recognized after five years in prison and a hardened look; to Anthony taking my liqueur workshop; to the car chases; the road detour, and shooting of Adam; the yellow pickup truck; and finally this. While waiting, I make notes and diagrams that keep expanding to more sheets of paper. I want to make sure to include everything.

After the evidence collection, which takes hours, I'm able to walk through the rooms with the detectives, pointing out what happened, and where. When I come out of the warehouse, I see Adam speaking with an officer. When he sees me, he sprints over and pulls me into his tight embrace.

More than a minute later, he leans back and looks at my cheek. I've already washed off the streaks of blood, but there is a distinctive, recently scabbed A.

"It could have been worse." I shrug with bravado I don't feel.

36

THE LETTER

"I knew he was a bad-boy," insists Mia. "But I like them that way." She looks slightly embarrassed.

We're talking in the lounge because my office still has Mandy Crawford's transmitter.

"Don't worry about it. Things happen." If she hasn't figured out things don't happen as often to people who follow the rules, then I'm not going to lecture her.

"I can't believe he did that to your face. It's so gross. It'll probably leave a scar and you'll have to wear it, like a bad dress, for the rest of your life," she starts off encouragingly. "I'll get the number of Mom's plastic surgeon, she uses him for all her lifts and tucks; he's the best." She sends a text to her mother before I get a chance to tell her not to bother.

"Thanks. So, if I can ask, why did you leave that review about seeing a rat in here?" I make sure the question doesn't sound accusatory.

"I'm soooo sorry about that. I was angry you kicked out Hector, you know?"

"Yeah. But since he did this to my face, maybe it wasn't worth doing that review for him. I also got your car back. Will you remove it?" I smile and look hopeful.

"Well. I could, but it's how I felt at the time. It was accurate *then*, even if it isn't now."

"It wasn't accurate. It was false. There weren't any rats in here. If you want to be more accurate, perhaps you can remove the part about the rat, and say you were upset because I kicked out your sexy, bad-boy who later stole your car?"

"You're right. I'll take out the rat. The manager at Seaside Resort said I should include that because the SEO, search engine optimization, targets that word."

"I'm sure it hits on 'stolen' as well, and it's more truthful. You may want to keep your review record clean, so your followers know you speak the truth."

"Yeah, that's a consideration. I'll change it right now." She pulls up the app, does a little erasing, and says I ordered her sexy car thief to leave. She proudly shows it to me before entering it.

"Thanks, that's perfect. Would you be interested in changing the star from 1 to 5?"

"No. After all, you did kick out my guest. I can write a new one after I stay a second time."

"Ok. I understand."

And no, she won't be staying a second time.

It's been two days. Two days with plenty of rest, home cooked meals courtesy of Quinn, and massive amounts of comfort. He feels guilty about leaving. I told him again and again that it wasn't his fault. He even left Adam here for my protection. I can't be monitored 24 hours a day. Maybe if it weren't so creepy, I'd have a GPS chip implanted in my arm like a pet.

My face still hurts. I've been sleeping on my right side, slathering vitamin E on my face, and a tube of something medicinal from the dermatologist. I'm hoping it doesn't leave a big scar when it heals. A little one will be okay, since it will fade like most of my others. At least I'm not a model. If I look at it another way, it will give me plenty to talk about while networking. I usually wear a small gold horse-shoe necklace that opens up the conversation. I'm not sure anyone will ask about an A on my cheek, but maybe I could wear a knife necklace—then when they comment, I can elaborate by pointing to my cheek. It could be a new way of individualizing myself. Am I serious about this? I don't know. I'm trying to stay sane when I'm not sure if I want to curl into a ball and cry.

I'd also like a tiny gun hidden in my boot heel like James West in the old TV show The Wild Wild West. It's hard to find the series these days, but worth it for the adventures.

Adam said if I don't heal completely, mentally and physically, he will always blame himself for telling me not to follow the DETOUR signs. I should have ignored him, but I wanted to prove the app was wrong—and I did. But I should have stood up for my opinion before taking the wrong turn. I take responsibility for not being more assertive. I like saying "I told you so."

So much for resting. I've been barraged with calls and texts, and bringing everyone up to date with my mental and physical recovery. That includes Mom; she didn't hit the roof—she never does. I inherited my common sense from her.

* * *

Quinn and I are going for a run. He's acting as my body guard. He says he isn't leaving my side until Hector Adriani is caught. The problem is, the guy is wealthy enough to get out on bail. I'll address that when he's caught. In the meantime, my first run is only a two-mile jog, but my endurance seems to have vanished, so I slow to a walk.

"I don't think it's physical. Your mind is exhausted." Quinn tries to be helpful.

"Okay. I'll work on happy thoughts and creative ideas."

"Why don't you get started on the hot tub project," he suggests while jogging next to me without losing his breath. "Search for designs you like. Have you decided on a stone or concrete path, whether it will be more rustic, or formal? Do you want to step up to it, or step down into it? Do you like a redwood deck, or stone, or built into the hill which will take grading and earth moving?" He keeps giving me options.

"I want it to blend into the hill, which means earth moving and digging, and is more expense than just plonking it down and walking away," I pant after that long sentence.

"Good idea and what else?"

"I know I want six-inch wood beams across the top, so I can run shade cloth across it."

"Painted or stained beams?"

"Maybe I could cover the columns with stone." I'm beginning to see a picture in my mind.

"Nice, and do you want a privacy screen?"

"I haven't figured that out yet. Since the hill is a good six-feet above the road, I think a low, stone wall will keep it private, so all you'll see are heads."

"Trees?"

"Yes, pretty ones, maybe jacaranda with purple flowers, if they can handle the salt spray."

I know he's trying to distract me and it's working. It gives me a dream, a plan.

"Thanks, Gorgeous." I reach over and not too elegantly touch his shoulder. I'm panting, and my arm is rising and falling in time with my steps. Nope, it isn't elegant, but it's good enough.

* * *

I always watch for the mail truck. Since the box is at the front of the property, I try to get out there to collect it as soon as possible to avoid theft. "I'm getting the mail," I announce and step out the door in my bare feet. I know it sounds dumb, but I like to walk across the gravel to keep myself from becoming a person who falls apart if they have to walk without their shoes. I'm not talking about crossing over cut glass, or hot coals; it's just a bit of gravel. Take it from me—you don't always get to wear running shoes when chased. Thankfully, that hasn't happened yet. I've tested it and I know I can't walk across sticks without wincing. I doubt I could run, but I'd rather not find out.

As I pull out a bundle of mail, my breath catches. The return address on the oversized, white envelope is from Meadowbrook Hotels Inc.

What does it say about someone when they rip open the Scotch taped end and dive right in, vs the person who quietly walks up the path, stops to chat with a guest for ten minutes, enters their cottage, then sits at the kitchen table and slices it open to neatly preserve the end?

I don't know.

But after running that scenario through my mind, I step away from the street, and a possible killer driver, and carefully rip open the top by sliding my finger under the end.

It's a single, unfolded piece of linen stock with a blue, embossed heading. I see they want to impress me with their fifty-cent paper.

___________________Meadowbrook   Hotels Inc.____________________

Dear Ms. Wilcox,

We have carefully reviewed your information package.

Upon the advice of our attorneys, the prestigious law firm of Lawrence, Lawrence & Eisenstadt, we would like to offer the following:

*Ms. Mandy Crawford shall be terminated as soon as practicable. Her ties to Meadowbrook Hotels will be severed, including all social and business connections.

*The electronic receiver which accessed your private office conversations shall be immediately destroyed.

*The misinformation given to the Cambria Public Works Depart-ment and the County Health Department shall be amended.

*The newspaper shall be contacted with the correct information about your Greenstone Cottages, and a retraction will be requested. At the very least, we will run a half-page apology for two weeks.

We deeply regret our employee has been anything but an exem-plary ambassador of the Cambria Seaside Resort. We hope that you will remain a valued neighbor and friend in our business community.

The transmitter you placed in our office has been removed and returned in a separate package. We request that you cease all covert listening activities.

We have complied with your wishes, and if this is sufficient to meet your needs, please do us the favor of a reply by signing the enclosed letter in the postpaid envelope.

We appreciate your willingness to solve this in a reasonable manner.

Sincerely,

Thomas Markowitz, CEO Meadowbrook Hotels Inc.

Thanks, Mr. Markowitz. It is indeed sufficient!

Mandy will be tossed out on her tail as soon as *practicable*. That's a fancy word for practical.

I feel like running up the slope shouting for Quinn, but I know that won't go over well. Instead, I resort to walking quickly, speaking with a guest for ten minutes, then charging into the cottage and waving the letter in front of him, screeching "we won!"

He leans back from his work on the table to read it. "They're taking all responsibility. I guess they don't want a law suit. I espe-cially like the part when they say they appreciate your willingness to solve this in a reasonable manner. That translates to mean, they're thanking the Man Upstairs that you aren't going after a few million and attorney's fees.

"I hoped they'd be smart about it."

"You gave them reasonable options. It made sense to accept your rational demand." He pushes the chair back and pulls me onto his lap. "Congratulations, sweetie."

I wonder if she'll go quietly.

37

THE CALLS

Lyle Stamford sends a text to see if I'm available to talk.

"Yes. Any time after 4:00." I always worry when people don't say what they want.

He calls at 4:10. I guess he was watching the clock. "Hello Jessica. Are you able to talk now?"

"Yes, I have plenty of time."

"I appreciate your hard work on my case. My wife and I are in the midst of an unpleasant battle." He pauses to let me assimilate what I already guessed was going to happen. "We're divorcing."

"Oh dear. That's a shame."

"Yes. I won't go into the details, but she is claiming I'm having an affair with the young lady at the hunt named Roxy. Do you remember her?"

How could I forget? She was glued to his side, then she got friendly with David Reynolds and snuck out of his dressing room after having sex. "Yes, I remember."

"She is claiming that I," he pauses while searching for the correct word. "She is claiming that I had an affair with her at the foxhunt. I know you were there for the last several rides. Is it possible you saw anything that may refute that?"

"Yes, I saw her come out of David Reynolds' dressing room after what I believe was an *interlude*."

He lets his breath out through pursed lips. "She is saying I was in there with her, not David."

"No. I heard them both and saw him come out."

"Would you be willing to tell other people what you saw and heard?" Meaning the court.

"Certainly."

"Thank you very much! I appreciate your hard work, and you're a lovely rider, too," he sounds grateful.

He mailed a $700 check as proof he hired me, paid for the hireling, and paid for my written report.

Unlike his wife who still owes me and won't get anything written.

* * *

I SHOULD HAVE TURNED off my phone. I don't want to speak to anyone other than family after 8 PM.

"Jessica! I have a problem. I need you to speak to my attorney," Georgina Stamford demands.

"Oh?" That seems to be my favorite stalling word.

"That husband of mine is claiming I'm having an affair with David Reynolds. I need you to tell them I'm not. You were there, you saw that skinny, blond woman chasing Lyle. Tell them he was sleeping with her."

"I saw them talking. She was with him while riding, and part of the time at lunch. Then she got friendly with David Reynolds and hung out with him."

"That little hussy. That's unacceptable."

"Well, that's what I saw."

"I hired you to get proof Lyle is having an affair with Roxy." She knows her name.

"Yes, and I took two riding lessons, and rode to hounds three times, and paid to ride Mr. Reynolds horse. But I have only been paid for one hunt and one rental."

"Oh. Uh, I'm sure my accountant sent it," she murmurs.

"I haven't received it, and you haven't responded to my texts and messages," I reply clearly.

"That man. He never gets anything right. I'll tell him to send it again," she huffs, ignoring the rest. "In the meantime, send me your written notes," she says with authority.

"I'll be happy to do that after I receive your check. I'm sure you understand, but I've had bad experiences in the past." She is the first one who hasn't paid.

"This isn't right. I paid, I mean I will pay you. Just send me what you told me," she insists.

"Mrs. Stamford, I have rules I need to follow."

"Fine." She hangs up.

I'm not sure if it's fine, she'll send the money, or fine she won't.

I've lost money on the Georgina Stamford case. The $700 cash she gave me the first day paid for renting David's horse—the hireling, and my ride. It didn't cover 552 miles of diesel fuel at $128. It didn't cover food and liqueur for the brunch. It didn't cover my second and third rides and rentals, and near death experience in jumping solid fences on a galloping horse. Nor the two riding lessons to make sure I knew how to safely navigate over the jumps. I'd like to make a little money on it, not just the experience. I'm worth the money. She even said I'm Lyle's type and I can ride. Go find another investigator who can do that.

And she's the one having an affair. She'll have a cow when she finds out I saw her. It goes to show, it's wrong to cheat your employees.

* * *

"Hey." A man sounds crabby on my voicemail. "You have my piece. I want it back. Call me."

Oh shoot.

No. Not shoot, that's the wrong word. I mean, "Oh no."

I get out of the empty bed. Quinn is probably with Adam in the RV, planning and researching.

"Quinn. I have a slight problem." I say in the living room which has surveillance when he's not here.

"How slight a problem?"

"It depends. Remember the guy in the yellow pickup—he wants his gun back. The one the guy in the SUV took."

"Buy it off him."

I opt to send a text instead. That way I can write it without getting a barrage of anger. "Hi. I appreciate the use of your gun. Unfortunately, the kidnapper took it from me. If the police find it when he is arrested, and if it's registered to you, you'll get it back. If you don't get it back, I'd like to offer to pay for it. I know this doesn't replace the gun. I hope it wasn't a cherished family weapon. Please let me know what you think. Jess."

"You want to know what I think? My father worked his fingers raw to buy it. He gave it to me on his death bed. My mother is crying every day since you stole it from me. It's worth $1,500. That's what I think."

Oh dear.

A phone call to Detective Roper is in order. I need to see if he has any info on the gun, and if the big suspect who took it from me has been arrested.

It doesn't take more than ten minutes to get my answer. "No I don't have any info on the gun. I haven't followed up on that yet. I'll send you his driver's license picture, the one associated with the registration of the yellow pickup. Tell me if he's the one who had it."

A minute later, I open the email and there he is. "Yes, that's him. What's his name?"

"Joe Beck."

"Can you see the guns registered to him? I'll try to get his dad's name to see if he told me the truth."

"Do you really think the guy who shoved a gun in your face registered it?"

"No. But who knows." I'm trying to keep an open mind instead of thinking the worst. "When I took it from him I said he could have it back. I'd like to keep my word, or at least pay him for it."

"Why would you pay for it when it's probably stolen?"

"Because I don't want another angry man chasing me."

"You live too far away."

"I won't take the chance."

"So pay him. If you get his dad's name I'll see if it's registered to him." His voice tells me he has other things to do.

"Thanks."

Now it's time to chat with Joe. I'm not oblivious, but I'm giving him a chance. This text has a different tone. I'm more assertive. "Hi Joe. The gun isn't registered in your name. Did your father register it in his?"

Much later, he replies, "You going to welch out on your promise?"

"No. I'll pay you for it."

"$2000."

He told me $1,500 a while ago. It went up, either by accident, or to teach me a lesson.

"Do you have registration papers or a photo depicting the weapon so I know it's the same one? I only got a quick look at it."

He sends a photo of himself in gang attire, flashing gang signs, covered in tattoos and looking mean. And the gun is in his hand, with his finger menacingly on the trigger. "Are you sure you want to mess with this?"

I send two texts, "Not messing." "What is your father's full name?"

When I receive his info I forward it to the detective. I could see if Quinn or Adam can research it, but they'd have to call in a favor. I'd prefer not to put them in that situation. In a few hours I'll know the answer. Joe Beck will have to wait.

* * *

A PEACEFUL NIGHT with Quinn in my bed, and Adam in the RV means I live to see the morning light.

Round two starts in the office after breakfast. A courier opens the door with one of those oversized cardboard envelopes in his hand. "Looking for Jessica Wilcox." He smiles.

"I'm Jessica." I turn away from the computer to sign the digital pad.

He leaves it on the counter. "Thanks, have a nice day." He's out the door in a flash.

I rip off the strip and look inside before reaching in. It's a check for $5,000 from Georgina Stamford. The note says it all. "This is enough to cover your expenses and your cooperation."

I worked out my expenses, and they come to $2982. That includes 55 cents a mile for wear and tear on the truck, and the full cost of the jumping lessons I didn't get to take. She has overpaid me. That would be nice, except for the typed note mentions my cooperation. I guess it's time for a phone call.

"Hello, Mrs. Stamford? This is Jessica Wilcox."

"You received my package." She knows it was delivered.

"Yes. There is more than my expenses. Will you explain the rest?"

"You were hired to find proof my soon to be ex-husband is having an affair. I'd like that proof."

"I see. I will send my photos and video, as well as a written statement, and I'll be willing to testify. However, I have no evidence indicating he cheated on you. In fact, he acted honorably toward me."

"As I said, the extra money is to cover your cooperation in proving he is having an affair."

"Cooperation," I repeat.

"Cooperation," she says again.

Silence...while I formulate my reply.

"I won't be cashing your check, because it's more than we agreed upon, and I feel there may be a misunderstanding regarding my services."

"If you don't cash it, there won't be another one," she threatens.

"That's interesting. I'll look forward in seeing you in small claims court."

Silence...while she comes to a decision.

"I see. What is the total amount I owe you? I expect an accurate accounting," she sounds frosty.

"I'll email you the correct amount, with receipts." I feel quite relieved, and oddly happy.

She hangs up.

Yes, I feel very happy. She was trying to pay me to incriminate an innocent man. Nope. Not doing that.

I'm also noting this conversation and keeping the recording. Yes, I recorded it. Did you think I wouldn't?

38

NEWS

Detective Roper calls with astonishing news. "I'm surprised, but the gun is registered to Joe Beck Sr."

"No way!"

"Yeah. One of life's little surprises that keep me on my toes."

"What is the gun?"

"A 6 inch, chrome, .22 Smith & Wesson revolver."

"Huh. Well, thank you very much. I'll see how much it's worth."

"He shouldn't have been carrying it on the street. He doesn't have a CCW permit," he says.

"I know. I'm just glad it wasn't a .357 or something that would have left a large hole in me."

"You don't think this can kill you? The bullet bounces around your gut, making spaghetti of your intestines because it isn't powerful enough to go straight through."

"Oh. Hell. I won't be having spaghetti any time soon." I feel ill at the thought of what could have happened.

"I'll let you know if we recover it."

"Any luck finding Hector Adriani?"

"No—none. But the cousin, Anthony Adriani, contacted us. He was cooperative, and the D.A is working on a deal."

"I guess he didn't want any part of my *demise*." I phrase it that way to cover my discomfort over the real word.

"Hey, and another thing, I have a lead on the two suspects in the SUV. They are hired muscle used by the family. Anthony Adriani spilled the beans on them. He'll be facing backlash from the family."

"Hector should be the one facing backlash for being a psycho," I fume.

"Parents usually overlook that."

"Are the parents involved now, or is it just him, his brothers, and cousin?"

"We're still digging into that."

"Thanks." We click off.

I step outside to let the cool air clear my head.

A white rat zips around the door jam and into my cottage! How brazen, he isn't even afraid of me. Now what? I wonder if anyone has a Rat Terrier I can borrow. I refuse to put down bait. Maybe I'll order ten electric zapper boxes. I step back inside and wake the cat. She can dine on fresh rat for dinner.

My phone dings with a text. I have no peace these days.

"I'm waiting." It's Joe Beck.

"Hi Joe. I heard back from the police. Your father shows as the registered owner. I researched the value of the Smith & Wesson .22 and it is $499. The police haven't located it yet, but guns don't remain lost forever. You'll probably get it back. However, I'd like to pay you double the value."

"You think that helps? I can't go out and buy one."

Why am I not surprised?

"I have a suggestion: get your mother to buy it in her name, then you keep the change, or upgrade to a more powerful weapon. This is a good opportunity." I originally typed "you can get a manlier gun," but I thought it might enrage him because it was his dad's.

"I'll think about it."

That sounds promising. I bet he would have sworn at me if it was unacceptable. I don't need another person seeking vengeance, so I'm definitely willing to pay double for it.

* * *

Janet hurries in the office waving a newspaper.

"Jess—great news. Look at this!" She slaps it down on the counter.

The headline says: "Cambria woman arrested in embezzlement scheme."

"Oh yeah?"

She points to the name part way through the article: Mandy Crawford.

"A routine, in-house audit by the luxury hotel Cambria Seaside Resort discovered multiple discrepancies to their accounting. Mrs. Mandy Crawford has been arrested for theft, fraud, and money laundering. The exceptionally well planned scheme included writing checks to herself, withdrawing cash, and making unauthorized purchases over a ten year period."

I skim a few lines. "1.2 million dollars! No wonder she has so much pull in town. She is rich."

"She was rich," Janet muses.

"Did they find this out because of my complaint?"

"No, see here, it says it has been a lengthy investigation."

"You're right. It would take time to dig into their books and get her arrested. This means she was on their radar before they knew about me."

"There's something you'll want to see on page 3." Janet turns to the half-page ad.

"Cambria Seaside Resort extends an apology to Ms. Jessica Wilcox, owner of the hotel Greenstone Cottages. It has come to our attention that our employee Ms. Mandy Crawford deliberately and illegally spread rumors and caused problems for that fine boutique hotel. Ms. Crawford has been removed from her position with the Cambria Seaside Resort. You can rest assured we treat our guests with the greatest of care and their personal information has not been affected."

There's a beautiful photo of Moonstone Beach with a blue sky and crashing waves. Their website and phone number are at the bottom in nice writing. They turned this into an ad for their own hotel, but I don't have a problem with that—I've been cleared.

"And there'll be another one in next week's edition too!" I rejoice.

Ahhh, things are finally settling down. Life is good. I look out the window to my cottage. What a wonderful place to live. I have a thriving business, a terrific man, and good friends.

* * *

ON THE WAY to the mailbox, I pause at the site of the future hot tub. I'm ready to get going on this. There's a local contractor Caleb recommended who sometimes stops in for a beer. He's a nice man with a family and comes with a wad of references. I think my plate is clear enough that I'll call him this afternoon.

I feel light. Mandy is getting her payback. I can't believe she was embezzling! I wonder if she was going to use the money to buy my place.

* * *

THE MAILBOX IS STUFFED TODAY, including a small box without a return address.

Traffic is slow on the road, but in keeping with my safety habits, I move out of harm's way. I wonder if I should open it. Do I have to be afraid of a bomb with a mercury switch? If I wonder about every package, I'll be living a life of fear.

I'll be careful. I place it on the ground, and pick off the tape.

It's a bottle of Limoncello packed in tissue paper for protection. The envelope contains a glossy card with a photo of a lemon. Inside it reads:

"I invited my cousin from Sicily and suggested he visit your hotel. *A.*"

A, just like the wound on my cheek. I read it a second time, hoping this isn't as bad as I think. I compose myself on the way to the RV where Quinn and Adam are working. I knock twice and enter.

"What do you know about the Sicilians?"

Find out as Jess waits for Hector's cousin, while helping a local restaurant with a New Orleans crawfish boil.

Coming in 2021: Mystery in Tawny Brown.

FREE ADVENTURE BOOK

Have you joined my list of readers who like reading about Jess and her adventures? I'd like to send you an email when I have a new release.

Plus, when I go to the wine country, I'd like to share my own adventures that may not make it into a book.

I've created the novelette **Mystery in Chianti** just for you.

Join Jessica for a fast-paced trip to Italy—where the wine is as intense as the men.

https://storyoriginapp.com/giveaways/0a5633cc-8bdd-11e9-bb9b-d7f6fe5abdf8

ACKNOWLEDGMENTS

Thank you, Molly Conway for your time and expertise. A foxhunter for decades and a former whipper-in, she is a wealth of knowledge about horses, hounds, and cheating husbands.

Her view on foxhunting differs from mine. I'd prefer to leave them, the wild hares, and the coyotes alone. I don't see sport in chasing them for mile upon exhausting mile. Although I don't have a problem with boar hunting. Apparently, they make good sausage and don't trigger my empathetic response.

* * *

The nice comments as told to Jess during her jumping lesson are the actual words of Ludger Thole during a lesson he was teaching one Saturday morning. It looked so fun, I may try it with Bunny—she's the athletic one. Remember, she helped me escape from the lion-masked bandits a few months ago. Juliette and I would crash for sure.

* * *

Thank you Dr. Angele Blanton for the first round of proofreading which caught a load of errors. Then Christy Norcross found another batch. Then Bev found a few more. It seems to take a small army to fix my creative words. Thank you!

ABOUT THE AUTHOR

I started as a horse-crazy kid. It took nearly five years of collecting my dad's spare change to save up for a horse. What kind of a horse can you buy with $415? A difficult one. I survived, and we later came to an understanding.

For several years, I bred and trained potential show horses. That's what I wanted, but didn't often get. I remember each one with either a sigh of regret, or happiness. That's what a horse will do to you.

For a time, I was on the Los Angeles Police Department. It lets me bring descriptive scenes from my experience while working patrol.

I've always been drawn to the wine country. It's close enough to go day-tripping, but Cambria is twice the distance. I have to load up on coffee to make it home in one piece. I'd like to go more often, but it's easier to take a virtual trip. That isn't the same, so maybe I'll go again this weekend. Maybe.

ALSO BY DIANA STONE

Mystery in Pink Formerly titled Dressed in Pink

Mystery in Green

Mystery in Blue

Mystery in Orange

Mystery in Black

Mystery in Red

Mystery in White

Mystery in Yellow

Mystery in Purple

Mystery in Light Blue: Jess inherits a B&B by the sea

Mystery in Pale Green

Mystery in Tawny Brown: coming Spring 2021